Leadville

Also by James D. Best

The Digital Organization
The Shopkeeper
The Shut Mouth Society

Leadville

James D. Best

A Steve Dancy Tale

Leadville

Cover design by Wayne Best.

Published by Wheatmark®
610 East Delano Street, Suite 104
Tucson, Arizona 85705 U.S.A.
www.wheatmark.com

International Standard Book Number: 978-1-60494-238-5
Library of Congress Control Number: 2008943382

For Leo and Eli
I finished *Leadville* in the hospital the day you were born.

Leadville

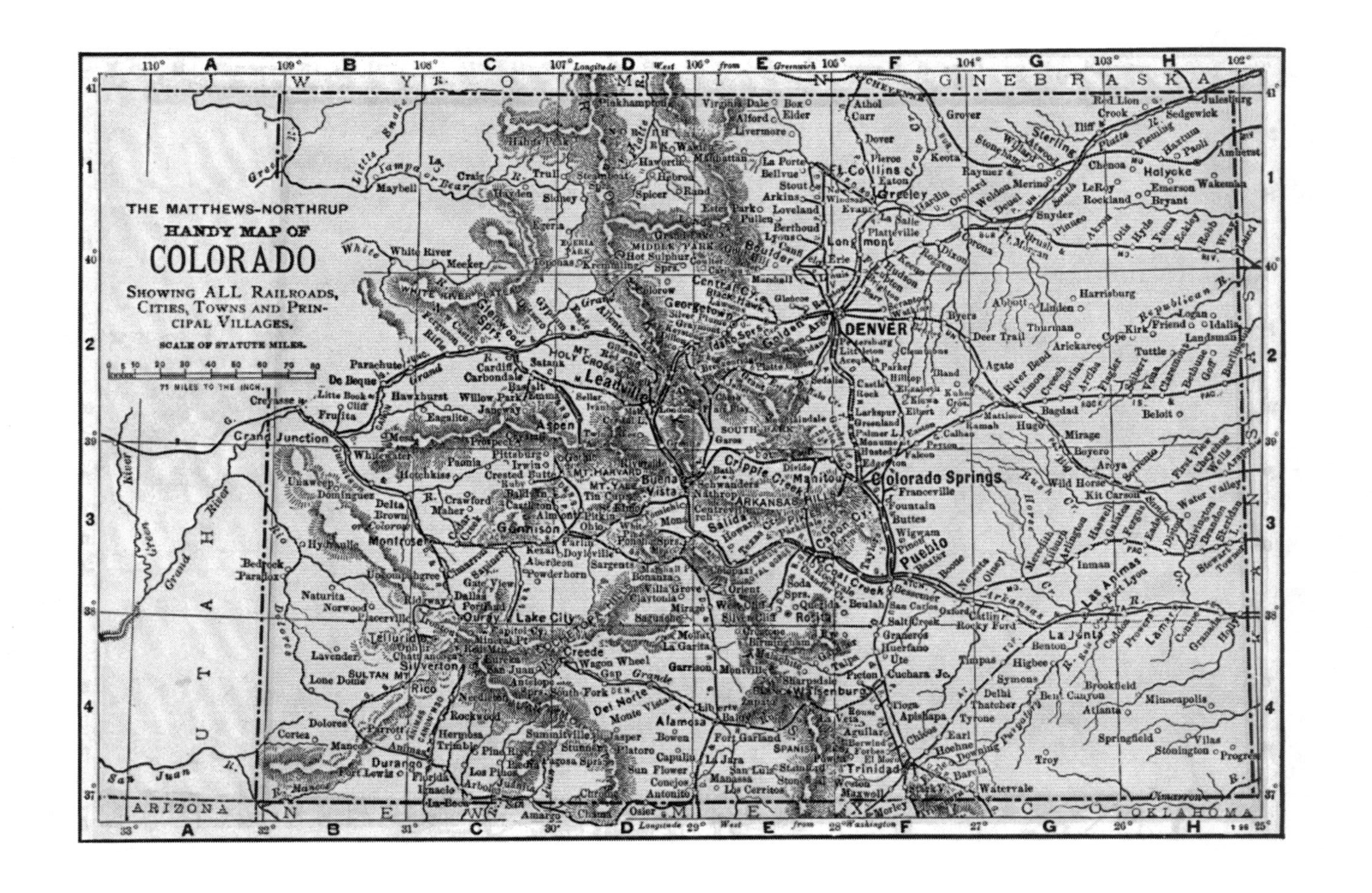
THE MATTHEWS-NORTHRUP
HANDY MAP OF
COLORADO
SHOWING ALL RAILROADS, CITIES, TOWNS AND PRINCIPAL VILLAGES.
SCALE OF STATUTE MILES.
71 MILES TO THE INCH.
DENVER
Colorado Springs
Pueblo
Leadville
WYOMING
NEBRASKA
KANSAS
OKLAHOMA
NEW MEXICO
ARIZONA
UTAH

Chapter 1

"Three."

"Days or weeks?" I asked.

"Days." Jeff Sharp squinted at the telegram as if it hid additional information. Rubbing the back of his neck, he added, "He can't make it. It's a six-day ride."

"If Captain McAllen says he'll be here in three days, we'd better have a room ready for him."

"A bath too." Sharp handed me the telegram. "What d'ya s'pose put such a charge under him?"

I read the telegram and absentmindedly ran my fingers through my hair. I needed a haircut. Although I had been out West for over a year, I remained vain about my sandy-colored hair. When it was neat and trimmed, I thought I looked the handsome gent, no matter how I dressed.

After a second reading, I shook my head. "Doesn't say much. He sent it from his Denver office, but I don't think it's Pinkerton business."

"Why not?"

I handed the telegram back. "He wouldn't ask our help on a professional engagement."

It was September of 1879 and we had lingered in Durango several days beyond the needs of our business visit. We were anxious to move on to our next destination, but now it looked like we would be delayed further. Sharp had come to Durango to hunt up mining investments in Silverton but decided against putting his money into any of the available enterprises. The gold and silver boom had driven prices far beyond what an experienced miner would pay, and Sharp lost all interest after he learned that the Denver and Rio Grande Railway had already started to incorporate the encampment into a town. Sharp preferred his investments and his beefsteaks rare, if not downright raw.

Captain Joseph McAllen was actually Sharp's friend. McAllen was a no-nonsense sort whom I guessed to be in his late thirties or early forties. I wasn't sure because you didn't ask McAllen personal questions.

I had recently employed McAllen and his team of Pinkertons in Nevada, and I felt we had developed a level of respect for each other. Not right away. It had been a dangerous affair, far beyond the bodyguard work I had originally contracted. At the time, I was fresh from New York City, and McAllen didn't appreciate my tenderfoot antics.

Dr. Dooley suddenly plopped into a seat beside us in the dining room of our boardinghouse. "I'm going."

"Figured," Sharp said.

Dooley was the third in our party. We had all ridden together from Nevada to southwest Colorado. Dooley was on his way to take a job at a consumption clinic in Glenwood Springs, and I had come along for the ride and to experience a new part of the frontier. I had come west to explore and make notes in my journal so I could one day return to New York City and write a rousing novel about my adventures. Exploring the West had been my profession ever since I had sold my shop in New York City on my thirtieth birthday. Most of my wandering had proved uneventful, but I had run into trouble in a mining camp called Pickhandle Gulch, and Sharp and McAllen had helped me escape alive.

Dr. Dooley was only a few years older than me, but he affected the image of a rumpled and seasoned doctor. Our friend Jeff Sharp had been to Europe and South America, worked mines, driven a stage, bossed cattle drives, and acted as an agent for a New York importer. Now, in his early fifties, he had settled on a career as a wealthy mine owner, although he dressed and acted more like a range boss.

We both knew what Dooley meant when he said he was going. Three days ago, a band of Utes had snatched a fourteen-year-old girl who had been exercising her colt in Mancos Valley, near Mesa Verde. The kidnapping had caused a stir, and newspapers demanded that the men in the community track down the renegades and recapture the girl.

Everyone in southwest Colorado was up in arms. The more reasonable citizens wanted the Utes brought to justice and publicly hanged, but most people just wanted instant punishment. A few rambunctious hotheads had already formed makeshift posses and raced into the San Juan Mountains, intent on being town heroes. One posse had taken time to provision properly, recruit a half-breed that spoke the Ute language, and get a mountain tracker to join the group. This same posse had asked Dooley to ride along with them in case the girl needed medical assistance.

"We won't be joinin' you," Sharp said. "A telegram from Captain McAllen asked us to wait for him. He says he'll be here in three days, an' you men might be gone for weeks."

"No matter; Grant has recruited plenty of men."

Bob Grant had organized this posse. I didn't know him well, but he seemed to be a take-charge man.

"How many?" I asked.

"At least a dozen. The Utes are rumored to number only about six."

"Something's wrong about this whole incident," Sharp said, with a distracted tone.

"How so?" I asked.

"Utes don't grab women, and renegades are even less likely to take on the burden of a white woman. These small bands move fast, an' they don't have any place to take 'em."

"Perhaps they wanted her horse," Dooley said.

"They'd take the horse, all right, but they woulda left her in the sage to fend for herself. The whole episode doesn't make sense."

None of us said anything more, so Dooley stood. "I gotta git." He started toward the door but had a thought. "Is McAllen coming because of this girl?"

"Doubt it," Sharp said. "No one's mentioned Pinkertons. We think it's personal."

"Well, if you need me, send a rider." Dooley charged out without waiting for a reply.

Sharp looked troubled. "What's on your mind?" I asked.

"You talk to this Bob Grant much?"

"You don't like him?"

"Too slick." Sharp stepped into the kitchen to fill his coffee cup from a pot on the stove.

We were staying at a boardinghouse in Durango because we couldn't rent private rooms in Silverton. The hotels and houses there put two or more men to a room, usually in the same bed.

After a major gold or silver strike, it didn't take long for saloons, prostitutes, and decent food to gather round the newly rich miners to siphon off a share of their wealth. In fact, Durango had grown up as a farming, ranching, and lumbering community to supply Silverton. That looked about to change. The railroad and a new smelter would make Durango the lifeblood of San Juan mining operations.

When Sharp returned, he added, "People talk about Grant like he's a town leader, but he's only been here a couple months, an' no one knows a damn thing about him."

"Seems an upright, friendly sort."

Sharp shook his head, as though trying to dislodge an uneasy thought. "Can't put my finger on it, but somethin' ain't bolted down tight with that man. An' he took his sweet time getting this posse on the trail."

"Jeff, one of the posses has already returned with tired horses and empty saddlebags."

"Yep, a trek into the mountains takes plannin', but there's a big difference between one hour an' three days. Grant looks to be stallin'."

The same thought had occurred to me. I may have been a newcomer to the West, but even I knew that trails grow cold, especially trails left by Indians.

It bothered me that Grant seemed so intent on raising money. He had met with all the town businessmen and elders, one at a time and always in private. I had no idea how much money he had gathered up, but he had certainly garnered a wealth of goodwill. Everyone praised his single-minded preparations and his unwavering vow to bring the girl home.

When not raising money, Grant had spent the last three days with the child's parents, who had fixed all their hopes on this paladin. The girl's father was the sole preacher in town, and his handsome wife taught in the only school. They were the civilizing force in this rough mining encampment, and their plight drew sympathy, prayers, and, I suspected, healthy cash contributions.

"Did you give Grant money?" Sharp asked.

I hesitated. "I set up a two-hundred-dollar line of credit at the general store."

Sharp laughed. "You don't trust the son of a bitch either, do you?"

I shrugged. "I never give money to strangers." Sharp and I were both well fixed, so I asked, "How about you?"

"Had to make a contribution, but I wasn't as smart as you. I gave cash."

I knew what he meant. Sharp ran the largest private mining operation in Nevada, and if he wanted to do business with the people in this town, he had to show sympathy for their troubles.

Suddenly, Dooley came bounding back into the dining room, gasping for breath. "Couple of men been asking about Steve Dancy."

"Asking about me?" I asked. "Why?"

Dooley bent at the waist and laid a hand across his belly. "Don't know more than that. One of the men in the posse told me they're asking lots of questions. Didn't sound right, so I thought you oughta know."

"Slow down. Are these men threatening me?"

"All I know is they're armed, strangers to Durango, and asking your whereabouts." He looked toward the door. "Gotta go. I'm holding up the posse."

Before I could say thanks, Dooley had bolted out the door.

Chapter 2

"She's my daughter."

"What?" Both Sharp and I spoke at once.

Captain McAllen sank deeper into the bathwater and let out an exasperated sigh. "Did you think I didn't like women?"

"No," Sharp said. "But I couldn't imagine a woman foolish enough to git in a family way with ya."

"Wives tend to think that's important."

With that, our mouths fell open, but neither of us uttered a word. Finally, Sharp slid his chair closer to the tub and said, "Joseph, in ten years, you've never mentioned a wife."

McAllen made a dismissive wave, flicking water droplets in our direction. "Never worthy of comment before. It ended badly, and in short order she married a preacher."

"The schoolmarm?" I blurted.

"Yep, Maggie's my daughter." McAllen looked around and then asked, "Steve, can you find me a whiskey? Been a hard ride."

"Sure." I got up and left the bathroom.

After I closed the hall door, I heard Sharp yell, "Get a whole bottle!"

McAllen must have ridden hard. Although he had made it to Durango in the promised three days, he hadn't arrived until well after dark. To our surprise, he had been accompanied by another rider, who had disappeared before McAllen even introduced us. When we asked if we should book a room for the second man, McAllen had said he could take care of himself. Kindliness had never been a McAllen virtue, but he had either the skill or the good fortune to gather around him tough, self-reliant men who didn't need coddling.

When I had first encountered McAllen, he and his men had all worn black vested suits and white shirts. The attire seemed impractical for the trail, but it identified them as Pinkertons, which might prove important in some circumstances, because they didn't wear badges. Tonight, though, McAllen and his riding partner had been dressed like ranchers, their heavy dusters covering coarse cotton shirts and trousers.

We had hustled McAllen into his room and a hot bath so he could scrub off the sweat and trail dirt. The boardinghouse bathroom had a single tub, but since he had arrived so late, we had the room to ourselves. After McAllen had settled into his bathwater, Sharp and I had pulled over a couple of straight-back chairs and sat on either side of him so we could learn what had made his trip so urgent. I couldn't have been more surprised when he told us the missing girl was his daughter. To call McAllen taciturn would be an understatement, but we had shared enough campfires that the subject of a daughter and a former wife should have come up at one time or another.

I bought a bottle of the best Kentucky whiskey in a saloon across the way and raced back with three glasses and a hundred questions. When I opened the door to the bathroom, I heard Sharp ask, "That man with ya a Pinkerton?"

"He's employed by Pinkerton at times, but he's here as a friend."

"Wives *an'* friends," Sharp hooted. "Next, you're gonna tell me you're a damn Mormon."

McAllen made a practice of ignoring offhand talk. "What's the latest news?"

"There's a posse out," Sharp said. "This one left three days ago. A couple of parties took off earlier an' returned empty-handed." Sharp leaned forward, rested his elbows on his knees, and intertwined his fingers into a loose fist. "Everyone assumes the renegades rode into the San Juan Mountains, but no one knows for sure."

"Any other raids or incidents?"

"Nope."

"North or south?" McAllen pondered his own question. "They know the terrain in both directions, and there's plenty of game migrating before winter sets in."

I poured bourbon at the sideboard and then passed the glasses around. After an appreciative sip, McAllen said, "Tell me about this posse."

"Left three days ago, fourteen men, well armed an' provisioned, with at least six packhorses," Sharp explained. "They haven't sent a rider back with any news."

"Doc Dooley's with them," I added. "Along with a Ute half-breed."

"Who's in charge?" The question seemed a natural for Captain McAllen, who ran his Pinkerton teams with an iron will and sure-handed know-how.

"Man name of Bob Grant … seems capable," I said.

"Capable of fleecing this town, at least," Sharp added in a sarcastic tone.

"You don't like him?" McAllen asked.

"Seems full of himself … and far too cautious," Sharp said.

McAllen seemed to think that through. "Bad combination to lead a pursuit. Steve?"

"Don't know the man, but he won the town's backing." I hesitated. "He did seem more intent on soliciting money than getting on their trail."

"What's he do?"

"Agent for Wells Fargo," I said. "I hear he heads the Leadville office, and he's here to check up on the company's operations and security."

"I've done work for Wells Fargo, so I can check him out. But that don't sound like a posse that'll bring back my daughter." McAllen put a hand on each rail edge of the tub and pushed himself to a standing position. "Hand me a towel." He stepped out of the tub and rubbed himself dry. "I need a decent night's sleep in a soft bed. I'll leave tomorrow." He paused. "Probably about mid-morning." He looked pointedly at me. "Steve, you ready for another adventure?"

I guessed he assumed Sharp would join him without asking. "Only if you'll teach me some wilderness skills."

"Seems a steep price, but it's a deal."

That was the first hint of humor I had ever seen from McAllen, and pretty weak at that. The captain dressed in a nightshirt without further word, so I asked, "Who'll join us?"

"A lot of men get in the way, so just the four of us. In the morning, rent two or three packhorses. Sharp'll help you buy supplies."

"What'll ya be doin'?" Sharp asked.

"Sleep late and then see my ex-wife." With that, McAllen grabbed the bottle of bourbon and a glass and marched out of the bathroom.

We sat there a moment, and then Sharp said, "We probably oughta go to bed as well, but how 'bout a beer?"

I stood. "Whiskey puts me more in a sleeping mood, but the captain's run off with our bottle."

Sharp remained seated. "On second thought, maybe ya oughta write Jenny a letter instead. We might be in them hills a long time."

I wasn't surprised that Sharp brought up Jenny Bolton. He had been harassing me for weeks to write her. I had dallied because the prospect scared me. I had left Jenny on her ranch in Nevada's Mason Valley. More accurately, she had sent me on my way, uninterested in my advances. Sharp still held out hope, but memory did not encourage me to revisit the pain of rejection. "Let's go over to the saloon, and I'll think about it over a drink."

Chapter 3

The next morning we made the local shopkeeper happy. Sharp bought so many provisions that we needed four packhorses. He seemed intent on emptying the shelves of ammunition, canned goods, dry goods, blankets, candles, and utensils. Sharp also bought two pair of field glasses, a lantern, an axe, a shovel, pliers, a twelve-inch file, and four heavy sheepskin overcoats.

"Why a lantern?" I asked.

"When yer close on the heels of yer prey, a low lantern ain't nearly as bright as a campfire... and ya can carry it around for light, if need be." Sharp looked at my feet. "How're yer boots?"

"Fine. Bought them a couple months ago in Carson City."

"Buy another pair," Sharp ordered.

"Why?"

"We could get an early snow or trudge through streams. Wet boots make a man miserable."

I spent a few minutes picking boots from a selection of only two styles, one being the square-toed stream-waders miners preferred. After I dropped a serviceable pair of riding boots onto the counter, I ruffled through the tall stack of blankets and canvas pads that were part of our order.

"Heavy coats, no fires, enough blankets to warm a small church congregation, and now you make me buy spare boots." I pointed at a wooden box filled with canned goods and sacks of foodstuffs. "How long do you expect to be gone?"

"Until McAllen finds his daughter." Sharp hefted the box of cans and tossed it into my arms. "And some of them blankets an' pads are to wrap the packhorse loads so they don't rattle an' bang. A quiet load makes for a calm horse."

I grunted under the load and turned a quizzical eye at the storekeeper. "I'll get a boy to help you," he said.

I turned and slid the box back onto the counter. "Two," I replied.

"Steve, there ain't no boys to hire in the mountains. Better get used to carryin' yer load."

"Right now, I better see to hiring some horses to carry these supplies." I turned to the storekeeper. "Have the boys bring all this down to the livery... oh, and Mr. Sharp will gladly pay the tally." I whirled and marched out, happy to see the chagrin on Sharp's face.

The liveryman was pleased to rent packhorses this late in the year. I had arranged for four horses by the time Sharp and two boys entered the livery burdened with loads that required them to peek around the sides to see where they were going.

Sharp dropped his load and examined the packhorses. "Good animals," he said. "Which one's the boss?"

"Boss?" I asked before the liveryman could answer.

"Horses are like dogs when they run together. One of 'em is gonna put the others in their place. Nature. Ya rue the day ya try to change the peckin' order." Sharp lifted an eyebrow at the liveryman.

"That big gray Morgan. Ya put him in front of the string an' ya won't have no trouble."

Sharp nodded. "Let's see yer pack saddles."

"Sawbuck or Spanish?"

"Spanish. Better on mountain trails," Sharp said.

"Goin' after them Utes?" the liveryman asked.

"Yep."

"Good luck. At least ya know what yer 'bout. Most of the men that went after 'em were miners, an' the rest had pint-size brains stuffed in big hats." He waved us to the back of the barn. "Saddles're back here."

Sharp sorted out the saddles and hitches and picked the ones he wanted. Then Sharp eyed the horses as he sorted the loads into four piles.

Before we saddled the four packhorses, Sharp explained, "The secret to a behaved string of packhorses is spreadin' the loads between the animals based on what they can carry. Then ya gotta make the loads snug, balanced, an' quiet, with nothin' stickin' out to get caught on a tree or rock. Ya see, a saddle horse carries a live weight, one that shifts with the circumstance, but a packhorse carries a dead weight, so it's gotta be balanced just so."

"Maybe we should get a wagon," I offered.

"A horse can pull more than it can carry, but a packed horse can go more places." He moved a gunnysack from one pile to another. After another examination, he said, "Come on, let's get this loaded. I'll show ya a proper diamond hitch."

We were done by mid-morning, but McAllen was nowhere in sight. The supplies had been bought, packhorses let, our own gear readied, and everything packed. Saddling our riding horses was all that remained, and this would wait until we were set to depart.

Sharp and I stood outside the livery corral kicking our spurs into the dirt. "Let's get a ham steak," Sharp said.

"Bit early for a noon meal."

"Hell, McAllen went to see his ex-wife. No tellin' how long he'll be, and we might not see a hog for months."

"You said something similar this morning when we ordered that glutinous breakfast."

"True this morning, true now. If ya hadn't hired them boys, you'd be hungry too."

"What if McAllen shows up?"

Sharp leaned around the corner of the barn and yelled at the liveryman, "If a gruff gent comes lookin' for us, tell 'im we're at the café." Sharp turned and gave me a pleased look.

"What if he comes before we finish our meal? You know McAllen."

"Then we git up and head for the hills."

"He said mid-morning. Could be a waste of money."

"Might be right." Sharp pushed himself away from the barn wall. "So you pay." And off he went.

I followed Sharp around the corner to a hardscrabble footpath lined with single-story ramshackle buildings. Mining towns had only two purposes: to dig money from the earth as fast as possible and then to separate that money from the miners even quicker. And all mining towns looked as if they had been thrown up yesterday with little hope that they would be needed tomorrow. Because Durango served the mining towns and operations in the nearby hills, the town had been cut from this same mold. Even with the railroad on the way and looming incorporation, Durango had the aspect and temper of a makeshift encampment that would never last beyond the gold and silver. Despite these off-putting flaws, I loved mining towns. You could count on high spirits, savvy men, savvier women who threw social norms to the winds, have-nots suddenly awash in money, and a frantic abandon that appealed to me for reasons I never bothered to examine. I liked the unbridled energy that made me wake up anxious to experience the day.

Sharp was in his element in mining towns. I had met him in a rough camp that made Durango look downright cosmopolitan. In Durango, people lived in respectable buildings, with water readily available. The miners in Pickhandle Gulch built rudimentary rock hovels, because wood demanded a higher price than silver. Water came even dearer. Sharp had built a mining empire centered in Belleville, about twenty miles from Pickhandle. I accidentally got mixed up with his biggest rival, which made us natural allies, and we had since become friends. An odd friendship. Sharp, in his early fifties, was twenty years my senior. I was an aspiring writer with the best education a rich New York family could buy. Sharp lacked formal education, but he had been all over the world and built his wealth with his own hands. These differences somehow made the friendship work. Or perhaps it was our aggressive natures and the common need to make our mark that brought us together.

Sharp's destination was the same dowdy café where we had eaten breakfast. He liked to eat at unrefined places where he might pick up mining gossip. I preferred eating at our boardinghouse, but this time it was prudent to stay close to the stables in case McAllen came looking for us. The proprietors had tried to dress up the café's unpainted walls and plank floor with red-checkered tablecloths and bright blue enameled plates. Deer antlers bracketed an American flag tacked to one wall, and a cheap grandfather clock kept up a relentless beat in the corner.

The owner's plump wife greeted us with surprise. "Thought you boys were heading out of town."

"Couldn't leave town without another of yer great meals," Sharp said. "Bring us a couple thick ham steaks with yams an' any other fresh vegetables ya got in the kitchen."

"And pie?"

Sharp laughed. "And pie, goddamn it."

"Comin' right up. Pick your seat." She scurried off.

The place was empty. I knew it was too early for the noonday meal. Sharp chose a table in the rear, sat against the wall, and then immediately leaned his chair back into his customary position. Sitting opposite, I said, "You sure McAllen will be late?"

Sharp snapped his chair back to the floor and yelled around the corner, "Greta, bring out the pie first!"

Her head appeared around the door frame. "Before the meal?"

"Yeah, keep us busy while you grill them ham steaks."

"You boys sure are peculiar." She disappeared again but soon returned with two outrageous portions of berry pie. "This ought to keep you busy."

Sharp gave her one of his *shucks, I'm just a good ol' boy* smiles and said, "Thank ya, darlin'." He grabbed his fork with a fist and shoveled in mouthful after mouthful. When I started laughing, he gave me a purple toothy grin. "Dig in, Steve. McAllen might show up any minute."

Sharp finished his pie before I was half done and excused himself to visit the privy. The ham steak appealed to me more than sweets, so I laid my fork aside and wiped around my mouth with a napkin. Remembering Sharp's berry-stained teeth, I took a healthy swallow of coffee, swirled it, and then ran my tongue over my teeth.

"Steve Dancy!" The menacing tone at my back alarmed me. I tried to maintain a casual posture, but I made no move to turn around.

"Dancy, ya son of a bitch, we're talkin' at ya."

Shit. More than one. I made up my mind. I grasped my plate, still half full of pie, and flung it across the room. At almost the same instant, I whirled off the chair, staying low on one knee, and drew my gun. As I came around, I saw two men with guns pointed in my direction. I could see the eyes of the one on the left shifting away from where the plate splattered against the wall and back toward me. I shot him in the middle of the chest. As I swung toward the second man, a gun flash scared me so much that I shot him three times before I gained enough control to switch my attention back to the first gunman. He was no longer on his feet.

The gunfight seemed like crawling time, but it had happened so fast, the plate was still clattering across the floor. During the fight, I had heard only the report of my own six-shooter. When the echo died down, I became aware of a woman screaming like a banshee. I stepped over to the two men and saw that neither would ever get up again. Whipping my head around, I decided that the screaming came from the kitchen. In a few short steps, I found Greta huddled on the floor in the arms of her husband. She was screaming so loud, I yelled, "Where're you hit?"

Her husband buried her face in his chest and said, "She's just scared. Goddamn it, what happened?"

Sharp came barreling into the kitchen from the rear door and yelled the same thing.

"I don't know! Two men just started shooting at me."

"You whole?" Sharp asked.

"Yeah." I looked around and saw where the second man's errant shot had gone through the wall, splintering the thin paneling. No wonder the woman was scared out of her wits. Thankfully, the bullet did not hit her or her husband. I pointed with my thumb at the front room. "They're dead. It's a mess."

Sharp started toward the door, nearly bumping into McAllen and another man I recognized as the marshal. McAllen spoke first. "Is everybody in here all right?"

"Hell, no," the husband yelled. "My wife almost got killed!"

The marshal turned to another man out of view and calmly said, "Jeff, get the doctor for her."

"Right away, Marshal," said the voice from the front room, and I heard boots clunk across the hardwood planks.

The marshal remained businesslike. "Who shot those men?"

"I did. They got the drop on me, and I was lucky they didn't kill me."

The marshal looked dubious. "Both got their guns out, but only one barrel is warm."

"I shot the first one before he fired his gun."

"Really?" He looked at the other three people in the room. "Anyone see this fight?"

"I was alone," I interjected. "Marshal, I don't make a habit of killing random customers that walk into a café."

"I'm unconcerned with your habits. What happened?"

"I was eating pie with my back to the door, and I heard someone behind me yell my name. It sounded like—"

"I heard that yell," the owner interjected, his wife now crying quietly into his shoulder.

The marshal held up two fingers. "Not now. I want to hear his story."

"It was a threat. I threw a plate against the wall and whipped around with my gun out. Two men had guns drawn and pointed at me, and I shot them. That's all there was to it."

The marshal did not appear convinced. "Who were they, and why were they hunting you?"

"I don't know and I don't know."

"I do." This surprising revelation came from Captain McAllen.

The marshal raised an eyebrow toward McAllen, but before he could explain, the doctor barreled into the kitchen with a deputy right behind him. Now there were seven men in a room already crowded with a hot stove, work tables, cabinets, and a sobbing woman. "Get out!" the doctor shouted. "Let me tend to her."

I was happy to see the marshal wave toward the back door. I was not eager to revisit the bloody bodies in the front room. When we gathered between the building and the privy, the marshal turned to McAllen and said, "Yes?"

"I recognize the men. They were ranch hands at the Bolton place in Nevada. We had a bad experience there. I'll explain in your office."

"Cliff and Pete!" I exclaimed.

Now it was McAllen's turn to look surprised. "You know their names?" he asked.

"The two men that raped Jenny. I was there when she fired them."

Jenny was the wife of a politician I had supported for governor of Nevada. After his murder, I helped Jenny secure title to his ranch. The politician's bitter mother had used the ranch hands to chase Jenny away before her daughter-in-law discovered that she had inherited her husband's ranching empire.

My entanglement in Nevada politics had been dangerous, but I had thought it was over. "Why would they come after me?"

"Someone sent them," McAllen said.

"Mrs. Bolton." The sudden realization hit me hard. I thought when I had dispatched the greedy old woman to San Francisco I was done with her.

"She's the one that deserves shootin'," Sharp added.

McAllen put a hand on the marshal's shoulder. "John, can we go to your office? I can explain all this."

The marshal looked uncertain but then said, "All right, but I want to look at the bodies one more time before the undertaker hauls them away."

After they left, Sharp gave a low whistle before saying, "That Bolton woman has the devil in her. Ya won't be safe till you deal with her."

I felt a sudden pang of anxiety. "Never mind me." I grabbed Sharp's forearm. "Jeff… this means Jenny's not safe.

Chapter 4

While McAllen talked to the marshal, I raced to the telegraph office. I needed to warn Jenny that her mother-in-law was still up to her evil ways. I had thought she was safely out of the way, but obviously the old battleaxe held a grudge against me. As I trotted toward the Western Union station, I grew increasingly alarmed that she might have nefarious plans for Jenny as well. The two women hated each other, and no venomous act was beyond that old woman.

The Western Union office had only two customers, so I wouldn't have to wait long. I immediately went to a stand-up writing desk and pulled a telegraph message form to compose my warning. I stopped. What was I thinking? The Bolton ranch didn't have a telegraph station. I had gotten so used to communicating instantly with people in cities that I forgot you couldn't send a message to someone on a remote ranch.

Panting, Sharp caught up with me, and before I could explain my dilemma, he said, "Let me send the telegram to Fort Churchill. The commander knows me, an' I can git him to send a rider out to the ranch."

Without hesitation, I slid the form over to Sharp. I had a reputation in Nevada as a man-killing gunman, but Sharp owned expansive mining interests in the state. He would surely get a better response from people in authority. It suddenly occurred to me that I had just established the same reputation in Colorado. Even gunplay in self-defense earned you notoriety in this untamed frontier.

"What should we say?" I asked.

Sharp thought a minute, his pencil poised above the form. "How 'bout: *Mrs. Bolton sent Cliff and Pete to murder Dancy. Be careful. Letter to follow.*"

"Fine, but add: *Dancy unharmed.*"

"Yep. Wouldn't want the little lady to think ya was kilt. Might get her thinkin' about other suitors." Sharp's laugh made me uncomfortable. "I also need to send a telegram to the colonel with instructions, so start a letter to Jenny with the full tale while I work on this."

"What'll I say?"

"Did ya write her before like I told ya?"

"No."

"Damn it, Steve." He looked frustrated. "All right, tell her something about the fight and about the situation with McAllen's daughter. Let her know we'll be gone awhile. Then finish up by tellin' her ya love her."

"Jeff!"

"Women cotton to men that cotton to them. Tell her, ya fool."

Without responding, I went up to the clerk and bought paper, envelope, and postage. The first part of the letter went easy, but I struggled with the finish. I was still standing at the writing desk when Sharp peeked over my shoulder.

"Cat got your tongue? I thought ya wanted to be a writer. Just tell her how ya feel."

"Rejected? Lost? How do I tell Jenny I love her after she sent me on my way?"

"With pen an' ink. Ya sure are thick, Steve. Just write it. Leave this office as a return address. Ya never know 'bout women. She could be regrettin' ya left an' be pinin' away for ya. What've ya got to lose?"

"My sanity. Hell, we'll be gone for weeks, maybe more. All the while I'll be torturing myself, thinking there's a letter back here that'll change my life."

"Only if she responds in kind. Otherwise, your life goes on as now, with ya mopin' about like some lovesick youngster."

Sharp made sense. It was better to know for sure and get this behind me if it wasn't going to work out the way I wanted. I bent over the paper so Sharp couldn't see and wrote furiously. I wanted this done before I changed my mind. Then I quickly folded the paper and slipped it into the envelope.

"Did ya tell her ya love her?"

"I told her I felt the same as the last time I saw her and that if she would entertain the notion, I'd like to return to court her."

"Damn it, Steve. I've told over a dozen women that I loved 'em, and it worked every time."

"Worked? For what?"

"To git what I wanted."

"Maybe I want more than you."

Sharp just stared at me. Finally, he said, "Well, if ya won't take the advice of an older, more experienced man, then I can't help ya."

I started to make a smart response but instead simply said, "In truth, only Jenny can help me... and only if she wants to."

Chapter 5

Not knowing what else to do, Sharp and I returned to the livery. After rechecking everything, we took up our old station against the wall and used our spurs to dig deeper holes in the dirt.

"Do you think that old hag will send more killers?" I asked.

"Those two were readily available ruffians. Mrs. Bolton don't move in those circles, so I don't think it likely... at least not soon." Sharp spun his spur in the tiny furrow he had dug in the dirt. "You ain't gonna like this, Steve, but them hands proves she ain't gonna leave this be. Ya took her ranch away an' gave it to the person that stole her son."

"Jenny's husband wrote the will. I just saw that it got properly executed."

"To that ol' shrew's way of thinkin', you messed in her business."

"What should I do?"

"Jenny knows her mother-in-law better'n us. She'll protect herself. Keep your mind on our business at hand."

In less time than I expected, McAllen and his friend from the Pinkertons marched up the street with more purpose than a couple of generals about to go into battle.

"Let's go. We're late," McAllen snapped.

"I'm free to go? No charges?" I asked.

"Not entirely. I'll explain on the trail," was all McAllen said.

Wordlessly, we saddled our riding horses and gave the packhorse loads a final tug to insure that they were secure. Swinging into the saddle, I rubbed Chestnut's neck and then pulled the reins lightly to guide him into the street. I had owned numerous horses in the East, but none compared with Chestnut for steady character, trail skills, and endurance. He had carried me all over the West for more than a year, and we got along just fine. The dime novels talked about how cowboys loved their horses. I could certainly see how affection grew between man and horse, but I still preferred humankind. Maybe I hadn't been in the West long enough yet.

We rode single file out of town, but as soon as we emerged into open country, McAllen turned in his saddle and waved me up. I trotted up the string of horses and settled into an easy walking gait beside McAllen.

"You'll face a hearing on our return."

"But the marshal still let me leave town?"

"In my custody... with my promise you won't bolt."

"So I'm your prisoner?"

"I'm just responsible for your behavior. You have to be back in nineteen days, when the judge's circuit brings him to Durango."

"What if we haven't found your daughter by then? Sharp bought enough supplies to get us through the winter."

McAllen glanced back toward Sharp but said only, "Nineteen days should be enough."

"Did the marshal buy my story?"

"After I vouched for you and explained the rest. Those two had made a nuisance of themselves around town, and a witness saw them hanging around outside the café until they saw you alone. I don't think you'll have a problem, but this ain't Pickhandle. They got real law here."

In Pickhandle Gulch, I had also killed two men in a street fight, but the town was so lawless that no one even questioned me. Before that incident, I had never even shot at a man before. I had learned to handle firearms growing up in my father's New York City gun shop. After he died, I ran the high-end shop and practiced or tested new models several hours a day. I became proficient with handguns, rifles, and shotguns.

"Are you going to introduce your friend?" I asked.

McAllen reined up and waited for all four of us to gather in a rough circle. "Jeff Sharp and Steve Dancy, I'd like to introduce Alfred Mathers, but he prefers to go by Red."

Red wore his black hair short, and his high cheekbones and sturdy-looking chin made him look formidable.

"Half-breed?" Sharp asked.

"My father was Shoshone, but I speak Ute. My Indian name is Red Oriole."

Sharp laughed. "That explains the absence of red hair." He reached out his hand. "Welcome to our little band." After handshakes all around, Sharp asked, "Known our cordial leader long?"

"I track for the Pinkertons. The captain an' I have done a few assignments together."

"What were you doing this morning?" I was curious, because I knew McAllen never allowed his men to sit idle.

"The captain—"

"Steve, you asked for an introduction. You got it. We're wasting time. I'll explain after we've made camp tonight." To punctuate his point, McAllen wheeled his horse around and resumed riding southwest.

Chapter 6

Because of the shooting at the café, we didn't reach our destination before nightfall. Red had ridden on ahead to scout the terrain, and by the time we caught up with him at dusk, he had trout cooking on sticks extended over a welcoming fire. We ate in near silence and bedded down early to escape the chill.

The next morning, we rode hard, and in about four hours, we arrived at the location in the San Juan basin where the girl was believed to have been snatched. McAllen had already explained that Maggie boarded her horse at her aunt's ranch, which we had passed an hour previously. Ever since she had finished her schooling, her father would occasionally ride her out in a buckboard so she could stay a week or so at his sister's place. Maggie loved her aunt, the ranch, and her horse. When the weather was clear, she would often go riding after her chores.

One of the early posses had found tracks in a broad meadow, and they believed that those tracks indicated the likely place where she had been abducted. We relied on their description and rode directly to the meadow. When we reached the spot, McAllen pulled up and lifted a hand to stop us. He nodded at Red, who dismounted and walked the ground ahead of us.

I looked around the pleasant field. It was ghostly still. In fact, the meadow seemed so peaceful that it felt like a place of worship. It was hard to believe that an abduction of a young girl had disturbed this tranquility.

"This may take a bit," McAllen said. "Unsaddle and let our horses graze free. Picket the packhorses in good grass . . . don't unload them."

Conversation had been minimal during the ride, and no one grew chatty now that we had stopped. Sharp and I pulled a western-style saddle off Red's horse, while McAllen kept a careful eye on his friend's investigation of the scene.

In less than an hour, Red quick-paced back toward us. "Useless. Too many horses trampled the site." He pointed. "The last posse headed southwest, along the mesas."

McAllen hefted his saddle by the horn. "Let's go. Without tracks, we follow the posse. Hopefully, their tracker knows what he's about. Steve, you ride with Red along the south side. Jeff and I will take the packhorses and scout the north. Stay within sight. If anyone sees a trail not left by one of those dunderfooted posses, yell out."

"And if we get attacked by Utes?" I asked, meaning it as a joke.

"Shoot back," McAllen ordered without humor. With no further ado, McAllen set off.

As we rode, Red focused on the ground in front of us. I couldn't tell the difference between posse tracks and a herd of elk, so I watched the cliffs. I thought I spotted something unusual high up in a cliff in one of the side canyons. The natural lines seemed disturbed by a squared pattern that appeared man-made. I couldn't be sure, because everything along the cliff line was the same color. I dug into my saddlebag and pulled out the field glasses that Sharp had bought. On closer inspection, I had no doubt that men had used rock blocks to build a shelter under a crescent-shaped overhang.

I pointed and asked Red, "What's that shelter built into the cliff?"

He didn't bother to look where I was pointing. "Ruins."

"How old?"

"Don't know." I thought this was all he was going to say, but then he added, "Bigger ones deeper in those canyons."

I wanted to go and explore, but I knew better. I'd have to come back after we rescued Maggie and hire a guide. "What's the name of that place? The bigger ones?"

"Don't know."

"Who lived in those cliff dwellings?"

"Indians."

"What tribe?"

"Don't know."

"What happened to them?"

"No one knows."

I belatedly took the hint and kept my remaining questions to myself. As a writer, I appreciate solitude, but I don't mind a little conversation on occasion. No wonder Red and McAllen were friends. I could see the two of them regaling each other with silence on those long rides into the wilderness. If either Sharp or I had tracking skills, we could have ridden together and talked as much as we liked. On second thought, Sharp would have harassed me about Jenny. Better to be teamed up with Red and his *Don't knows.*

In a couple hours, the sun had set, and twilight made it increasingly difficult to see. I was also hungry. Breakfast had been slight, and our noonday meal had been apples eaten in the saddle. Suddenly, out of the gathering gloom, I saw McAllen and Sharp ride toward us. I hoped we were still distant enough from our prey that we could have a campfire to ward off the chill. I needed to get used to the hardship ahead, but I liked comforts. City upbringing, I guess.

"Anything?" McAllen asked.

"No." That was the eighteenth word Red had spoken since we had separated. I had been so bored, I had counted.

"How about that chasm for the night?"

We all looked where McAllen pointed, but it was getting so dark I could barely make out two rocky ridges protruding into the narrowing valley about a quarter mile ahead.

"I'll scout it." With that, Red galloped away to secure us a cozy abode.

"Do Indians attack at night?" I asked as we walked our horses leisurely behind Red's dust trail.

McAllen gave me an irritated look. "Only Easterners and dime novelists think Indians quit fighting when the sun goes down." After a few paces, McAllen added, "They do like to use the cover of darkness to sneak up and attack at first light. Probably where the myth came from. But don't worry. We're only hours out of Durango. The Utes are far away."

McAllen walked for another minute before saying, "Most men bed down deep in a canyon, thinking they've found safe haven. Problem is, Indians can scurry alongside the ridgeline and catch you unawares. I prefer to encamp at the mouth. Good line of sight, but you can fall back if attacked."

This almost amounted to a speech for McAllen, so I presumed he took seriously his promise to teach me wilderness skills. I had to ask. "Fire tonight?"

"No, but it should be safe to have a small fire in the morning for coffee."

Just as I had feared. At least we would have hot coffee to wake up to. As soon as the sun went down, the autumn air in these foothills turned brisk. I decided to sleep in the fleece coat Sharp had bought.

When we caught up with Red, he merely nodded to signal that no danger lurked nearby. In short order, we had unpacked and unsaddled the horses and used loose brush and branches to fence the end of the chasm as a crude pen. I had no fear of Chestnut wandering away, but McAllen explained that our rented packhorses might head back to the livery if we failed to corral or picket them.

After we had laid out our bedrolls, Sharp made my night. He got permission from McAllen to cook some beans at the back of our little gulch.

"Can I help?" I asked.

"Ever done much cooking?"

"No."

He threw me two cans. "Then carry these tins. Ain't no boys for hire out here."

I laughed and started off, but Sharp began digging around in the burlap sacks, so I ended up waiting awhile. When he stood, he had a paper-wrapped parcel, a small bottle, and a heavy sack. He shoved them all in a cast iron pot and hung it over my arm.

After he had given me the entire load, Sharp said, "McAllen may know how to track dangerous men, but he can't cook worth a shit. Let's go."

Sharp arranged rocks in a small circle and then piled wood on top and set the whole thing ablaze. As the fire burned, he opened the tins with his knife and poured them into the pot. The paper parcel hid bacon, and he tore six slices into tiny bits and threw them in with the beans. He took a fistful of sugar from the heavy sack and dumped that into the pot. The small bottle held Lea & Perrins Worcestershire Sauce, and Sharp splashed the surface with a generous covering. After making a self-satisfied grunt, he used his knife to stir the concoction.

"Looks like we get our pig, after all," I said.

"Yep. Ya kinda ruined our noonday meal yesterday. That woman was so scared, she's gonna be useless in the kitchen for weeks."

"I'll try to behave more civilized in the future."

Sharp used his knife to knock all the embers inside his small rock circle and added a few more pieces of kindling. Next, he settled the pot on his makeshift rock grill.

"Will that work?" I asked.

"Hell, them rocks an' embers are hotter than a stove top. Done this lots of times. Later, we'll bury the rocks under our bedrolls to help keep us warm."

A couple of small boulders served as convenient seats to watch his handiwork. We were inside the pen, but the horses ignored us as they tried to find their own meal between the rocky outcroppings. We both pulled out tobacco, Sharp to roll a cigarette and me to tamp a load into my pipe.

Sharp licked the edge of the paper and sealed an expertly rolled cigarette. After watching his beans for a while, he hooked a thumb behind him. "Chestnut handles this wilderness like he was born to it."

"He feels different under me since we ventured off the road." I grinned at Sharp. "Fancy-free and unfettered, I guess."

"Probably bored ridin' them dull roads ya hold him to."

"I suspect you're right." I drew on my pipe. "Chestnut probably thinks I'm too citified as well."

"Well, do me a favor … don't start behaving civilized just yet."

Chapter 7

I had lugged the fixings for dinner to the back of our sheltering outcrop, but Sharp proudly carried the pot containing his concoction back to camp. Using his handkerchief to hold the hot handle, he reminded me of a priest swinging a censer before an expectant congregation. I, of course, brought along the sugar, bacon, and Worcestershire sauce. When we got back, McAllen was sitting alone on his bedroll with his back against his saddle.

"Took long enough."

"After ya taste these beans, ya'll quit eatin' 'em cold out of the can," Sharp retorted. "Where's Red?"

"He said he was going to scout around, but he took paper with him, so I suppose he had other duties."

The reminder of our primitive facilities did not delight me. While Sharp got out some tin plates and forks, I stuffed the sundries back into the gunnysacks and found the hardtack. Soon, we were ready for our feast.

Red returned wordlessly, and we all set upon eating. I may have been overly hungry, but I devoured the beans, which tasted better than I had expected. After I emptied my plate, I went back to the pot and was disappointed to see it empty.

"Since you finished first, you wash the pot," Sharp said with a malicious grin.

Evidently the newcomer got the menial tasks. I started toward the canteen, but Sharp yelled, "Hey, use dirt."

"Dirt?"

"Yep. Just grab handfuls of dirt an' rub 'em around the pot till the dirt falls out dry. Use yer 'kerchief to finish the job."

I looked at McAllen, but his nod told me this was not some tenderfoot joke. I did as Sharp said and was surprised when the pot appeared clean after I had finished.

When I handed the pot to Sharp for inspection, he whistled and said it looked just dandy for the morning coffee. That didn't sound appealing, but Sharp had already proved his skill around a campfire, so his coffee would probably be good as well. I guess a little dirt never hurt anyone. As I snapped my handkerchief in the air to rid it of dust, my three companions started laughing uproariously.

"Did I do something wrong?"

"You did just right," McAllen said. "Tell me, when you were on your own, did you use precious water to wash up after a meal?"

When I left New York, I had traveled by train to Denver and then bought myself a horse and appropriate gear for the road. I rode alone from Denver through the Rockies and Utah until I reached Nevada. The trip taught me how much I didn't know about how to live outdoors. "Mostly I found towns or inns, but if I couldn't, I ate cold—right out of the tin."

"Stayed on roads, I bet."

I couldn't understand why McAllen found this amusing. "I came to explore the frontier, not the wilderness."

"Our quarry prefers the backcountry," McAllen said.

"Indians don't like to be penned like horses," Red muttered to himself. This comment caught me by surprise. The sentence could almost have counted as a soliloquy for Red.

McAllen made a guttural noise to pull our attention back to him. "This morning I had Red send a few telegrams to get the story about a Ute uprising that happened up north last week. The White River Utes attacked an army troop. Killed plenty. Then it appears that yesterday they wiped out the Indian Agency on the reservation, murdering a man named Meeker and seven of his staff. More to the point, they stole Meeker's daughter—a sixteen-year-old girl—and her two children."

"How far away?" Sharp asked, suddenly interested.

"Over two hundred miles as the crow flies. Further around the mountains."

"Doesn't sound like our renegades," Sharp said.

"Nope. Hard five-, six-day ride away." McAllen kicked at the dirt a few times. "This is a separate band, but Meeker's the one that got the Utes riled." McAllen kicked again. "Forget what happened up north. We gotta track this band."

"Problem is those other posses messed the trail." Sharp looked at Red but got no response. He turned back to McAllen. "Lot of territory."

"We'll find 'em." McAllen's tone was flat, not confident.

I didn't want to think about if or when we did. Four against six or seven didn't sound promising. And how were we supposed to rescue the girl without endangering her?

"What riled the Utes up north?" I asked to get my mind off the coming fight.

"Meeker tried to turn them into Christian farmers," Red said, with a note of distaste.

Red didn't say which part of that sentence offended the Utes more. The only Indians I had encountered lived in towns, and they seemed like despondent castaways. I assumed that when in their own element, Indians were of a different character. Savages? They certainly fought savagely, but my experience in the café the other morning had not been particularly civilized. Sharp once said that Indians had the same faults as us. Without firsthand knowledge, I'd take him at his word. I was learning about a part of the West I had not yet considered. My journal had concentrated on the rough-hewn towns, and I had completely ignored the original inhabitants of this vast country. I suddenly realized I could collect valuable material for my book on this trip. For the first time, I grew somewhat excited about our venture.

"D'ya think the two snatches are connected?" Sharp's question snapped me back from my musing.

"Red doesn't think so," McAllen said.

"Why not?" I blurted out before thinking.

"Indians don't have telegraphs." Red said these words in a matter-of-fact manner, but I still felt like I had again exposed my frontier ignorance.

"Rebellions don't start overnight," McAllen explained. "These angry braves probably jumped the reservation earlier." Another kick at the dirt. "I sure hope to hell those boys don't hear 'bout this uprising."

"Why?" I asked.

"Because they'd kill the girl so they could race back to the reservation to help their brothers," Red said. "We need to find them before they learn that the Utes up north need their help."

Reminded about our grim purpose, my newly found excitement for our odyssey dimmed. I might learn more than I wanted about the savagery of small-group warfare in remote environs where white men were newcomers.

"Turn in. I want to start at first light," McAllen ordered.

"Do ya have a plan?" Sharp asked.

"A shaky one. The other posses probably drove the Utes deep into the mountains. Winter's coming, so I think they'll avoid the high country to the north." McAllen kicked the dirt again. I realized that the calmest man I had ever met was nervous. "After we pass through this valley, we'll head southwest. Red'll pick the route. Hopefully, the instincts of his Indian half will put us on the right trail."

I looked at Red. "Were you raised a Shoshone?"

"I lived with my father's family until we were forced onto a reservation, then he sent me to my mother in Denver. When I was old enough, I returned to my father for a few years, but it wasn't what I expected."

"You didn't fit anymore?"

Red met my eyes for the first time. "I fit with the Pinkertons." When Red finally spoke, he seemed to have a few burrs.

Sharp used a light tone to change the subject. "Gonna think with yer Indian half tomorrow?"

"Like a Ute, not Shoshone. They're mountain people."

McAllen returned to his bedroll, scooted down, and threw a blanket over himself. The three of us followed suit. After a few quiet moments, Sharp said, "Killin' troopers, wiping out an Indian Agency: at least those acts kinda make sense. Hurt the ones that hurt you. But stealing this girl? It just gets men chasing ya for no purpose."

"They have a purpose," Red said out of the dark.

"What purpose?" I asked, leaning up on an elbow.

Red stared at the stars. "Don't know."

Chapter 8

The next day we ran across no tracks, no people, and no decent game. We stopped in the late afternoon, and McAllen told us to set up camp below an imposing mesa. The quiet meadow took my breath away. The valley narrowed at this point, with steeply sloped gorges heading off in any number of directions. A thin waterfall splashed against some rocks at the base of our cliff and then disappeared into the ground.

We were surrounded by towering rock faces but still had vistas between the valley walls that extended out to the flatlands for tens of miles. The brown and gold hues and unlimited horizon made the whole scene seem unreal to someone raised in the East, where impenetrable walls of green trees blocked an extended view. It suddenly occurred to me that the big sky, vast landscape, and soaring monuments gave westerners a sense of freedom and boundless opportunity not shared by their eastern neighbors, who could seldom see a thriving community less than a mile away.

It was beautiful, and I wanted to make entries in my journal, but it had also gone from brisk to downright cold. I wondered if I could hold a pencil steady enough to read my own writing when I got warmer.

As I was wondering if I would even have time for my journal, McAllen ordered, "Set up for a few days."

"The horses?" I asked.

"Probably won't run back now, but picket the packhorses a good distance apart in good feed. Let our saddle horses graze free."

McAllen and Red walked off to speak in private, so Sharp and I unloaded the packhorses and started arranging our supplies behind some huge boulders that had fallen down from the cliff. I glanced up but didn't see any fissures that seemed ready to drop a new load onto our heads. It took about an hour for us to get the three packhorses hobbled by the front foot on picket lines and to get the equipment and supplies stowed in some type of order.

When we started to unsaddle our mounts, McAllen yelled from a distance, "Leave Red's horse alone!"

"What's going on?" I asked Sharp.

"Red's going to scout those gorges an' try to pick up their trail. We'll wait here for him until he can tell us which way to go."

"Days?"

"Unless he gets real lucky."

I looked around at the terrain. "They think the Utes came this way because there're so many routes they could take out of this valley. Rocky surfaces too."

"You're learning, Steve. 'Fore long, ya'll be a regular frontiersman."

I hooked a thumb at the rest of our party. "What're they talking about?"

"Probably how far Red should track 'em if he finds signs."

"Wouldn't it be dangerous for him to approach alone?"

"Not if Red's father taught him well. Damn sight safer than the four of us and seven horses pounding after 'em."

"Then we may be here awhile," I mused.

"Yep. Good place too. Can't come at us from behind, an' these boulders'll stop any bullets they throw at us from the front."

I looked up and down the still valley. I saw no life, and the only sound I heard was a distant crow making an ugly squawk like something had jerked its leg. Otherwise, it was dead quiet, and our camp felt as lonely as a graveyard in an abandoned town. "I bet they're long gone."

"Probably, but ya can't be too careful."

"Of course you can … but I guess that means no fires."

"No fires." Sharp swung his arm around. "See them ridges? Easy to spot even a small fire from up there."

"Then they've probably already seen us."

"Not necessarily. Indians have a low opinion of whites. They know we like fires when it's cold. They might take a peek over that ridge at nightfall but otherwise ignore this valley."

"Sounds careless."

"Not from their point of view. They surely got a bead on that other posse, so occasionally, they'll just check to see if there's another group of pursuers. A second party's not their first concern."

"Thinking like an Indian?"

"Thinkin' like someone pursued." Sharp unbridled one of the packhorses and gave him a swat on the rear to move him out of his way. "That other posse messed the trail, but they'll also keep that Ute band busy. 'Bout time those boys lent us a hand."

Our riding partners meandered back and, without a word, Red mounted and walked his horse away from us along the cliff line. McAllen looked over our handiwork and offered no suggestions. He hefted his saddle and laid it up against a boulder. Then he did something I copied. With both hands, he started pulling out the long grass and throwing it where he intended to put his bedroll. I guessed they decided Red would track the Utes all the way to their lair. If we were going to be here awhile, might as well get comfortable.

It took us half an hour to pull enough grass for our crude mattresses. The sun had slid behind a mountain peak, turning the rock formations red and gold with a scattering of green splotches from the low-lying junipers.

McAllen seemed to mull something over and then said, "Gather up some dry wood for a fire in the morning."

Sharp looked puzzled. "A fire can be seen from above."

"Only from the north if we build it close to the cliff." McAllen examined the mountains to the north of us. "Hell, if they went that way, they've eluded us already."

Sharp and I trudged off to search for loose wood that wouldn't require the noise of a hatchet. "Has he lost hope?" I asked, noticing that the air had grown so cold I could see my breath.

"He's a realist. Our chances are slim."

"But—"

"Listen. We're late. He's bettin' his daughter's life that they went south. If he's wrong, we'll never find her. Let's just get some wood."

I wasn't going to argue. I was cold.

We returned with armloads of wood and picked a spot directly under the high cliff. I arranged everything so that only a match would be needed in the morning, and Sharp brought over the sacks that contained our food supply. About thirty feet away, McAllen sat cleaning his rifle against one of the boulders that fortified our new home.

"How 'bout fish for dinner?" Sharp asked as he went over to our pile of gunnysacks.

"I see a waterfall, but I don't see a stream," I said.

"Sardines . . . canned."

"Sounds better than cold beans. I'm not sure I'd enjoy them out of a can after that gourmet meal last night."

"Exactly. Pales by comparison."

With that, Sharp pulled out three cans of sardines and some hardtack biscuits. Now I understood why Sharp had been eager to eat at Greta's again. Then he tossed me three apples that I barely managed to juggle. "Dessert," he said.

When we had finished eating, McAllen said, "We need to post a sentry. Steve, you take the first few hours, I'll take the middle, and Jeff the last."

"What am I looking for?" I asked.

"Nothing. You won't see shit with this moon. Listen. Try to pick out any unusual sounds."

"Don't get mad if I wake you because one of our horses decides to night graze."

"I'll be mad if you don't. Them horses'll give us our first warning."

I nodded, well aware that I had been given the easiest hours. No one seemed to have anything more to say, so I got out my own rifle to clean in the remaining light.

"You're handy with a pistol and steady in a fight, but I don't expect any close-in work. Ya any good with that long gun?" McAllen asked.

"Better."

"Sounds boastful."

"I don't think you want a demonstration. Might be a bit noisy."

"Nope. Take you at your word."

I carried a Winchester '76 that used 45-75 cartridges. My model had the standard extended magazine that held twelve cartridges, plus one in the chamber. Being a gunsmith, I had modified the rifle, just as I had improved my factory Colt. I started with the pick of the litter, lightened the trigger pull, attached a custom target sight, and added a lighter hammer spring. The ammunition was my own load, using English powder for a cleaner burn. It was a fine weapon, and my skill had been honed by practice in my gun shop and in the field. Like my father, I seemed to have a natural way with guns.

I thought about what McAllen had said. His question about my skill with a rifle meant he intended to ambush the renegades. I knew the numbers dictated surprising the Utes, but shooting men from a distance bothered me. It seemed less like a fight and more like murder. I knew enough about McAllen to know he was tough, but he was not ruthless, and he operated according to a strict code of honor. Still, I wondered if I could trust his judgment when his daughter was involved.

As I finished cleaning my rifle, Sharp and McAllen crawled into their bedrolls. Not knowing what else to do, I grabbed my saddle and carried it to the other side of a boulder, leaning it against the rock for a backrest. McAllen had been right about the moon, something he probably kept track of in his business. When the sun had completely set, I could not see more than a few yards.

I rested my Winchester in my lap and listened for all I was worth.

Chapter 9

Our four-day encampment could not have been less eventful. Sharp cooked a respectable breakfast each morning, we ate out of tins in the evening, and, while they lasted, we ate apples midday. Between meals we gnawed on jerky and occasionally sucked a peppermint stick.

For the most part, I spent the time writing in my journal. When I reviewed my notations, they seemed to dwell on how uncomfortable I was rather than on the breathtaking country. And it was beautiful. The high meadow was exceptionally quiet, except for a soft whistle that came each afternoon with the gentle breeze. The rust-colored mesas that soared above our heads looked grand and ethereal. Misshapen junipers clung precariously to naked cliff faces, while most of the flat ground seemed to be covered by low-lying gamble oaks. The fall colors ran mostly to browns and dull reds instead of the myriad colors I was used to in the East. At first, my prejudices told me that autumn was prettier in New York, but the muted colors of this high desert blended perfectly with the red rocks and dusty green plants.

This was grander than the nature that Thoreau wrote about. I should've been enthralled, not pining for a comfortable chair, a hot drink, and an even hotter fire. I would have reprimanded myself, but I knew that Thoreau's idealized Walden Pond was actually only a short walk to these same accoutrements that he enjoyed on a regular basis at his friend Emerson's house. I was about to make a notation along this theme when it struck me that easterners thought Walden Pond was raw nature, unsullied by man. In contrast, we were two days' ride from a rustic encampment that offered few human comforts. Thoreau risked mosquito bites to experience nature. We were hunting men bred to the wilderness, so we could kill them—or perhaps be killed by them. In the West, nature was beautiful and imposing, but it was also dangerous.

My respect for McAllen's fortitude grew by the day. He showed no outward sign of impatience when Red did not return. In his place, I would have paced and probably cursed the heavens, worried that Red had been killed or captured. The previous day, I had asked McAllen about Red's return, and he had simply said that we wouldn't see Red until he located our band of renegades.

McAllen appeared to have picked our campsite offhandedly. Four days had taught me how impressions can be wrong. Sharp had found a recess in the rocks to build his morning fires that could not be seen from above. The boulders gave us protection from attack and shelter from the chilling wind. We had climbed through some rocky shale to enter this shelflike plateau, and the horses seemed content not to challenge the loose rocks downhill as long as there was ample grass nearby. Even the little waterfall had unanticipated benefits. I could rinse my dirt-scrubbed pots and plates without sullying my handkerchief.

In fact, I was doing just this chore when I heard Sharp say that he could see Red riding toward us. I hastily shook the water free, threw the plates into our do-everything pot, and scrambled to watch Red ride in. He looked as fresh as if he had been out on a half-hour ride, but his face told me nothing, so I checked McAllen's expression. Nothing there either.

Red dismounted and walked straight up to McAllen. "I found them."

"And?"

"The girl is not with them."

Chapter 10

Through tight lips, McAllen asked, "Where are they?"

"Half day's hard ride . . . in a small valley, a ways up Sleeping Ute Mountain." Red pointed. "Probably went there because they feel safe. Legend says the sleeping Ute is a great warrior-god that will slay the enemies of the Ute."

McAllen didn't bother to look toward the mountain. "No sign of my daughter?"

Red uncharacteristically looked away and then met McAllen's eyes. "They have her horse . . . and I saw them using her dress for a sack."

"A sack?"

"They tied the neck with the arms and used it to collect berries."

Only McAllen's eyes changed. "How many?"

"Seven. One's a young brave."

"Tell me the rest."

"After two days, I had found no tracks. I picked up the other posse on the first day, so I went back and followed them, hoping they had discovered the trail and covered it over with their own horses. They led me straight to the Utes."

"They have a tracker with them," Sharp offered.

Red nodded. "They camped two miles from the band. Only one horse went back and forth . . . at least twice. Looks like they powwowed."

McAllen paced back and forth. Finally, he stopped in front of Red. "Same rider or different riders?" McAllen seemed to think this was important. "The half-breed might have approached first and returned for instructions. Another rider might have gone in to negotiate."

"The tracks weren't clear enough to be sure, but my guess is two different riders."

"Damn!" McAllen paced some more.

"That posse was het up," Sharp said. "Why would they let the Utes go free if they killed your daughter? The Utes must have turned your daughter over to them."

"The band was not wary," Red offered.

"See, they released her," Sharp said encouragingly.

"Naked?" McAllen spit the word with so much anger, he frightened me.

We all stood silent until Sharp had the courage to say, "Perhaps they had other clothes for her?"

"Less valuable than a berry sack?" McAllen's voice showed frustration with this line of thought. "Jeff, take Steve back to Durango."

"You need us," I protested.

"This is gonna get brutal. I don't want a do-gooder along."

"An odd handle for me after what we've been through together."

McAllen gave me a hard look. "I ain't looking for a fair fight."

"What *are* ya lookin' for?" Sharp asked with an edge. "Revenge?"

McAllen swung around on Sharp. "Answers. This stinks. I want to know what happened and why. We're gonna take two alive and get answers."

The number worried me. If McAllen wanted two, it meant he thought one might not talk before he lost the ability to talk. This *was* going to get brutal. It seemed that both McAllen and Sharp harbored serious doubts about this abduction, so I turned to Red. "How does this affair strike you?"

Red took so long to answer, I thought he might refuse to respond. Finally, he said, "The Utes up north are on the warpath, but these braves probably jumped the reservation weeks or months ago. They don't act like a war party. No other marauding. A tribe will raise whites as their own but not renegades. Renegades wage war or hide. These look to be hiding."

"Is it likely they would kill the girl?" I threw a sideways glance at McAllen but continued anyway. "After they were through with her."

Red swallowed. "They would have used her and killed her right off... or kept her for the winter." He hesitated and then added, "I believe these Utes jumped the reservation merely to live the way of their fathers. How they got involved with the girl looks strange. I don't understand it."

"Damn it, those Indians ain't gonna stay put forever!" McAllen yelled. "I want to scout their camp before nightfall, so you two get going... or wait here. I don't give a damn either way."

With that, McAllen went to his bed and began to roll it up. Sharp looked at me with a raised eyebrow. I nodded and went to pack my own gear.

When McAllen saw we intended to go with him, he said, "No packhorses. Take food for two days in saddlebags and hide the rest. Pen the packhorses, and we'll pick everything up on the way back. Jeff, show Steve how to collect our horses."

"Can I holler?" I asked.

"What?"

"Can I make a loud noise?"

"Sing for all I care," McAllen said. "That band of Indians is hours away."

I walked over to our food bags and rummaged around until I found a carrot. Walking a little way out of camp, I cupped my hands around my mouth and yelled, "Chestnut!"

When my horse started walking in our direction, I snapped the carrot. Chestnut immediately trotted right over. When Sharp looked dumbfounded, I said, "So … how do you collect your horse?"

Despite the situation, Sharp laughed. McAllen did not. He just picked up his lariat and went after his own horse.

Chapter 11

In five hours we were on a rise above the Ute camp, peering down at them through field glasses. We had left the horses behind a ridge and scurried low until we took shelter behind some brush overlooking a small meadow. The Utes were digging in for the winter. They had constructed shelters out of branches and covered most of them in hides. Three of the men were dressing a deer. They hung the skins to dry and carved off the meat in thin strips and hung them as well. In a few minutes, a teen Ute emerged from the woods toting the dress with something inside that weighted it down.

"I count five," McAllen said. "The other two are probably hunting. We wait for all seven." McAllen handed me the field glasses. "Are you as good a shot as you said?"

"What do you want me to hit?"

"I want you to shoot two of the Utes in the shoulder or leg… from here."

I didn't put the field glasses up to my eyes. "Tough. About two hundred yards." I thought about it. "The shoulder's risky, and a man hit in the leg can still have a lot of fight."

"Then go for the leg. They're not carrying weapons."

"Have to be fast. The second man might be moving." I was talking to myself.

"Boy."

"Boy?"

"Shoot one of the men first, and then go for that boy."

"I don't know if I can shoot a boy."

"For God's sake, Steve, we're gonna kill the rest."

"Don't give me that, Captain. You want the boy because you think it'll be easier to make him talk."

"Damn it; just tell me… can you do it?"

"You're going to kill them from ambush?" I asked. "The other party *talked* to them."

"Someone in the other party was in cahoots with them."

"What?"

"Tell 'em, Red."

"If they'd murdered the girl, they would kill anyone who approached and run. Probably the same if they still had the girl. And they wouldn't parley with a white if one of their own was in the party."

"You don't know that, and you aren't even sure two different riders went into their camp."

"Look at them," McAllen said. "They show no fear of reprisal. This meadow may be hidden, but it's low. A good place to ride out a winter, but too close to travel lanes for fugitives. They're not afraid."

"The posse came directly here," Red added.

"An' the posse didn't attack," Sharp threw in. "Odd—whether they got the girl back or not. Those men tramped out here to be town heroes."

All of them seemed convinced. "Say you're right. Then the real culprit is back in town, the one that wanted your daughter abducted by these Indians."

"Damn it, Steve. This is why I told you to go back. You're headstrong and always go against my counsel. You did it in Nevada and now here." McAllen turned his face to the ground and took a deep breath. "Listen, those Indians didn't ride up and snatch her. She rode into them. Her mother told me she rode the same trail every day, through that pastureland below Mesa Verde—the main route to Colorado from the West. She was an expert rider on a good horse. A band of Indians couldn't catch her in that open ground. Did you notice that swale close by where she got grabbed?"

I thought back. "Yeah."

"They waited for her. Renegades hiding along a heavily traveled route to capture a girl when she rode into them." McAllen pounded his fist in the earth. "They knew her routine."

I picked up the field glasses to examine the scene and to give myself time to think. Sharp had held reservations from the beginning. McAllen and Red were experienced with Indians, and their Pinkerton jobs forced them to think like criminals. They must be right. I had been forewarned this venture would be brutal, and there was no reason to argue further.

I pushed the glasses away from my face. "Captain, for me to

wound them, we need to exchange rifles. Mine's designed to kill buffalo."

McAllen nodded and we switched rifles. I made a quick examination of his Winchester Model 1873 and then went back to watching the Indians prepare for winter.

A sharp noise. Damn. The two absent Utes were behind us—directly behind us.

Chapter 12

Everybody went into action. As Sharp and McAllen rolled onto their backs, blazing away, I dropped the field glasses and picked up my rifle. I trusted the others to deal with the two behind me and pointed the rifle at the meadow. The first target that came into my sights was the boy. I shot him in the hip. I shot a second Ute in the upper leg, but he continued to limp toward some objective. I aimed to shoot him again below the waist, but just as I squeezed the trigger, his leg gave out and he fell. A spume of blood exploded from his head. I searched for any others and saw two Utes go down from a series of shots that came from Red. I spotted a lone brave racing toward one of their shelters, and when I squeezed off a single shot, a volley hit him or threw up puffs of dirt behind him. All four of us had shot at the last man. I flipped on my back to check the two who had been behind us. They were dead. All seven of the band were down. To my knowledge, no Ute had fired a shot.

"Come on!" McAllen yelled, as he leaped to his feet and bolted down to the meadow.

When I rose, my legs felt shaky, but I forced myself to run after the other three. Then I saw McAllen's concern. The only moving body was the youth. He seemed determined to crawl to the same point that was the focus of the second Ute I had shot. He was going for a weapon. McAllen ran thirty yards ahead of me, but he would not reach him in time. I stopped and fired two shots into the ground ahead of the boy, but he didn't stop. If he reached a rifle, he would be killed. I hesitated just a moment, and then shot him again in the leg. He uttered no sound that I could hear, but thankfully he quit crawling.

When I caught up, the three men had formed a rough circle around the youth as Red talked to him in a quiet tone. I saw the knife. He may have been crippled, but he still had fight. Red said a few more words, and the youth finally flipped the knife away. McAllen and Sharp immediately left to check the other Utes. While I kept my rifle on the boy, Red picked up the knife, went over to a shelter, and cut a long strip of leather from a hide the Indians had used to cover the branch structure. He brought it back and used it as a tourniquet on the boy's leg. The hip wound would be more difficult. Red was cutting open the dress when McAllen returned.

"What are you doing?" McAllen demanded.

"Making a compress," Red said.

"Not with my daughter's dress. Find something else."

"Captain—"

"No, goddamn it!"

Red looked about to drop the dress on the ground, but he quickly curbed the impulse and handed it to McAllen. Then he walked off, evidently to find other material.

McAllen turned his wrath on me. "I told you I wanted two alive."

"Well, you got one. Better make the most of it." The fight had made me edgy as well.

"Damn it. I meant to threaten to kill the boy if the brave didn't answer my questions. Now, I gotta get my answers from that child."

A child he was. From a distance, I had guessed he had reached his teen years, but up close he looked as young as ten or eleven. I felt ready to explode, but suddenly fatigue, and perhaps the relief of still being alive, washed over me. "Captain, I tried."

McAllen's hard face softened. "I know... sorry, Steve." He looked at the ruined dress in his hand and sadness seemed to overwhelm him. "Things don't always go the way you want in a fight." If possible, his expression became even more forlorn. Before I could think of any words of comfort, he turned and walked away. As I watched him retreat, I saw McAllen smell the berry-stained dress.

"Ya know about treatin' wounds?" Sharp pulled me back to our situation.

"Not much."

"Then I'll help Red. Why don't ya check those shelters for any sign of the girl?"

I started off toward the first shelter, thankful for something to do.

Just as I stepped away, Sharp added, "Be careful. Enter rifle first. Could be more'n we thought."

I found no more Utes. Of the four partially built shelters, two were living quarters, and the other two held supplies and food stores for the winter. When I returned from searching the camp, McAllen and the others stood talking about ten feet away from the wounded youth. The captain waved me over. "Find anything?"

"I found her saddle and bridle. No personal stuff. No shoes, hat, coat." I shrugged. "Nothing."

Red and McAllen looked at each other. "You look everywhere?" McAllen asked.

I was about to give a snippy answer but caught myself. "Yeah, all four shelters. Other than her gear, no other sign of your daughter." McAllen looked puzzled so I added, "I found some things that might be normal, but they struck me as odd."

"What?" McAllen demanded.

I pointed at the two far shelters. "Inside I found canned goods, tobacco, sugar, whiskey." I thought a second. "A couple pots, a saw, an axe… stuff I didn't think Indians packed with them." I glanced at Red. "At least not Indians that want to live like their forefathers."

"I 'xpect you paid for those supplies," Sharp said.

"Me?"

"That two-hundred-dollar credit you set up at the general store."

"Jeff's right," McAllen said. "The posse probably traded those goods to the Utes."

"For what?" I asked.

"That's what Red will find out from that boy."

I looked at Red and then at the youth. "I'll go get our horses."

"Thanks," McAllen said. "Don't forget to pick up the field glasses."

Without a word, Sharp hitched up alongside me, and we both walked to the rise where we had first observed the Ute camp. I pulled out my watch and was startled to see that less than an hour had passed since the two returning hunters had surprised us.

"Will it go bad for the boy?" I asked.

"No worse than if he had been caught by Shoshone."

"Are you justifying what's going on back there?"

"Nope. Just somethin' that's gotta be done."

"Why are you with me?"

"I'd rather not be a demon in that boy's nightmares."

Chapter 13

Sharp and I each led two horses back to the Ute camp. As we approached, McAllen marched toward us looking so grim and threatening that I had to suppress an impulse to mount up and ride away.

When he got within earshot, he yelled, "We're returning to Durango. Now!"

I looked at the sky. "Captain, we can't—"

"Now, goddamn it!"

Without another word, Sharp and I stepped into our saddles, and by the time we had gathered up the reins, the rushing McAllen had reached us and swung onto his horse without a moment's hesitation.

"Jeff, run Red's horse down to the camp and tether him. Move it!"

As Sharp trotted down to the camp, I asked, "Red's not coming with us?"

"He's staying with the boy for a few days. He'll catch up later."

I felt relief that the boy was still alive. We watched Sharp in the distance lean off his saddle and flip the reins of Red's horse around a drying rack and then wheel his horse about and race back to us at a full gallop. I thought when Sharp reached us, we would get some explanation, but McAllen rode off before Sharp arrived. Soon, we made a single-file line and retraced our path from earlier in the day.

We rode hard for about an hour, and then dusk slowed us down to a walk. We were not on a trail, and the mountain terrain was rough going. Without Red to guide us, I wondered how far McAllen would continue to push on in the dark. In another half hour, I got my answer.

McAllen pulled up under some rocks in a flattish space no bigger than a one-room cabin. "We'll wait here until light," he said.

I noticed he didn't say sleep. After we dismounted and unsaddled the horses, I realized this would be a close space for three men and three horses, but it was too dark to find another place for the horses. Perhaps McAllen didn't intend to sleep.

"Build your goddamn fire," McAllen said with bitterness. "We ain't hiding from anyone now."

McAllen normally kept his thoughts to himself, and his current mood certainly did not invite questions. Sharp and I gingerly felt our way in different directions to gather up some wood. Soon we had a decent fire, but that was all. Coffee and anything that might be improved with cooking had been left at base camp. We sat around the light and warmth of the fire, gnawing on jerky and hardtack between sips of Kentucky whiskey from our flasks. It had been one hell of a day.

Sharp went to his bag and pulled out a small burlap sack. As he stood over us, he popped raisins into his mouth. Finally, he dangled the sack by its tie string in front of McAllen. "Raisins, Joseph?"

I wondered for a moment whether McAllen would draw his gun or accept the offer. Eventually, he reached up and accepted the sack and then spilled some of the raisins into his palm. "Sit down, Jeff. I'll tell you two what happened."

Sharp plopped down close to the fire, and we exchanged glances as we waited. I suspected that McAllen might be crying. After a long moment, he tossed the burlap bag over the fire to me and wiped his eyes with the back of his hand. "She's dead."

"I'm sorry." It was all I could think to say.

McAllen slammed his fist into the dirt. "Murdered." Sharp and I waited, and when McAllen spoke again, he seemed to have regained some control. "A white man paid the Utes to seize and murder my daughter. He told them when and how. Nothing was spur of the moment."

"Was it one of the men in the posse?" Sharp asked.

"The boy doesn't know. He wasn't allowed to hear the men talk." McAllen threw the handful of raisins into his mouth and chewed. "He knows that a man entered their camp loaded down with supplies and left with her scalp and a necklace." McAllen's voice broke with the last word of that sentence. After a minute, he continued. "I gave her that necklace last Christmas. I know that was the one the Indians gave him, because she wrote to me that she wore it every day."

"The body?" Sharp asked.

"The boy has no idea. Somewhere back along the trail. He was sent away from the camp to hunt when they murdered her."

Sharp seemed to think things over. "Could be the man just haggled to get her effects for the family, but it don't sound right. Why didn't the posse just kill 'em all an' simply take her stuff?"

"Stuff?" An edge had come back into McAllen's voice.

"Sorry, Joseph. Poor choice of words."

"Forget it," McAllen said. "But you're right. Two big questions. Why did the posse barter instead of attack, and who paid the Utes to do this?"

"You think we can get the answer in Durango?" I asked.

"Yes. From that posse. We'll leave at first light and ride down to the base camp to gather up our supplies and the packhorses. I want to be in Durango by nightfall."

That will be a hard day's ride, I thought. "When will Red join us?" I asked.

McAllen made a motion with his hand, and I threw him the bag of raisins. After chewing a mouthful, he said, "We didn't hurt the boy. He saw no reason not to tell us what little he knew." McAllen had understood the real intent of my question. "Red will stay with him until he's well enough to fend for himself or possibly take him back to Durango. The boy's choice."

Sharp put another stick in the fire. "Ya said there were two big questions. I think there's three."

"What else?" McAllen seemed nervous about what might come next.

"Why did someone do this?"

"I don't give a damn why."

"Joseph, I don't think preachers and schoolmarms make a hell of a lot of enemies."

"Meaning what, exactly?"

"Meaning, the person who did this probably meant to hurt Captain Joseph McAllen."

Chapter 14

When we rode into Durango the next evening, not a single person could be seen on the street. We stopped in the middle of the road and looked around for some sign of life. It felt ghoulish until I heard a hymn coming from the church.

"Could the whole town be in church?" I asked.

McAllen spurred his horse forward. "They're conducting services for my daughter."

The only church in town sat at the end of the lane, and the entire area around it was crowded with carriages, buckboards, and horses. After we corralled the packhorses at the livery, we tied up our horses in front of a saloon about seventy yards away from the church. As I stepped out of the stirrup, I could see only four or five people inside the saloon instead of the normal bunch of rowdies just off their shift.

McAllen immediately marched off toward the church. I followed reluctantly. I smelled bad after nearly a week in the wilderness, I needed a shave, and my clothes were covered in filth. When McAllen opened one of the church's double doors, a sea of men's backs blocked our entry. McAllen pushed his way in, and we followed. Once inside, McAllen continued to push his way to the front, but Sharp and I remained standing just behind the last row of pews.

The hymn ended, and it didn't take long to discover that we had arrived at the end of the service. I could hear wailing at the front and sobs from all over. After a final prayer by a layman, Sharp and I jostled our way out of the church and returned to where we had tethered the horses.

Walking our mounts over to the livery, I asked, "Did you see Doc?"

"Too many people. Let's get the horses quartered an' go find him."

The liveryman was at the services, so we unsaddled the horses ourselves, pitched fresh hay into their stalls, and made a quick pass at grooming them. After seeing to our mounts, we unloaded the packhorses and stacked our supplies and gear in a corner of the barn. I brushed each packhorse while they ate and then returned them to the corral. I would have preferred to spend more time brushing Chestnut, but we wanted to get back to the church so we could ask Dooley what had happened when the posse came upon the Ute renegades. A few more pitchforks of hay thrown into the corral, and we were walking back to the church.

Dooley was not hard to find. There must have been about forty people talking quietly outside the church, and Dooley stood with a couple other unattached men. We caught his eye and waved him over.

"Sad day for the town," Dooley said.

"Sadder for Captain McAllen," Sharp said.

Dooley looked puzzled, so I explained. "McAllen used to be married to the schoolmarm. Long time ago. The girl was his daughter."

"Oh, my God. I had no idea."

"What happened out there?" Sharp asked.

Dooley turned his back to us and whispered to himself. "So that's why McAllen rushed here."

"What happened?" Sharp repeated in a commanding voice.

Dooley returned his attention to us. "We got there too late . . . damn it, Grant should've gotten off sooner."

"Doc?" Sharp was getting impatient.

Dooley wiped his forehead. "The half-breed tracked us right to them. He went in to parley—to see if he could barter for the girl—but they had already killed her." Dooley went in another direction again. "Did you hear about that Meeker massacre up north?"

"Yeah, go on," Sharp insisted.

"Well, Grant went in with a bunch of supplies and got her, uh . . ."

"Scalp," Sharp said with a sharp tone. "Why didn't ya attack and kill the sons a bitches?"

"They had already joined up with a bigger war party. The half-breed said there had to be over thirty of 'em. It woulda been suicide."

Sharp and I looked at each other. Finally, I asked, "Did Grant say that there were over thirty, or just the half-breed?"

"What? Why?"

"Damn it, just tell us. Did they both confirm a large war party?" I was getting as frustrated as Sharp with Dooley's obfuscation.

Dooley rubbed the back of his neck. "No, I don't think Grant said anything about it, as far as I can recollect."

"When we came on 'em, there were only six braves and one boy," Sharp said.

"Maybe they split up after we left."

"There were no signs of a larger party," I said. "I searched the camp myself."

"You checked the camp? How? Had they left?"

"In a way of speakin'," Sharp said. "We killed 'em. All but the boy."

"Oh, my God."

"Doc, no war party camped in that meadow." Sharp had lost all patience. "Only a ragtag band of renegades. Now, where's this half-breed and Grant? I want to talk to 'em."

"Gone."

"Gone? Gone where?"

"The half-breed left us on the trail. Said his work was through. Grant paid his respects to the family and left for Leadville yesterday." Dooley looked back at the crowd in front of the church. "Grant said he had urgent business, but everyone assumed he was actually embarrassed by our failure."

"We better find McAllen," I said.

Dooley looked back at the church again. "He's still in the church. We're waiting for the burial service."

"Burial?" I asked.

"The minister bought a coffin and put her, uh, remains in it. They're going to bury her in a few minutes. As soon as the wife is a bit more under control." Dooley looked beaten. "Damn, I'm sorry. Grant seemed such an upright fellow."

Sharp put his hand on Dooley's shoulder. "Not your fault. He had the whole town buffaloed."

"Jeff, what're we going to do?" I asked. "We've got to get after Grant and this half-breed. I think they're both in this up to their necks."

"I know. We'll deal with 'em, but first we gotta help our friend bury the dead."

Chapter 15

About two hundred people attended the burial, and even though I had never met the girl, the somber mood caught me. Evidently, she was well liked and her parents respected. It brought to mind my father's funeral. I was just twenty-four and his death jolted me. With his passing, I inherited his business interests, his substantial bank account, and his greed-driven family. I had no siblings because my mother had died in childbirth. By the time I was old enough to understand there should have been people who cared about me from her side, we had lost track of her family. I became convinced that my father's side had pushed them away. After all, they were barely middle-class, and we were among the elite of the New York City social set.

My father and I were friends. Although he had many business interests, we spent most of our time at his gun shop. He loved guns, especially expensive European shotguns. The shop catered to rich bird hunters, and we used every sale as an excuse to escort our client into the countryside to test his purchase. After his death, I grew to understand that he had no more use for his family than I did, and he used his enthusiasm for guns to escape their meddling.

My father's brothers and sisters were all the family I knew, but we did not get along before his death, and a heated feud developed afterwards. At first, they just seemed obsessed with marrying me off to some appropriate girl to seal a business partnership between two social register families. Then they dragged me into nefarious business dealings that always seemed to involve some large bribes to shady politicians. No thank you. I headed west.

A chorus of *amens* brought me back to the burial. Captain McAllen didn't stand beside his ex-wife and her current husband. I wasn't sure if it was out of respect for their relationship, or if there was ill will between them. After everyone had walked by and thrown a handful of soil into the grave, Sharp and I joined the other people moving down the hill and into town. At the bottom, Sharp stopped and glanced back up the hill. I assumed he wanted to wait for McAllen. I felt self-conscious because we looked like a couple of unwashed trail hands too ignorant to find proper dress for a funeral. As the crowd passed, we just stood there making solemn nods to people we didn't know.

Eventually, McAllen came down by himself. When he saw us, he came right over. "They want some time alone at the graveside," he said.

"What about you?" I blurted.

"I'd just as soon be by myself as well. That's the way I always saw her. I'll go back after dark."

"Did you see her often?" I asked.

"Once or twice a year. My ex-wife was always polite, but I knew I wasn't welcome. She had a new family, and I had become an intrusion."

Without a word, we started for the livery to collect our belongings. We waited for McAllen to open the subject of the Utes and the abduction. At the camp, he had seemed vengeful and anxious to get to the bottom of things. Now he kept his thoughts to himself as we worked for about an hour collecting our stuff and storing it in my room. Because Sharp had thought that we might be gone for a long time, the unused supplies took up both available corners.

As we stacked the supplies, McAllen said, "Steve, the circuit judge came around early, so they already held an inquest. No charges were filed against you. Deemed self-defense." He threw another sack onto a pile. "If you haven't written Jenny, I suggest you do it tonight."

"You too?" I threw my own sack. "Isn't it enough that Jeff keeps haranguing me about Jenny? Well, I already wrote her, but we got back too soon for a reply to arrive."

McAllen grabbed my forearm. "I don't care about any damn love letter. Write her and tell her what happened. She needs to be warned her mother-in-law ain't just socializing with the Nob Hill crowd."

Chagrined, I simply said, "I did. Jeff and I also sent a telegram before we left town."

"We need to check with Western Union," Sharp said. "She may have responded to our telegram."

We finished our work, and the three of us stood looking at my cluttered room. "I didn't pay for all this," McAllen said, "but if you don't mind, could we donate what we don't need to the church in my daughter's name?"

"Of course," Sharp said.

I gave Sharp a sideways look and said, "Jeff, we better get over to the Western Union office."

Sharp made a move toward the door, but McAllen stopped us by finally broaching the subject. "Did you find Dooley?"

"Yep, but ya won't like what we found out," Sharp said.

"I already know Grant left town. What else?"

We told him. McAllen eyes grew dark and mean, but he merely nodded. After a moment, he went to the window and looked out. "It's dark," was all he said. Then he turned to face us. "Let's get a soak and a beer. There's nothing more that can be done tonight. Besides, I need to see my ex-wife again this evening, and I think my request will be better received if I clean up."

"What do you want from her?" Sharp asked, confused.

McAllen headed for the door. "The necklace."

Chapter 16

Jenny had indeed sent a return telegram, but, as we predicted, no letter had arrived yet. The telegram was terse. It simply said, *No problem here. Being careful. Glad Steve unharmed.*

She had used my first name. Was that a good sign? I told myself not to get my hopes up. She had only responded to the warning of danger, not my more personal letter, which she may not have received yet. After I got through with my wishful thinking about her feelings toward me, I took comfort in her statement that there were no problems at the ranch. Hopefully, Mrs. Bolton would aim her wrath only at me. Then I realized that would be completely out of character for Mrs. Bolton. If she had resumed the warpath, Jenny would undoubtedly be a target.

After we returned to our boardinghouse, Sharp and I found McAllen and commandeered the bathroom. I paid the owner's son to run across the street for some chilled beers. Few things in life felt more comforting than slipping into a hot bath with a large tankard of beer in hand. The common bathroom provided little privacy, so I tipped the boy to keep the water fresh in the single tub and to shoo away any other tenants.

The stove used to heat the bathwater kept the room warm, so after our soaks, we sat in straight-back chairs with towels wrapped around our waists. After the boy had fetched our second beers, McAllen got down to business.

"Any of you got any answer other than that Grant planned this?"

"Nope," Sharp said. "He led the posse right to them. Might have been good tracking, but my bet is he knew exactly where they'd be. We know he lied about the number of Indians in order to keep the posse away from 'em."

"And the half-breed lied as well," I added.

"Yep," Sharp said, "so the two gotta be in cahoots."

McAllen took a swallow of his beer. Then another. "We know a white man paid the Utes and told them how to pick her up. The boy said nothing about any half-breed, but the two of them musta been partners."

"Does the town think this was part of the Ute uprising?" I directed my question to McAllen because he had had more contact with townspeople at the funeral and burial.

"Yep, and no use getting the people worked up about some conspiracy we can't prove." Another swallow of beer. "Besides, they all think pretty highly of this Grant fella."

"You ever have a run-in with Bob Grant?" Sharp asked.

"Not that I recollect," McAllen answered. "What's he look like?"

"Big guy, good lookin' with brown hair… what he's got left of it," Sharp said. "Looks to be about forty, probably six-two, heavy built, dresses like a city feller, an' carries a shoulder gun under a frock coat. Walks heavy-footed. Ready smile, especially for the ladies."

Sharp's description impressed me. For some reason, I had difficulty describing a person unless I had already made notes about them in my journal. Grant had not warranted an entry. Until now. I suddenly realized the book I planned about my trek through the Wild West would include at least one chapter on this nefarious character. At the next opportunity, I had to catch up my journal on recent events and make some notes on Bob Grant.

At first, McAllen remained silent after Sharp's description. Then he asked, "Any scars?"

"None that I noticed," Sharp answered.

"He has a scar." I was glad to be able to add something. "Right hand. Went from his thumb almost to the back of his wrist."

McAllen flung his tankard against the wall, splattering beer and glass shards everywhere. "Goddamn it!"

The boy burst into the room at the sound. He looked at the mess and said, "Yer gonna pay for that."

"Shut the hell up!" McAllen yelled.

"I'll pay," I said. "Please, step back outside."

He hesitated but bolted when McAllen leaned over for his gun that lay on the floor. "Go down and get us more beer!" McAllen yelled through the closed door. I heard boots immediately thud against the stairsteps.

After a long moment, McAllen said, "The man's real name is Jim Vrable. Shit! That son of a bitch. This time I'm gonna kill that bastard."

We waited. The frightened boy opened the door just enough to get his head around. "I have your beers, sir." We waved him in, and his boots made a crunching sound as he walked across the glass-strewn room. "Should I clean this up?"

"No. Leave it... and us. Now!" McAllen ordered.

His departure disappointed me—I wasn't eager to step out barefooted onto broken glass.

After the door snapped shut, McAllen said, "I gave him that scar. He came at me with a knife, and I cut him. Shoulda killed him." When McAllen continued, his voice broke with anguish. "I'm the one. I brought this down on my daughter."

I knew there was nothing to say, so I just studied the opposite wall until McAllen started talking again.

"The last time I saw Vrable, he worked for the Denver and Rio Grande Railway. Superintendent. Slick son of a bitch. Had everybody fooled. But I found out he beat the hell out of his wife and kid, and I helped them escape his clutches. And after the knife fight, I used my contacts with the railway to get him fired." McAllen slapped his hand against his thigh. "It all fits. Vrable comes across as somber-minded and capable, just how the townsfolk describe Grant. But let me tell ya: He only appears normal. Under the surface, Vrable's as crazed as a rabid dog."

"You think he killed your daughter for revenge?" I asked.

"Yep." McAllen's voice was quiet now. "That bastard thinks it fair retribution for me taking his wife and son away from him."

Sharp turned to face McAllen. "Can I ask ya somethin'?"

"Go ahead."

"Joseph, you're a tough hombre with a powerful organization behind ya. Why did Grant think he could get away with this?"

"Probably expected me to find out by telegram. If we hadn't gone in right after the posse, there'd be no way to know different from what they said." He shook his head. "If I hadn't been in Denver when I heard about this, I would never have gotten here in time. Vrable woulda got away clean."

I started to understand. "Do you think when he got back, Vrable learned you were out chasing the Ute band, and that's why he took off so quick? Before you returned and recognized him?"

"That's the way I got it figured," McAllen said, and then he yelled, "Boy!"

After the boy gingerly opened the door, McAllen said, "Sweep up this glass, so we can get the hell outta here."

After he went for a broom, McAllen turned to us. "Sort out enough of those supplies for a four-day ride. No packhorses, so take only what we need to get by. We're traveling light and we're traveling fast. We leave first thing in the morning."

"Breakfast?" Sharp asked.

"If you get up early enough, eat as hearty as you like."

"Where're we going?" I asked.

"Leadville."

Chapter 17

Dr. Dooley met us in the morning at the livery stables. "I'd like to join you men, if there's no objection."

"None here," Sharp said.

"Nor here." I slapped Dooley on the back, and all three of us looked at McAllen.

When some time had elapsed, McAllen sensed that we were waiting for his response. Without turning from his work, he said, "When a man says, 'if there's no objection,' and I don't raise one, he shouldn't push further to get permission."

All three of us had gotten up early enough for a predawn hot meal. At breakfast, McAllen had been sour company, and his mood had not improved. "Saddle up, Doc. We're about to get under way," Sharp said.

Glenwood Springs was less than fifty miles from Leadville, but because of mountains, they were fifty impossible miles. Dooley intended to catch a stagecoach east from Leadville to Denver and then take a train traveling west again to Glenwood Springs. This circuitous route was better than the direct route through the Rockies, which could prove dangerous to a lone rider, especially since the consumption clinic at Glenwood Springs was close to where the Meeker massacre had occurred only a little over a week before.

Sharp told me that Leadville, at over ten thousand breathtaking feet of elevation, held the title as the highest town in the United States. We were already at eight thousand feet, but to get there we would have to make a couple of mountain ascents, then drop into a high valley on the other side, only to climb over yet another peak. We could look forward to two hundred and fifty miles of cold weather and rough terrain. I reached over and scratched Chestnut's forehead. We had a hard ride ahead of us.

When I bought Chestnut, I had been looking for a big strong horse, because I carried a Winchester, a shotgun, two handguns, and a gunsmith's toolset. Add my own one hundred and seventy pounds to all this hardware, plus food and clothing, and I needed a sturdy horse. Chestnut would not win many races, but he could walk or trot all day under heavy load. I had recently discovered that Chestnut also handled backcountry with aplomb and a sure foot.

The night before, Sharp and I had sorted out the food for our four-day ride. Sharp wouldn't be applying any of his culinary skills to beans on this trip. We were carrying minimal supplies and using no packhorses. The remainder of the stockpile we had lugged over to the preacher's house and stacked on his porch.

Now I heard a voice from around the barn door. "You drop those supplies off at my house?"

"I thought someone in the congregation might use them," McAllen said over his shoulder. "There're a gift from these two gentlemen, Mr. Sharp and Mr.—"

"Thank you. I'll see that someone needy gets them." The preacher directed the acknowledgement at us, cutting McAllen off.

"Do with it what you will." McAllen continued to cinch his saddle.

The preacher turned back to McAllen. "You have your necklace, Captain. Now please go. *My* wife and I need some time alone." With that, the preacher turned his back on us and marched away.

Curiosity gnawed at me, but I kept my mouth shut. Sharp did not. "For God's sake, Joseph, did ya tell 'em Grant held a grudge against ya?"

"No." McAllen grabbed his saddle horn and tugged it to and fro. Satisfied, he picked up his saddlebag. "We never did get along, but this weasel thinks I hold him responsible for not protecting my daughter."

"Ya can't leave it that way."

McAllen's tone turned angry. "He shouldn't have let her ride all by herself."

"You told him that?"

McAllen grunted something and threw his bulging saddlebag over the back of his horse. "He said she didn't ride alone. She rode with God at her side."

"Joseph?" When Sharp got no response, he prodded, "Do ya really hold him responsible?"

"Him . . . and his almighty God." McAllen swung onto his horse. "Let's ride."

We all mounted our horses and trotted after McAllen, who had not bothered to wait for us. This looked to be a tense ride. I felt sympathy for McAllen, and I probably owed him my life, but this man who had always appeared controlled seemed unable to think straight. If there had been less history between us, I probably would have sent him on his way without me.

Leadville had always been the next destination for Sharp and me, but we had planned to leave almost a month earlier, when late summer weather was more predictable. Now, as we rode off into the high Rocky Mountains, we risked the surprise storms that sometimes endangered travelers in October.

After riding for almost an hour, Dooley said, "You want to know something strange?"

Sharp and McAllen rode ahead of us, out of earshot. I was thinking through a storyline for my journal, so I answered absentmindedly. "Sure."

"That half-breed seemed more in charge than Grant."

Dooley had grabbed my interest. I swung around in my saddle. "What do you mean?"

"I mean, whenever anything came up, Grant and the half-breed went off together to talk private, but it looked like the Indian told Grant what to do, not the other way around."

I thought about it. "The half-breed probably knew more about the wilderness."

"I'm not talking about on the trail. Even in town, it appeared to be the half-breed's show."

"What did he look like?"

"Big ugly brute. Dark skin, oily black hair, pockmarked face, and scarred bad. Face and hands were all I saw, but he must have run into some serious trouble one time or another."

I started to ask another question but instead yelled, "Hey, Captain, Jeff, hold up!"

McAllen still looked sour, so I wasted no words in relaying what Dooley had said. I could actually see McAllen thinking through the possibilities. When he spoke, his voice sounded uncertain. "You sure 'bout that description?"

"Yep, and I'm sure Grant was afraid to cross him."

"Goddamn it, the man's name is not Grant!" McAllen's compressed lips made a straight line across his red face. "You want to talk to me anymore about this, you call him Jim Vrable."

"Well, I don't," Dooley said.

"Don't what?" McAllen nearly yelled.

"Want to talk to you anymore." With that, Dooley spurred his horse and galloped away.

McAllen looked at us with eyes that burned with anger. Sharp and I just wheeled our horses around and gave chase to Dooley.

As we rode away, I heard McAllen yell, "Jim Vrable, goddamn it! I'm riding to Leadville to kill Jim Vrable."

Chapter 18

We met a small cavalry force about dusk on the second day. McAllen stopped and signaled us to arrange ourselves single file behind him. I presumed he wanted to look unthreatening to the soldiers. A lieutenant rode slowly forward and pulled up when his horse stood nose to nose with McAllen's.

After a curt nod, he said, "Lieutenant Miller. You gentlemen coming up from Durango?"

"We are," McAllen answered. "I'm Joseph McAllen. Your troop from Leadville?"

The lieutenant made no attempt to shake hands. "Yes, sir. On our way to protect the citizens of Durango against this Ute uprising."

"Have you passed any other riders?"

"Bob Grant, yesterday. The fool was riding alone, so I sent two troopers to escort him to Leadville."

"I thought your orders were to protect the people of Durango?" McAllen spoke with a harder edge than I thought appropriate. "It doesn't look like you have enough men to send two of 'em off to keep one man company."

The lieutenant sat more upright in his saddle before speaking. "My men and I can handle the Utes."

"All six of you?" McAllen's tone turned derisive.

"My other men will catch up in a couple days." The lieutenant cocked his head and gave McAllen an appraising look. "Are you with Pinkerton?"

McAllen nodded.

"Why didn't you introduce yourself as the celebrated captain of Pinkertons?" The tone did not reflect the respect of the words.

"Because I'm not on company business." McAllen kept both hands folded on his saddle horn, but I got the sense he could explode at any moment without warning.

"What kind of business are you on?"

"I suggest you carry out your orders and leave other people to their business." McAllen made a show of looking over his troopers. "I also suggest that in the future, you keep your force all together so you can carry out those orders."

The lieutenant seemed taken aback. "I am following the intent of my orders. You may not know it, but Bob Grant's an important man hereabouts."

"How so?"

"He works for Wells Fargo, which makes him a key man in the Tabor and Routt operations. They rely on him."

Sharp reined his horse around until he was level with McAllen. "Horace Tabor and John Routt?"

The lieutenant puffed up. "Yes, sir, the Carbonate Kings. Richest men in Leadville. Grant handles the security for all their gold and silver shipments."

Sharp and McAllen traded knowing glances. Sharp turned back to the lieutenant. "Ya say he was riding alone? He left Durango with a half-breed."

"A half-breed? No. Grant was alone for sure." The lieutenant gave Sharp a baffled look. "He doesn't normally hang with half-breeds. You might have your men mixed up."

"No," McAllen interjected. "I know the man." He gave the lieutenant a casual salute. "Well, we better be getting on."

"Are you about to pull up for the night? We could make camp together."

McAllen nudged his horse around the lieutenant's. "We're in a bit of a hurry. I reckon we'll ride as long as we got some light."

"Suit yourself, but during these dangerous times, there's safety in numbers."

As McAllen rode away, he said over his shoulder, "I'm sure you and your troopers will—"

"—be a great comfort to the people of Durango."

I almost laughed when Sharp interrupted McAllen before he could offend the cavalry officer again. As I pulled past the lieutenant, he looked confused by the exchange. Partly to distract him from taking offense, I asked, "What riled the Utes?"

The lieutenant looked at me for the first time. "Meeker, the Indian agent. Not a bad man, just ignorant." The lieutenant shrugged. "A political appointment."

I had a sudden thought. "No outside provocation?"

The lieutenant screwed up his eyes at me. "What do you know of this affair?"

"Just town gossip."

After a moment, he said, "We suspect that a Mexican might've encouraged the uprising. What have you heard?"

"Some think what happened in Durango may not be connected to the problems in the North." I couldn't think of anything else to say to keep the conversation going.

"They were Utes, weren't they? Must be connected." The simple thought process of a soldier.

McAllen must have had good ears, because he turned around and trotted back to us. "What's this Mexican's name?"

The lieutenant obviously did not want to respond to McAllen, but he eventually said, "Bane."

McAllen looked like he had been hit with a piece of lumber. "Bane's dead!"

"Nope. Lots of rumors of that sort, but you can't kill the devil's spawn."

McAllen turned toward Dooley. "That half-breed? Could he have been Mexican?"

"Hell, I don't know," Dooley said. "Coulda been, I guess, but I never heard of a Mexican that told people he was a half-breed."

"What did Grant call him?"

Dooley thought before answering. "Nothing that I ever heard."

The lieutenant held up his hand to stop the talk. "Grant would never associate with Bane. And if you knew Bane, then you'd know he'd never be seen with Grant… except maybe to kill him."

"Unfortunately, I do know Bane," McAllen said.

The lieutenant seemed dubious. "How?"

"Actually we met only once, but I hunted him for months." McAllen still looked awestruck. "My God, I shoulda killed him when I had the chance."

"You never had a chance," the lieutenant said arrogantly. "Lots of men thought they did… until they tried. Bane's meaner than a coiled rattlesnake, and he's wild crazy. You men are barking up the wrong tree. Grant and Bane have nothing in common. Nothing."

"Yes, they do." McAllen voice sounded muted, as if his thoughts were elsewhere.

The lieutenant looked completely incredulous. "Oh, and what might that be?"

"They both hate me."

Chapter 19

We rode away without giving the troopers an explanation. Once out of earshot, I asked Sharp, "Why do they call them the Carbonate Kings?"

"They mine lead and refine the silver out. A good find is one hundred and sixty ounces of silver per ton. Sell the lead too. But smelting costs are so high, many prospectors can't afford to develop a claim, so they sell out to one of the Carbonate Kings. They just keep getting bigger."

That sounded like a lot of work to extract a small amount of silver, but they must have the process down if these men had become wealthy.

I glanced over at McAllen. He looked grumpy, but I decided to chance a question anyway. "Do you think Vrable's half-breed was Bane?"

"Later," McAllen said. I thought the troopers wouldn't be the only ones to proceed in ignorance, but then McAllen added, "I'll explain when we camp. The horses got a good rest while we palavered, and that's no small hill in front of us. We'll ride hard until the light's gone."

Without waiting for a reply, McAllen spurred his horse and charged up the hill. Sharp gave out a small cowboy yodel and took off after McAllen. With a nudge from my spurred heels, Chestnut chased after Sharp and McAllen. I glanced back and saw that Doc Dooley lagged behind, but I enjoyed this race too much to pull up my reins. McAllen had an especially fine horse, one Chestnut might never catch on flat land, but on this steep incline, Chestnut kept gaining as we made our way up the hill. After a few minutes, Chestnut's solid gait pulled ahead of Sharp's mare and continued to close on McAllen's.

We had cleared a rise and started across a plateau that extended for almost a mile before the next incline On the fairly flat terrain, Sharp pulled abreast of me again, and McAllen sprinted further ahead. We were not running the horses full out because everyone understood that we would ride until the twilight faded. Chestnut continued to trudge along in a steady rhythm that reminded me of a steam engine. As we started up the next slope, I could feel Chestnut's firm stride, and I knew we would outlast them all. When the slope steepened, Chestnut pulled away from Sharp and then flew by McAllen.

"Damn you, Steve! This ain't no Sunday race."

McAllen's rebuke should have deflated my joy in victory, but instead I felt exhilarated. I knew McAllen felt depressed and angry about his daughter, and I should have been respectfully restrained in my own emotions, but I could not suppress my pleasure in winning. Chestnut had run with heart, and despite McAllen's denial, the captain had been racing. Perhaps not against me, but he was running away from something.

We pulled up at the top of the hill. Dark had started to descend on us, but from the top of the ridge, I could see enough to make out that this mountain just kept climbing. McAllen made the same determination and said, "We camp here."

After we made a rudimentary camp with a decent fire, we ate our sparse meal of hardtack and cold bacon, washed down with sips from our bourbon flasks. The chill had turned into a brittle cold. All four of us huddled by the fire in our sheepskin coats, with bedrolls across our laps.

McAllen no longer seemed surly, but he remained intense. I tamped and lit my pipe before saying, "Bane doesn't sound like a Mexican name."

McAllen looked up, coming out of some reverie that had placed him somewhere else. "It's not."

"First or last?" Dooley asked.

"What?" McAllen still seemed distracted.

"Is Bane his first or last name?" Dooley clarified.

"Only name. Far as I know, he chose it himself. No one knows his real name."

"Ya gonna tell us about him?" Sharp asked.

McAllen folded his arms and tucked his gloved hands in his armpits. "His background's murky, but according to the story I heard, Utes captured him as a youth. Treated him bad. Like an outcast or a slave. But as a youth, he became a great warrior and earned respect in the tribe. In a bloody battle with the Shoshone, he was captured again. The Shoshone treated him even worse. Tortured him for days and then left him to die in the wilderness."

McAllen took a sip from his flask. "But he's tough. Somehow he survived. When he tried to return to the Utes, they shunned him because they believed he could never have escaped without telling the Shoshone about their secret encampments. He tried the mountain towns but didn't fit with the white man or the Mexicans. So he became a solitary mountain man. Not only was he alone for years in these mountains, but there's some evidence he killed anyone that happened upon him. He hates people. The lieutenant said he was mean as a coiled rattlesnake, but a rattler coils when it's afraid. Bane has no fear and he kills instinctively, with no remorse. You meet the man and you're dead before 'howdy' leaves your lips."

"Why did you hunt him?" I asked.

"He killed a friend of mine. Another Pinkerton. I got permission from the agency to track him down. The idea was to bring him in for trial. Make him an example of why it's a bad idea to murder a Pinkerton. My boss assigned Red and a few others to my team." McAllen started to take another sip from his flask but instead turned it straight up and gulped it down until the flask was dry. "We quit the search after we heard he had taken two shotgun loads from another mountain man." McAllen shook his head. "How does a man survive two shotgun blasts?"

"Only one way," I said. Everyone looked at me, so I added, "The shotgun had to be loaded with light birdshot."

"Birdshot'll kill ya," Sharp said.

"Only if you're close enough. Over twenty yards—maybe less with a heavy coat—it'll hurt like hell, and you'll bleed some, but they won't penetrate deep enough to reach a vital organ."

"But a man's gotta bleed to death, don't he?" Sharp asked.

"The pellets are so hot, they cauterize themselves. The ones that hit bare skin will eventually puss up and work their way to the surface. In years past, I've been hit several times bird hunting. Only, in my case, it was over forty yards. Hardly worse than getting hit with gravel thrown by a wagon wheel. Birdshot at a distance can hurt, but it's not lethal."

Sharp turned his attention back to McAllen. "Who'd ya hear this story from?"

Good question, I thought.

"I know you're thinking Bane made up the story to get me off his trail, but it happened at a trading post in front of witnesses. Bane rode up, and this other mountain man just unloaded on him with no warning. Bane was hated with such passion that someone else roped his legs and drug him behind a horse. I was told they left him in the woods for the wolves to feed off." McAllen hesitated before continuing. "If Bane's still alive, I think Steve's got it right. That mountain man hit him with birdshot, probably through a heavy coat."

"Steve's right about the damage birdshot will do," Dooley said. "I suspect those wolves went hungry. Seems this man has cheated death more than once."

McAllen reached his hand out, and Sharp passed his flask over. This time he only took a sip and passed it back. "You're probably all afraid to ask about when I had my chance to kill Bane. It was before he killed my friend. I saw this scarred up, ugly brute beat a man to a pulp in Grand Junction. Most men would call it self-defense, since the stupid miner swung first, but it was so brutal a beating that I drew my gun to stop it. For a minute, I thought the bastard was gonna take a bullet to get at me, but in the end he just laughed and walked away. I shoulda shot him right there … then maybe my daughter would still be alive."

"Joseph, ya had no idea. Don't be so hard on yourself." Sharp offered his flask again, but McAllen waved it away.

McAllen folded his hands in front of him and hung his head. When he started speaking again, he did not lift it. "I knew the kind of man Bane was, so when I went after him, I purposely made him angry. I wanted him to come after me, because I didn't believe I'd ever find him in these mountains. I knew when I chose that course that one of us would end up dead. When I heard he was killed by someone else, I shoulda searched for his remains to make sure."

"What'd you do to make him angry?" I asked.

"From the stories, I figured Bane prided himself on his courage. I had the Denver papers portray him as a coward. Then I got the story printed all over the region. They quoted me as saying he showed yella at Grand Junction. The articles also said he blubbered like a baby when captured by the Shoshone. I had the story bylined out of Glenwood Springs, and the article said I was there on a long-term engagement.

We set a trap for him, but he was killed on his way to our carefully planned ambush. Or at least, we thought he was killed."

We sat quiet for a long time. McAllen had not talked this much since I had known him. I felt bad for him, but I had no idea what I could say to lessen the hurt. The cold started to bite, so I threw some more wood onto the fire. The only sound was the crackling of the dry wood and my chattering teeth.

I cringed when Dooley asked, "How do you suppose Bane or Vrable found out about your daughter?"

Instead of getting angry, McAllen continued in a dry tone. "No secret. I may not have told you boys, but I visited her once or twice a year, and it was common knowledge in Denver. I just never thought my work would endanger my family."

"There's no reason you shoulda," Sharp said.

"Thanks, Jeff, but in my line of work I make enemies of bad men. A good father would've taken steps to protect her."

"What steps?" I blurted.

"Secrecy, for one. So many years had gone by, nobody would've guessed."

"Then you would never have been able to see your daughter, and she would have missed knowing her father," I said. "You may have seen her only once or twice a year, but I bet those were important events in her life."

We fell silent again, but soon McAllen started talking to himself. "When we get to Leadville, I'll search out Vrable and take care of him. I'm sure he's the masterminded behind the abduction. As for Bane—" McAllen's voice trailed away.

"Vrable needed Bane to pull this off," Sharp said. "How do you think the two of 'em got together?"

"Vrable's good at sidling up to people to get what he wants. The man doesn't lack for charm. I'm sure he searched Bane out and drew him into his scheme."

"But Bane musta been like handlin' nitroglycerine." After a pause, Sharp added, "Vrable may be a snake charmer, but he doesn't sound like a match for Bane in a fight, so they must have separated peaceably… and if they did, do they have some more mischief in mind?"

That caused McAllen to sit up. Finally, he said, "You're right. Bane kills without thought. Friend or foe. For them to quietly separate means there's more at stake. Damn it."

"What?"

"I need to question Vrable. I need to know what else he has in store."

After a moment, I asked. "Does anyone know about us?"

McAllen looked away from the campfire and caught my eye. "What are you suggesting, Steve?"

"That the three of us ride into Leadville and scout out the situation. You come in separate and stay out of sight till we figure out what's going on."

Sharp immediately said, "Steve's right. Don't charge into town until we know the lay of the land. Vrable might bolt."

McAllen picked up a rock and twirled it in his fingers. "I want to go in and kill the bastard, but . . . you're right. I need him alive." He flipped the rock into the fire. "We'll do it your way. At least at first."

"Can you hide in Leadville?" I asked, thinking it was too cold for even McAllen to stay outdoors.

"Yeah, no problem. Leadville's almost thirty-five thousand people. On second thought, I'll wait in Twin Lakes at the Inter-Laken Hotel. It's about twenty miles from Leadville. You come get me when you know something." McAllen's voice took on an edge. "But if I don't hear from you in two days, I'm coming in. Understand?"

"Yep," Sharp said. "Now that we got a plan, can we crawl into our bedrolls?"

No one waited for an answer. We stoked the fire with plenty of wood and took up positions as close to the flames as we dared. Just as I pulled my blanket up around my ears, Dooley asked, "Where'd Bane go?"

McAllen pulled his own blanket up and said, "That's one of the questions we need to answer."

Chapter 20

I awoke to gray. And cold. Everything around me was shrouded in a heavy fog that made it hard to discern the features of the landscape. I wore my sheepskin coat over two wool shirts and a bristly pair of wool long johns. I had kept my boots on and had jammed my hat between my head and the saddle that I used as a makeshift pillow. Still, the cold made me reluctant to throw off my blanket and face the day. Rolling over, I saw Sharp putting the last of our gathered wood onto the fire.

"Get yer butt outta that bedroll, Steve. The day's a wastin'."

"You sure it's day?"

"Sun rose over a half hour ago. Get moving. You'll feel better."

I rose to a sitting position and tried stretching, but every joint seemed frozen in place. "Where's McAllen and Dooley?"

"Saddling up. McAllen wants to ride off as soon as we finish with coffee."

I made it to my feet. "At least we get coffee."

"As soon as I get it boiling, but I had to threaten McAllen to get him to wait."

"How'd you threaten him?"

Sharp laughed. "I told him I'd sing all day if I didn't get hot coffee in me before we left. By the time ya get Chestnut saddled, it'll be ready. Jump to or McAllen might change his mind."

I reached down and grabbed my blanket, saddle, and rifle. My muscles still resisted moving, and everything seemed twice as heavy as normal. We had let the horses forage free, and I turned in a circle looking for Chestnut. I could see nothing in the fog.

"Why don't ya just call him?" Sharp laughed.

"Because the words'll freeze before they get ten feet."

This got a respectable laugh, and I trudged off in search of my horse. I followed the muffled sound of voices until I found McAllen and Dooley. "Seen Chestnut?" I asked.

"Call him," McAllen said.

I was too weary and bone-chilled to repeat my quip, so I bellowed,

"Chestnut!" After two more tries, Chestnut slowly emerged from the fog like some otherworld apparition. I said good morning by rubbing the front of his chest, and when I walked over to where I had left his bridle and my other gear, he followed me without being bid. I smiled to myself when I saw the look on McAllen's face. It was obvious he suspected that the prior exhibition had been a fluke. I hadn't been quite sure myself. After the first few months, Chestnut seldom failed to respond to my voice, but I had never before owned a horse that showed dog-like devotion or appeared to understand verbal communication. Chestnut not only responded to the bit and spurs, but he seemed to sense my moods, and a couple of times, I needed only to catch his eye to beckon him.

McAllen grabbed the reins of his saddled horse and led him back to the campfire, Dooley following close behind. I glanced around, saw no other gear but my own, and concluded that Sharp must also be ready to ride out.

McAllen yelled back at me. "Hurry it up, Steve! We leave right after breakfast."

Hardtack and coffee hardly seemed like breakfast. I rubbed Chestnut's neck and consoled myself that any town of thirty-five thousand people would have plenty of comforts for those with the ability to pay. As I lifted the bridle over Chestnut's head and fitted the bit in his mouth, I realized I wanted to hurry as well. The sooner we got to Leadville, the sooner I could get out of this biting cold.

It became still and quiet after McAllen and Dooley had gone. The eerie fog made everything so damp that when I shook out my blanket, it felt rigid and stiff, like it would permanently freeze into whatever untidy mess I dropped it into. After I got the saddle and bridle to my liking, I slipped my rifle and shotgun into the scabbards on either side of the saddle. The only things remaining were my saddlebags and Colt, which I had left fireside. Once Chestnut was ready to ride, I wandered off a few yards to relieve myself.

I had just re-buttoned my pants, when a twig snapped beyond the curtain of fog. The snap had been so loud, it may even have been a branch. I froze. Damn it. I was unarmed. Straining to see through the gray screen, I saw nothing, I heard nothing. After at least a full minute, I swiveled my neck to see how far away Chestnut stood. He had decided to seek out his own breakfast and grazed on some new grass about twenty yards away. I faced the mysterious noise again but still saw no danger. I told myself that Indians moved quietly, so if anything was out there, it was probably just a deer.

I couldn't stand there all day, so I started to slowly retreat in the direction of Chestnut and my rifle. After two steps, I saw the outline of a huge hulking mass low to the ground. It looked like a boulder rolling silently toward me. I froze again. What the hell was that?

Then I saw—and it saw me. A grizzly bear. A huge grizzly. It hunkered on all fours, its massive head hung low to the ground from a thick neck. My hand brushed my leg, but I had left my knife with my Colt.

We each stood motionless and stared at each other until something happened that froze me—not in caution this time, but in utter fear.

The grizzly reared up on his hind legs, bared its teeth and claws, and gave out a monstrous roar.

I wanted to run, but my legs refused to move.

The bear fell back onto all fours, threw its head, and roared again.

I sensed it was seconds from a charge, but I still could not move. Suddenly, Chestnut neighed menacingly at my side. He reared back with his front legs kicking the air furiously and looked to be ten feet tall.

I regained my senses and stepped under Chestnut to grab the reins and pull him back to earth. I had to get to my rifle. He landed hard on his front hoofs, but immediately wrenched himself free and reared again. I glanced at the growling bear as he stood with his front paws also whipping the air.

As Chestnut dropped to ground once again, I sidestepped, grabbed the saddle horn, and leaped onto his back with a single bound. My butt had not slid into position before Chestnut reared again. With only a left-handed hold on the horn, I kicked my feet furiously to find the stirrups while I reached for my shotgun on the right side of the saddle. I grasped it but couldn't get it out of the scabbard at this angle without getting a foothold in at least one stirrup. At a loss, I used my grip on the stock to flip the shotgun up and caught it by the barrel before it slipped back into the scabbard or fell to the ground.

Just then, Chestnut pounded onto his front hoofs so hard, I tumbled over his head and onto the ground. I rolled uncontrolled into a tree trunk and spun around on my butt toward the threat. The grizzly was charging me!

I still had the shotgun in my hand.

Reflexively, my left hand gripped the stock, my right slid back to the trigger, and my thumb cocked both barrels.

Bang! Bang! Two blasts!

The grizzly came on.

I ducked just enough to avoid being battered with his teeth, but not before one of his claws mauled at my arm. I thought this was my end, but in a moment, I realized that although I had an enormous weight on me, the bear was not moving. I put the flat of my hands against his chest and gave a mighty shove. The brute hardly moved, but it was enough for me to slip sideways out from under him.

When I stood, both of my hands were covered in blood. I wiped them off on the bear and looked around for Chestnut. He stood only a few feet away, snorting and throwing his head side to side in a gesture of triumph. I ran over and threw my left arm around his neck as I pulled my rifle out with my right. The embrace was fleeting, because I wanted to make sure the bear was dead.

I walked over to the grizzly and shot him in the head.

"I don't think that was necessary," McAllen said from behind me. "That animal was already dead."

McAllen and Sharp stood behind me, rifles at the ready.

"Yep," Sharp added. "Don't look like ya keep birdshot loads in your shotgun."

I started to laugh but instead collapsed to the ground, with my leg muscles shaking like loose shingles in a northeaster. Dooley came running up and immediately knelt beside me.

"Gawd, you're a mess." This was not my desired prognosis from a doctor. After a few minutes of inspection, Dooley used his handkerchief to wipe the front of my coat. He showed me the handkerchief. "This ain't your blood, except on the arm. Lucky you had this sheepskin coat on. You only got deep scratches."

"Check my heart. It might be dislocated. I think I feel it in my throat."

"You're lucky," McAllen said. "I've seen what a grizzly can do to a man."

I lifted my uninjured arm. "Give me a lift up, Doc." When I

regained my footing, I said, "Luck had nothing to do with it. Chestnut saved my life." I walked over to my horse and laid my head on his left side, wrapping both arms around his neck. This time I made more than a fleeting embrace. After a moment, I pulled the reins slightly until his head was even with mine. I looked Chestnut in the eye and said, "Thank you."

When I turned, my three friends were watching me. Sharp pointed at the bear. "Ya want the head?"

"The head?" Then I got his meaning. "Nope. You want it, you take it. I'll see that grizzly's head every time I close my eyes. I don't need to see it when they're open."

Leading Chestnut gently by the reins, I started to walk back toward the campfire. "Jeff, I hope that coffee's ready. I sure could use a cup."

Chapter 21

We rode into Leadville in the late afternoon of the fourth day. The surrounding Rocky Mountains inspired awe and humility. The thin air, at over ten thousand feet, lent a hand to the breathtaking grandeur. High peaks hemmed us in from every side, cropping out much of the expansive blue sky that I had come to expect in the West. In fact, the mountains loomed so large over us that I felt Lilliputian.

We had left McAllen in a foul mood at the hotel in Twin Lakes, which was over an hour's ride outside of Leadville. We promised the impatient captain that we would meet him for dinner the following night at the Inter-Laken. McAllen would not be a congenial guest, and I had more than a little sympathy for the unfortunate staff that would have to deal with him.

Leadville was a substantial, though crude, town. Two- and three-story brick buildings lined intersecting streets, and construction on every block confirmed the explosion in mine operations. The building frenzy wasn't the hasty clapboard variety that I had encountered in other mining settlements, but instead the materials of choice seemed to be brick and mortar. I presumed the winters at this altitude called for solid protection against the elements. It was only early October, but the wind already made the autumn chill cut right through our heavy layers of clothing.

After several days tensing against the numbing cold, I longed for a fireplace, a glass of good whiskey, a hot bath, and a warm meal. "What's the best hotel?" I asked Sharp.

"I think the Tabor Grand is still under construction, but we'll give it a try. Otherwise, our best bet is the Carbonate. I just hope we can get a room ... anywhere."

I hoped so, too. People milled everywhere, and many had the prosperous look that probably meant the best hotels were full. The front of the Tabor was choked with wagons hauling bricks and other construction materials. Without discussion, Dr. Dooley and I followed Sharp further down the street until we pulled up in front of the Carbonate Hotel. After I hitched Chestnut, I inspected the hotel.

The rather plain three-story, square brick structure had a sidewalk in front so narrow it wouldn't even accommodate a chair. Most of the hotels in the West had a porch or balcony. An involuntary shiver reminded me why this hotel had been built for indoor living.

The nondescript exterior hid a lavish interior. The handsome décor's heavy masculine flavor reminded me of my father's club in New York. The large lobby bustled with self-important men and a few expensively dressed women. My heart sank. The hotel looked busy, and I doubted they had any rooms.

At the reception desk, two hotel employees were arguing in low tones with a dapper man in his fifties. I eased over to the counter to overhear the discussion.

"Mr. Brannan, must I remind you that you agreed to our terms in advance. I made it clear that your deposit for these rooms would not be returned under any conditions."

"I'm a good customer. Would you like me to take my trade elsewhere?"

"I appreciate your patronage, Mr. Brannan, but we have many good customers waiting for rooms, customers we turned away because of our commitment to you. Now you wish to renege on your side of the commitment."

"You're going to resell the rooms. At a higher price, I might add. I'm doing you a favor by releasing the rooms."

I leaned against the counter and tapped Mr. Brannan's forearm to get his attention. "How many rooms do you have?" I asked.

The hotel manager answered in a firm voice. "The reservation is not transferable."

I slid a single eagle under my palm toward the manager. "May I speak to Mr. Brannan alone for a moment?" I lifted my hand so he could see the coin.

The manager casually reached out his hand, and I withdrew mine in an easy motion so he could cover the gold coin with his palm. "Of course," he said, as he made a *come with me* motion to the other hotel employee.

I took Mr. Brennan by the elbow and led him out of earshot. "How many rooms do you have reserved?"

"Four, but they'll cost you. Rooms are going at a premium."

"How long do you have them for?"

"Ten days. I reserved them for investors from Chicago, but they pulled out."

"What kind of investors?"

"The rich kind."

This man was beginning to irritate me as much as he had the hotel manager, but I wanted the rooms. "Are you selling an interest in a mine?"

"I'm a broker for a number of ventures," he said pompously.

"Mining ventures?" I let irritation creep into my tone.

"Of course, why else would anyone come to Leadville? Certainly not for the climate."

"Exactly. That's why my companions and I are here. We want to look at mines for investment." I pointed out Sharp and Dooley. All three of us were crusted with trail dirt and looked pretty raggedy. My unshaven face and ripped, bloodstained coat from the bear incident probably didn't project the right image to this dandy.

With a condescending expression, he said, "Sure, I'm supposed to believe that and give you the rooms. No dice. You pay *my* price for the rooms or sleep in your damn bedrolls."

"Did you see what I passed the hotel manager so I could talk to you?" I didn't wait for a reply. "A single eagle." I paused for that to sink in. "We have the means." I pointed at Sharp. "That man may not look like it at the moment, but he's the largest mine operator in Nevada. We look like this because we just rode up from Durango, where we saw a lot of mines but didn't see anything we wanted to buy." I paused again. "So, do you have anything that might interest us?"

I didn't like the look on his face. He actually looked scared. Then I realized I had made a mistake by bragging about Sharp's knowledge of mines. Brannan was a swindler, not a legitimate broker. He wanted investors who knew nothing about mining. The Chicago boys probably pulled out after someone whispered in their ear that Brannan wasn't reliable.

After a moment, he said, "I got something you're interested in: four rooms in the best hotel in Leadville. If you want them, pay me three hundred dollars, right now. All four rooms for ten nights."

I did and he settled his remaining tariff with the hotel manager for what I assumed was a heady profit.

It cost me another single eagle to get the hotel manager to pretend that we were Brannan's investors. At first, three hundred and twenty dollars seemed an outrageous toll, but then I thought that maybe it was a reasonable fee to get rid of that pest Brannan. Three hours later, I was sure. Our rooms, though not large, were well appointed. In short order, we were fed, clean, and warm. Doc soon excused himself to retire early to a warm soft bed, but Sharp and I went to the lobby for a drink. As we settled in front of a roaring fireplace in comfortable chairs, sipping an excellent Scotch whiskey, I suddenly realized I was very tired and looked forward to a good night's sleep in a comfortable bed.

"How do ya suppose we go about findin' Vrable?" Sharp asked.

"Ask, I guess." I looked around the lobby. "Stupid of me. I should have asked that Brannan character. He probably knows all the shysters on this mountain."

Sharp winced before saying, "If he's known here, it's probably as Bob Grant."

"What's the matter?" I asked.

"Toothache. Gettin' worse." He rubbed the side of his face. "I better get it pulled."

"Doc Dooley?"

"Doc don't do teeth, but he might know a good barber or dentist. Maybe tomorrow."

I lifted my whiskey glass. "I'd sure like to climb into a warm bed after another one of these, but I guess we better make a few inquires before we call it a night."

"I wonder if the Wells Fargo office is still open," Sharp mused. He swallowed the last of his drink and threw himself out of his chair. "Let's go find out."

Chapter 22

Although the sun had slid below the mountain peaks, the Wells Fargo office was not only open but would stay open for another hour to provide service to miners who conducted business at the end of the day. As we entered the spacious office, it felt good to step into warmth again. In Leadville, autumn days were cold, but once the sun slid behind the mountains, a wintry chill took over that made breathing painful.

Sharp sauntered up to the counter and casually asked, "Is Bob Grant available?"

A clerkish man flipped a glance and a thumb at a large man in a brown suit who was seated at a cluttered desk facing the counter.

The big man lifted his head from his papers. "How can I help you?"

Now what? We had never talked about actually finding Grant sitting nonchalantly at a desk in the Wells Fargo office.

Sharp jumped right in. "Do ya remember us? We donated funds to outfit yer posse in Durango."

Grant stood and walked over to the counter. "Sad turn of events, I'm afraid, but the donations were used to put a large group of men on her trail." He spread his arms out wide. "I have none of that money. If there is any left, you'll find it in Durango, not here."

"Forget the money. We have a friend who wants to meet ya," Sharp answered.

Not knowing what to expect, I slid my hand off the counter and let it hang beside my gun.

Grant just gave us a broad smile. "And who might that be?"

"Joseph McAllen."

Not even a flinch in the friendly smile. "I've been waiting for him to call. I'm surprised he sent you boys instead of coming himself." His expression turned sympathetic. "The news about his daughter must have been hard on him."

"You knew Maggie was his daughter?" I blurted.

"Of course. Everyone in Durango knew."

Sharp glanced at the clerk, who seemed interested in the conversation. "Mr. Grant, I didn't expect ya to welcome news that the captain was lookin' for ya."

"That's because you don't know the full circumstances."

Sharp pushed further. "He says he knows ya by a different name."

Grant smiled again. "Many things are not as they seem."

"Excuse me, but—"

Grant cut me off. "This is far too sensitive to discuss here. Tell the captain he has my condolences, and I want to meet with him as well." His expression had changed to sincere compassion.

"When?" Sharp asked firmly.

"Where are you staying?"

"The Carbonate."

"A fine choice. I'll meet the captain for breakfast in the dining room. Say seven?"

"I'm afraid McAllen hasn't arrived yet," Sharp said. "He sent us on ahead, but he might arrive by dinner tomorrow night."

Grant looked disappointed. "Tomorrow for dinner then. Would you tell the captain he needs to hear what I have to say? It'll change his understanding of events." He paused and then smiled again, but somehow it didn't come across as friendly this time. "Tell him that his family is still in danger. Everything, and I mean everything, can be set right if we come to a proper understanding."

I started to object to the threat, but Sharp raised his hand. "We'll see ya tomorrow night at eight. The Carbonate dining room."

"I'm sorry, perhaps you misunderstood. I'll see the captain alone... or not at all."

"That'll be McAllen's decision," Sharp snapped. "Unless ya want to meet him under different circumstances." Sharp paused dramatically. "I might add, he's in a foul mood."

Again, no flinch. "I'm afraid we forgot introductions. Who might you be?"

"Friends of McAllen."

"I see." Grant looked at the clerk, who had been closely following the conversation. "If you'll excuse us. This is a security matter I cannot discuss in front of you." The man walked a discreet distance away, but Grant still leaned over the counter until his mouth was beside Sharp's ear. "Tell the captain that if he wants to see his family whole again, he'll see me tomorrow night—alone. Understood?" The smile had vanished.

"No," Sharp said in a normal voice the clerk could easily overhear. "McAllen hasn't got any family. What are ya talkin' about?"

Grant pushed himself away from the counter. "Just tell him what I said." Then he turned and disappeared into a back room.

We left the office and stepped into a frigid breeze. Without pause, Sharp marched to our hotel, which I appreciated. I would rather talk about this incident in front of a big fire. The bitter cold made me shiver, and I hooked the top button of my coat and raised the sheepskin collar. Hopefully, our chairs beside the fire remained unoccupied.

When we arrived back at the Carbonate, the seats by the fireplace were taken, but we found two easy chairs in an alcove that actually provided more privacy.

After we had whiskey glasses in hand, I asked, "What do you think Grant meant?"

"Been thinkin' on that." Sharp took a sip and then a large swallow of the whiskey. "I'm not positive, but I think he was hintin' that McAllen's daughter is still alive."

Chapter 23

Early the next morning—with only coffee to sustain us—we rode out to Twin Lakes. Sharp, a man who never complained, grumbled the entire twenty miles about his toothache.

The Inter-Laken appeared rustic on the outside, but the lobby furnishings said that the hotel catered to wealthy patrons looking for a romantic interlude. Since it was still early, Sharp peeked into the restaurant before going to the registration desk. Sure enough, McAllen sat at a table by himself, looking as grumpy as when we had left him.

"What are you men doing here?" McAllen looked surprised as we slid into the extra chairs at his table.

"We missed yer cheerful company," Sharp said. "How's breakfast here?"

"Expensive. Did you find Vrable?"

"We found Grant, big as life, sitting comfortable as you please at a big desk in the Wells Fargo office."

McAllen started to get up. "Tell me on the trail."

"Joseph, we need to eat, and we already set up a meet for tonight. Lots of time." Sharp unsuccessfully tried to signal a waitress to come over. "Let's talk a bit before ya ride off in a snit."

McAllen looked ready to bolt, but he settled back into his chair. "What time tonight?"

"Can we—"

McAllen cut off Sharp. "No."

Sharp sighed theatrically. "Eight o'clock at the Carbonate. Grant insists on meeting you alone … for dinner."

"Dinner?" McAllen mulled that over. "Obviously there's more if you left Leadville without a meal."

"There is," I answered. "But we're not sure what it means. We got here early so we could talk it over."

"Then let's get breakfast ordered for you men." McAllen tapped his coffee mug with a table knife until he had the attention of a waitress, and then with a curt gesture, commanded her to come over to our table. As soon as she arrived, McAllen ordered gruffly, "Coffee immediately. Then get two orders of chops and eggs for these gentlemen. Move quickly if you want a gratuity."

After she scurried away, McAllen said, "All right, you have your meal on the way. Tell me exactly what happened and what he said."

Sharp told about our encounter with Grant, while I filled in a few details that he forgot to mention. Neither of us offered any speculation about what it all meant. As we had previously agreed, McAllen should be allowed to draw his own conclusions.

McAllen didn't hesitate when we were done. "So Vrable kidnapped my daughter and merely pretended that she had been murdered by Utes. Probably matted an old scalp with fresh blood from an animal."

"That's what we concluded," I said. "But why?"

"He wants something from me," McAllen said, as if he already knew what Vrable wanted.

"Something more than revenge?" I asked.

"He wants that too, but first he'll force me to help him steal a silver shipment. *Then* Bane will kill my daughter."

"Ya think Bane's got her?" Sharp asked.

"The two of 'em cooked this up. Bane's got her."

"How do you know he wants to rob a silver shipment?" I asked.

"Because the Carbonate Kings are careful. They engage both Wells Fargo and Pinkertons to guard their shipments. Hard to corrupt both parties at the same time. Vrable controls security for Wells Fargo, and he thinks I can handle the Pinkertons."

"Ya figured that out pretty quick," Sharp said.

"Been thinking hard on it—ever since we left Durango. Bane and Vrable are an odd pair to get together in the first place, and Bane would never split up peaceful unless he had further business with Vrable." McAllen looked pointedly at me. "Steve, you said Vrable seemed more intent on fleecing the town than getting out on the trail after Maggie. That's the Vrable I know. A goddamn swindler."

"How'd you figure out that your daughter was still alive?" I asked.

"Hoped, more like it. I was sure they paid them poor Utes to grab her, and it made no sense to go to all that trouble just to kill her. Lots of easier ways to do that." McAllen glanced around the dining room to make sure no one was eavesdropping. "This deal smelled from the start. Vrable volunteered to lead that posse. That didn't make sense. He knew I'd guess his real identity, and it wouldn't take much more thinking to figure out that he was part of the deed. Bane and Vrable are a couple of nasty characters, but they aren't stupid. If they didn't have something to hold over me, they knew I'd hunt 'em down and kill 'em."

I was still confused. "How could Bane get your daughter away without the posse spotting them?"

"I figure Bane circled back after the posse left and took her from the Utes before we arrived." McAllen shifted his attention back to Sharp. "Figuring out the rest of their plan wasn't that difficult. If you put Wells Fargo together with Pinkerton in Leadville, you got silver shipments. Vrable's the kinda man that would go after the money first and then get revenge."

We all sat quiet a minute and then Sharp asked, "What do ya plan to do, Joseph?"

McAllen scooted his chair away from the table. "Ride into Leadville and kill that son of a bitch."

"Joseph, no!" Sharp grabbed McAllen's arm, as if he could stop his gun hand. "If Bane still has your daughter, he'll kill her."

"Damn it, Jeff, he's gonna kill her anyway. They'll set things up so I'll be the one hanged for robbery... and probably murder. They'll kill her while I sit helpless in jail waiting for the hangman's noose, because they'll want me to know she's dead before I climb the scaffold. That's their whole plan."

"You can't be sure," I protested.

Completely out of character, McAllen looked ready to cry. Instead of continuing to rant, his voice sounded forlorn. "I'm sure."

For more than a minute, the three of us just sat there. Then I asked, "Where's Red?"

"On his way here... why?"

"Can he track Bane?"

"Thought of that." McAllen paused before adding, "Maybe." Then he shook his head. "No. We traded telegrams once I got to the hotel, and I told him to leave Durango immediately. It'll take him four days to get here, and then he'll have no idea where to start. If there's a trail to follow, it's back in the San Juans."

"Does he know these mountains?" I asked.

"What's on your mind, Steve?"

"Stall. We need time for Red to get here so we can try to find your daughter."

"You'll never find her, and if you do, Bane would kill the lot of you. He'll hide in a protected niche, and he's more dangerous than a crazed grizzly."

"I've killed a grizzly," I added weakly.

"You're a good man in a fight, Steve, but you're a tenderfoot in the wild."

"Red's not . . . and I've had some lessons of late."

Sharp jumped in. "Give us a chance," he pleaded. "What difference does it make if ya kill Vrable tonight or later?"

"The difference is he'll be alone tonight. Soon he'll surround himself with men in his pay. No, goddamn it. Later I might not be able to get to him."

The two men glared at each other, and then Sharp said matter-of-factly, "Your decision, Joseph. Do ya want to give your daughter a chance or not?"

McAllen looked ready to pounce across the table after Sharp, but then I saw his anger seep away. After a moment, he said, "Jeff, thanks for speaking plain, but even Red wouldn't have a chance of finding her. Those mountains are vast and deadly cold."

"Do you think Vrable knows where Bane's got your daughter?" I asked.

"Grab him and beat it out of him?" McAllen paused to think it through. "No . . . never work. Bane's too wily to let Vrable know his whereabouts. Nope, Vrable doesn't know."

"Doesn't Vrable need to tell him when you've agreed to cooperate? Or if you don't, he'll need to tell him to kill the girl." I leaned across the table. "They must have some way of getting messages back and forth. What will Vrable do if you insist on proof that your daughter's still alive?"

McAllen sat straighter. "Damn. I've let my anger cloud my thinking."

I thought it might have been grief, but I kept that thought to myself. McAllen went quiet, and we gave him time to think. In the meantime our breakfast arrived. I didn't get the breakfast I would've ordered. My eggs arrived undercooked, and the chop overcooked, but at least the biscuits were fresh from the oven, and the restaurant had a decent selection of preserves.

After we had dug into our food, McAllen said, "You're right. They must have some way to communicate, and it sure ain't by telegraph, because Bane would never feel safe in a town, especially not with a hostage. I know the man would never tell Vrable his location, so he must have a messenger he trusts. And that messenger is probably hanging around Leadville until needed. The trick is to spot him."

"And then we trail him," Sharp said, as he rubbed his sore jaw.

"Yes. They would need to get messages back and forth in short order, so I'm guessing Bane brought my daughter up here from the San Juans. Damn. I bet he's less than a day's ride away."

"We need time," I said. "Red's four days away, and even if we spot the messenger, we can't track him without Red."

"Steve, quit beating around the bush. What are you thinking?"

"Don't show up tonight. Vrable doesn't know you're close. We'll pretend you must have left late or took longer on the trail than we expected. Wait here a couple nights. When you finally see Vrable, tell him you telegraphed your Pinkerton resignation from Durango, and you need a few days to trade telegrams with Denver to see if you can get your job back. Stall until Red arrives, then insist on proof that she's still alive."

"What proof? They'll never bring her close enough for me to see her."

"Do you recognize her handwriting?"

"Of course."

"Then tell Vrable to bring you a letter written in her hand. Insist that it has a current date. That'll send the messenger out before the robbery, and we can trail him to your daughter."

McAllen frowned but only for a moment. "Steve, that might work. Worth a try anyway. If you were one of my Pinkertons, I'd give you a bonus."

I felt myself blush. For McAllen, this was high praise. I also felt pretty proud of myself, because I had come up with most of the plan between bites of food.

Sharp brought up something I had missed. "What instructions did ya give Red? We don't want people to know he's with us."

"I told Red to stay low. I meant to kill Vrable before he arrived. I wanted him here in case I failed. He won't sashay up to me or you men, if that's what's worrying you."

"It is." Sharp pushed his empty plate away. "So, do we have a plan?"

"For the moment. But if anything goes awry, anything, I kill that son of a bitch on the spot and go after Bane myself."

"Understood," Sharp said. "Then we'll see ya in two days?"

"Looks that way." McAllen looked around the dining room. "Damn, I wanted to get outta this place."

"Looks to be a decent hotel," I offered.

"I'm the only goddamn man in this hotel without a woman. The staff treat the honeymooners like royalty and the unweds with discretion. They don't know how to handle me."

"Hell, I've known ya for ten years, an' I don't know how to handle ya," Sharp said.

McAllen didn't laugh, but at least Sharp's quip raised a slight smile. Under the circumstances, that was an accomplishment. At least we had given him some hope.

"Listen, Captain, I know nothing's sure, but if it's at all possible, we'll get your daughter back." I didn't know how to convey my other concern, so I just added, "She's young and she's a McAllen. She'll recover."

"She's a McAllen all right. Tough girl, but she won't need to recover from what you're thinking. The Shoshone castrated Bane."

Chapter 24

After breakfast, McAllen told us to ride back to Leadville before we were missed. When we arrived at the Carbonate Hotel, we didn't see Vrable or anyone else that appeared interested in us. In fact the town looked quiet, and then we remembered that it was Sunday morning. The faithful were in church, and the sinners were sleeping off their Saturday night wickedness.

We left our horses at the stable and walked around to the back entrance of the hotel. Using the rear staircase, we went to our rooms to drop off our coats, scarves, gloves, and hats. I also scrubbed my face and combed my hair at the washbasin. After checking my appearance in the commode mirror, I decided I was ready to find Dr. Dooley.

Sharp stepped out of his room at the same time as me. Despite his scruffy clothes, he looked presentable; at least as presentable as I had ever seen him.

"Hey, when you strike silver, are you going to buy new clothes?" I asked.

"Already own lots of producing mines." Sharp tugged the sleeve of his shirt. "These ain't worn out yet."

"Matter of opinion, Mr. Sharp. Most people think threadbare is cause enough to throw something away."

"That's why most people ain't got two silver dollars to rub together. 'Sides, buyin' clothes takes too damn much time. Come on; let's see where the good doctor has run off to."

Sharp started toward the staircase, and I just stood there. When he failed to hear my following footfalls, he turned around and impatiently asked, "Well, ya comin'?"

"Naw, you go on ahead. I think I'll knock on his door to see if he's still in his room."

He turned around and trudged back up the hallway. "Shit, Dancy, sometimes yer a pain in the ass."

"Glad to hear it's only sometimes." I knocked on Dooley's door.

"Yep?" came the answer from behind the door.

I enjoyed the look on Sharp's face as I answered, "Steve and Jeff. We need to talk."

"Well, come on in then. The door's not locked, and your arm ain't broke."

Dooley sat propped up on his bed, fully clothed, reading the thickest book I had ever seen.

"Why're ya holed up in yer room on such a gorgeous day?" Sharp asked.

Dooley looked baffled at the odd question but then said matter-of-factly, "Reading. This book's too damn heavy to lug around."

"What is it?" I asked. "You didn't bring that up from Durango, did you?"

"Bought it from a doctor yesterday—used." He lifted the tome above his outstretched legs. "Steve, I don't think we'll be sharing this book, unless you have a desire to learn about consumption."

Dooley and I had been sharing books ever since we met in Pickhandle Gulch. I sure didn't have any interest in a medical book. As I thought about it, except for *The Autobiography of Benjamin Franklin*, all the books we had traded had been fiction. On second thought, I suspected that a good piece of Franklin's work might have been fiction as well.

Since Dooley made no attempt to get off the bed, I pulled over a chair, and Sharp grabbed a stool.

"Do ya know any dentists?" Sharp asked as he lowered himself onto the stool.

"I'm going to write John Holliday as soon as I finish this book. But this man's a killer, not a healer."

I scooted forward to the edge of my chair. "Doc Holliday? Damn, the real Wild West."

Sharp gave me an odd look. "You're pullin' my leg, right? What the hell do ya call that ruckus back in Nevada?"

"Washburn was a local hoodlum. Doc Holliday's famous all the way to New York City."

"Famous? For what, for God's sake?"

"Toughness ... gunplay ... knife fights ... roaming free, doing whatever he wants, and taking guff from no man." I decided I had to meet him. He'd get top billing in my book about the West, and my publisher would probably print another ten thousand copies. "Where is he?"

"New Mexico," Dooley said.

"Who cares? He's a wheezin', scraggy drunk," Sharp said. "Sober, ya wouldn't pay him any mind; drunk, ya don't want him to pay you any mind."

"You know him?" When would Sharp quit surprising me?

"I know the sober Dr. John Holliday. Thankfully, I've never met the inebriated Doc Holliday."

"How well do you know Holliday… the sober one, I mean?" I asked excitedly.

"I played at his table a couple of times. Few years ago. Holliday runs an honest faro game. He may occasionally get involved in a con with the Earps, but he keeps that away from the table."

"A con?"

"Yep. The boys like to strip greenhorns of their money. They're known for pullin' off low-level swindles. Sometimes they just take an unsuspectin' sucker for free drinks. Mostly, they do it for the fun of it rather than for the money."

"Tell me about it. I want it for my journal."

"Later," Sharp said. "Steve, I got business here." He turned to Dooley. "Doc, I got a terrible toothache. Ya know anyone in town?"

"No, but I can ask around." He studied Sharp a second. "I don't normally do teeth. Too much yelling for two dollars. But Jeff, if it pains you, I'll take care of it right now."

"I'd be obliged."

"You'll be in debt for two dollars is what you'll be." Dooley set his book on a side table and swung his legs around to get off the bed. "I'll get to it. Need a stretch anyway."

"Now?" Sharp exclaimed. "Maybe it don't hurt that bad."

"Hell, don't be a baby. I'm leaving on tomorrow's stagecoach. I want to get to Glenwood Springs before the first snowfall. Open your mouth, and let's get this over with."

Dooley took only a few seconds to examine Sharp's teeth. "Gotta come out." With no further ado, he rummaged around his black bag until he came out with a wicked-looking pair of pliers. "This ought to do. Open wide."

"Goddamn it, Doc. You done this before?"

"Naw, but I always wanted to pull a tooth. Now open up."

Sharp, a man I had never known to show fear, looked white as the pillow on Dooley's bed, but he opened his mouth as a single tear leaked out of his right eye.

I couldn't believe it when Dooley put his foot in the middle of Sharp's chest and immediately yanked for all he was worth. After a short scream of pain from Sharp, Dooley held aloft a bloody tooth like he had plucked a piece of silver from a streambed.

"Gotta do it fast. That's what separates the quacks from a skilled dentist."

"Thought ya never done this before," Sharp said as he examined the empty space with his tongue.

"Just joshing," Dooley said. "Done it dozens of times. Just don't like it. Rather set a leg or stitch a cut."

Sharp got up on shaky legs. "I thank ya, Doc. Now I need whiskey to clean the wound."

"Before you leave, aren't you forgetting something?"

He turned from the door. "What?"

"Two dollars."

"Doc, that tooth got gold in it?"

He wiped the blood away and looked. "Yep."

"Consider yerself paid."

Chapter 25

After we finished a whiskey in the lobby, I asked, "How're we going to flush this messenger out?"

"Don't know," Sharp said. "We've got to find this go-between, or our plan ain't worth shit. The captain'll be arrivin' night after tomorrow, and he'll want answers." Sharp got out of his chair, rubbing his jaw. "This feels pretty good. Let's start by walkin' around the seedy parts of town." He smiled. "Get a feel for the place."

I stayed seated. "Jeff, it's cold outside."

"I don't think we'll find our quarry in the hotel lobby, so go back to your room and get wrapped tight."

"What about Vrable?"

"Let him stew a while. Come on. Let's go. Get yer gear back on. It'll be fun."

I stood reluctantly. "Only you think it's fun to cavort with cutthroats and whores."

"What the hell're ya doin' out here if ya prefer to socialize with gentlemen?"

I smiled. "Lead on. I couldn't ask for a more experienced guide to the underside of a mining camp."

We walked for over an hour. Leadville was a series of broad avenues with narrow boardwalks. Most blocks were half filled with one- to four-story brick buildings. We walked in traffic lanes, because many of the empty lots were under construction, the building materials spilling from the boardwalks onto the streets. Everywhere, workmen barked orders. Even on Sunday, frenzied construction consumed the town—everybody wanted to beat the first snowfall. We had seen several shabby lodgings, but we didn't go inside. We didn't want word to get out that we were searching the town.

Finally, we entered a dodgy café to get warm. Boisterous and ill-clad men filled both sides of long tables that looked in dire need of a scrubbing. We sat opposite each other in the middle of one of the tables and ordered coffee from a girl no older than fifteen. My eyes scanned a blackboard with the day's offerings, but I saw nothing that appealed to me.

"Let's just order coffee and eat after we get back to the hotel," I suggested.

"Might be nightfall." Sharp laughed at the look on my face. "I've eaten in this kinda place lots of times. It'll be fine, just don't order stew. Ya might get surprised."

"That's what I'm afraid of."

"Well, I'm orderin' a meal. If we're gonna find what we're lookin' for, it'll probably be in a place like this."

"What *are* ya lookin' for?" This came from a big, rough-looking man who sat beside me at the long table.

Before I could think of an answer, Sharp said, "A guide. Someone who knows these mountains an' knows somethin' about prospectin'."

"Hell, that's easy. Half the men in this room claim to fit that bill."

"Like yourself, I suppose?" I asked.

"Naw, not me... hell, I could do it, but I got my own diggin's. 'Sides, only a fool would go into the mountains now. You'll freeze to death."

Sharp reached across the table, extending his hand. "Jeff Sharp. This here's my partner, Steve Dancy. Our mine in Nevada looks about played out, so we're lookin' for a new venture."

The man nodded. "Samuel Washington, but everyone calls me Pie."

"Pie?" I swung around to get a look at the man beside me.

The big weathered man shrugged. "I eat a bit of pie."

The man's nickname reminded me of my fight in Durango. I probably owed my life to that flung plate of pie. Perhaps I should adopt pie as my favorite dish as well.

"Anyone ya might recommend?" Sharp asked.

The man studied the room and repeated his question. "What're ya lookin' for?"

"Somethin' rare, I 'xpect," Sharp said. "A man that knows these mountains like the back of his hand... an' maybe knows a bit about prospectin'. An' someone that knows the local Indians. Don't want no trouble."

"Kinda late in the year, ain't it?"

"We tried Durango first and wasted too much time, but I figure we got a couple weeks before the first storm. That's why we need someone good. Maybe a half-breed? Someone who grew up in these mountains? Knows the terrain … and the weather."

"Couple a weeks, huh? Well, good luck to ya."

"You don't have anyone to suggest?" I asked.

"Nope. Ya go into those mountains this time of year, and ya'll probably die. A honest man'll just tell ya that right out. If ya want my advice, buy a producin' claim close to town. Plenty about, and ya'll likely see spring that way."

"Nope," Sharp said firmly. "That's how we wasted time in Durango. I'll not be suckered. I stake my own claims."

The big man turned to me. "What's yer part in this?"

"I'm the money."

"Have ya been in the mountains this time of year before?" He stared at me. How did Westerners always know I was citified?

Sharp answered. "I have. We got good gear an' good horses. All we need is a good guide."

"An' a hell of a lot of luck. Ya think ya can find a claim in a couple weeks? Some men traipse through these mountains for years with nary a strike."

"I've been lucky all my life," Sharp said. "I know there's silver and maybe gold out there. I want to get a look and a feel for the lay of the land before it goes all white."

Pie gave Sharp a hard stare. Finally, he said, "The men ya see here have come in for the winter. There's only one man I know of that ventures into these mountains this time of year."

"Who might that be?" Sharp asked.

"Don't rightly know his name. He's a full-blood Ute. Mean as hell. Some have used him as a guide, but he's a savage, not one of yer civilized-like Indians. I ain't recommendin' him, hear. He'll probably slit yer throat while ya sleep and leave ya naked in the woods to feed the bears."

"Where do we find him?" I asked.

Pie looked at me and shook his head. "You loco? Ya don't go off into these mountains this time of year guided by a savage that's got no more use for ya than a lame pony. Whatever's up in those hills, it'll still be there come spring."

"We got our minds set," Sharp said.

"Ya *are* loco," Pie said. He shook his head again and then added, "If ya want him, I hear he's encamped up on the rise at the north end of town—with all the other Indians."

"What've you heard about the Ute uprising at the reservation?" I asked.

"At least that ain't a worry for ya. The local Utes weren't a part of that mess, and the army corralled the ones that was. I met that Meeker once—a self-righteous son of a bitch. I'm guessin' he provoked 'em. Naw, if this Ute kills ya, it's for yer gear, not 'cuz he's part of some damn rebellion."

Sharp made a show of thinking through the possibilities. After a moment, he said to me, "Pie's got a point. Maybe it's too late in the year. Let's eat ... see how we feel in the morning."

I took Sharp's lead, and we changed the subject. The coffee was hot and not bad, but the steak I ordered came burnt and grizzled. I was not surprised.

At the end of the meal, the young girl brought our new acquaintance the biggest piece of apple pie I'd ever seen.

"Is that a single slice?" I asked.

"Naw. I'm known hereabouts." He winked. "Gotta keep up appearances, or I might lose my nickname."

Sharp reached across the table to shake Pie's hand. "We'll be goin' before you dig into that, but I want to thank you. Sometimes I get dumb ideas in my head. Ya straightened me out."

"If yer real grateful, ya'll buy my lunch."

"I think my partner can handle that. Pay the young lady, Steve.

Before I could pull the coins out of my pocket, Sharp had disappeared outside.

I found him at the end of the block, puffing on one of his cigars and gazing up the street to the north. I walked up beside him and pulled out my pipe. "We could've had our smoke inside where it's warm."

"In New York, did ya stay indoors all winter?"

"Most winter days in New York aren't as cold as this ... and people around here call this fall."

"Ya get used to it." Sharp seemed distracted.

"Do you think this Ute's our man?" I asked.

"Might be." Sharp puffed a moment, continuing to look up the street.

"What's bothering you?"

"Too easy. We've been lookin' for less than two hours. The reason most miners aren't successful is that they spot a showin' and commit their life to it. They'll chase a bum lead all the way to the grave." Sharp dropped his cigar and crushed it under his heel.

"Afraid this is a bum lead? A false showing?"

"Like I said, too easy. If a claim don't pan out, ya gotta move on. Look somewhere's else. And the sooner, the better, so ya don't waste time."

"You're saying we need to find out for certain... and without wasting too much time."

"Yep. Time we ain't got."

I lit my pipe and stared down the street as well. "Think anyone in town knows Bane?"

"Not likely, and we don't want to be askin' too many questions. 'Sides, we'd probably never find a white man that could tie Bane together with this Ute."

I assumed that Sharp's answer meant he thought we could only learn more from another Indian. "Red will be here in a couple days," I offered.

"I've been tryin' to decide if we can wait. McAllen will be here in two nights, an' he'll sure as hell want answers, not guesses." Sharp turned his attention away from the hill and back to me. "Steve, go back to the hotel. I'll meet ya there in a couple hours."

"Jeff, I just like to gripe about the cold. I'll go with you."

"No... one white man askin' questions makes 'em nervous; two shuts 'em up tighter than one of them drums they beat on."

"I don't think I look very threatening," I offered.

"That blood-soaked coat won't make people feel friendly."

I had forgotten about the grizzly blood. I had brushed the coat and stitched the rips, but most people would still recognize the splotch across the front as a bloodstain. "Shit, I forgot. I guess I better buy a new one."

"Buy one now, an' I'll meet ya back at the hotel."

Sharp obviously wouldn't accept any more objections, so I just said, "Don't push questions so hard you draw too much attention."

"I won't. Have a fine bottle of whiskey waitin' for me by the fire."

With that, Sharp turned his back on me and walked up the street in the direction of the town's Indian encampment.

Chapter 26

The haberdashery next to the hotel had the masculine feel of a New York City men's club. It looked expensive, but my mouth fell open when I checked the tag on a coat not dissimilar to the one I was wearing.

"There's an emporium down the street that may have something more in your price range."

The handsome female clerk—who probably made less than a constable—wore a perfectly tailored charcoal dress and a snooty expression. I, on the other hand, was dressed in filthy trail clothes that told her I spent my time on top of a horse, not inside a money-spewing mine.

I checked the tag again before asking, "Can you explain why this coat costs twice what I paid in Durango?"

The clerk lifted her chin. "Perhaps you should retain the one you're wearing. It looks to be broke in. A Chinaman might get those stains out."

The woman's attitude irked me. "Cleaning's been tried, and I don't like wearing the blood from one of my kills." I was rewarded with the wince I was trying to invoke. "Can we talk about a *reasonable* price for that coat?"

The haughty clerk caught her balance faster than I expected. "Our prices are not negotiable."

"They aren't reasonable either."

"As I already mentioned, there's an emporium down the street," she said, with her nose pointed at the patterned tin ceiling.

I didn't like her. She was in her mid-twenties and attractive, but she reminded me of the women my family had tried to match me with in New York. Well-spoken, obviously educated, and pretty in a restrained manner that signaled that she had class and an upper-class upbringing. Except that she was a haberdashery clerk in a mining town, which meant that she pretended to be the type of woman I disliked. And a fake was even worse than the real thing in my book.

She put on airs that she believed would appeal to the nouveau riche in this rustic town. I was unimpressed.

"May I speak to the owner?"

She stiffened. "I'm sorry. He's unavailable."

"Make sure."

She offered me a condescending smile. "There's no need for you to speak to the owner. Mr. Cunningham entrusts his business affairs to my charge."

"Really? You look like an underpaid clerk dressed in a store-loaned dress."

The woman responded in a heartbeat. "I hesitate to say what you look like, sir."

"Good decision. Hold that tongue. Now fetch the owner. Right away, please."

She didn't budge. "I'm the senior clerk. You may deal with me."

"Very well." I held her eyes for a long moment. "What price for the entire store?"

"All the contents? Very amusing, sir."

"Not the contents—everything. You're the highfalutin senior clerk. Give me a price."

"Don't be ridiculous." She started to turn away.

"Don't *you* be ridiculous."

I stepped toward the clerk. When our faces were inches apart, I added, "If you can get that kind of price for a standard sheepskin coat, then I want to own this store—or one like it. I came to Leadville to invest in mines, but I'm a shopkeeper by trade, and suddenly I realize I ought to stick to what I know. Shopkeeping appears to be a hell of a lot more profitable than I imagined... possibly more profitable than mining."

The unruffled clerk seemed bewildered and unsure for the first time.

"Now, give me a price... or do you need to go get the owner?"

She straightened her shoulders in an attempt to regain her composure. "The store is not for sale."

I walked to the front of the store and looked out the window. A new building was going up directly across the street. "Where's the telegraph office?"

She looked confused by the question, so I added, "I want to send a telegram to my associates in New York City." I pointed out the window. "I should be able to fully stock a haberdashery in that building across the street before the first thaw."

"You're serious?"

"I'm serious."

The clerk's haughty manner collapsed. "The owner of this store owns the Carbonate Hotel. You can find Mr. Cunningham in his office behind the reception desk."

"Good. I have four rooms at the Carbonate, so he probably won't treat me as dismissively as you did."

"Four rooms? How did—" The clerk threw a furtive look at the store entrance. "I apologize, sir. Obviously, I misjudged. Perhaps we can work a discount for that coat, after all."

"I no longer want just the coat. I want the entire store, or I'll open a competing store directly across the street. I owned several carriage trade shops in New York City, and I know how to run a pretentious enterprise."

I gave the clerk an appraising look. Her dark dress, cinched at the waist, showed off an excellent figure, and she carried herself with assurance. "If I buy this store, perhaps I'll even retain you as my senior clerk. You're certainly snooty enough."

"I come more expensive than you may think... and this is not a loaned dress. Besides, I would never leave Mr. Cunningham's employ. He's a gentleman."

"Not even for a piece of the business?"

That question got the reaction I wanted, but I suddenly wondered what the hell I was doing. I guess my business instincts had taken hold, but I wasn't in Leadville for business, at least not for my business. It was more than that. She had nettled me from the time I'd entered the store. All the women I knew in New York looked with disdain at anyone without money. I hated their condescension toward servants and riffraff they encountered in their daily lives. I came west to escape them and their so-called gentlemen friends. Perhaps that was why Jenny appealed to me. She was everything this type of woman was not. Jenny was uneducated but smart as a whip. She had been raised by a tenant farmer and had grown up working with her hands. A man might describe this clerk as beautiful, but Jenny was pretty—simpler and fresher, with an engaging smile.

I had to extricate myself from this situation, but I decided to take advantage of having placed doubt into the mind of this clerk. "I'll pay half for the coat."

"No, sir." Her voice was firm. "Twenty percent is the absolute best we can do."

"We?" I looked around. "I don't see anyone else."

"I meant the store." She waved her arm around like the dry goods were participating in the negotiations. "That's the best the store can do. Prices are sky-high in Leadville. Transportation costs are set at extortionist levels. Everything costs dear ... but you already know that if you aren't lying about having four rooms next door."

I decided that I had let my pride get the better of me. There was no way I wanted to own a business in Leadville. Without any further dickering, I said, "I'll take the coat. I'm sorry to have bothered you with my nonsense."

Chapter 27

My encounter with the store clerk had delayed me, so I had just finished ordering a bottle of whiskey when I heard Sharp call to me from across the Carbonate's expansive lobby. One glance in his direction and I rushed over. He had been beaten badly. Sharp was a sturdy-built man with a solid demeanor, but his swollen left eye and blood-caked nose and lower lip made him look his age and a bit fragile.

"Damn it," I said, as I rushed up. "I knew I should have gone with you."

"If ya want to help, grab that bottle of whiskey and help me up to Doc's room."

I turned to see a bewildered waiter standing behind me with a bottle and two glasses on a silver platter. I signaled him to come over. "Take that bottle and three glasses up to room 302."

I turned my attention back to Sharp. I began to pull his arm across my shoulder, but I hesitated for fear of hurting him. "Where're you hurt?"

"Mostly my ribs. That Ute pounded me with the handle end of his knife. Promised to use the other end if I came back."

I let Sharp lean his weight against my shoulder, and then we moved with a halting pace toward the stairs. It took us probably ten minutes to climb the two flights. Sharp's grunts and pants restricted our conversation to me saying "careful" and Sharp repeatedly exclaiming "shit."

Dooley, who had been alerted by the hotel steward, met us at the top of the landing. I was worried, but the doctor looked curious, like a blacksmith sizing up a broken wagon. He stopped us and quickly examined Sharp's injuries.

"Sit him in a chair in my room. Keep him upright so I can wrap those ribs. The rest of his wounds just need to be cleaned and dabbed with iodine. He ain't hurt bad."

"Glad to hear it, Doc. Now that I know that, maybe this pain'll go away."

"Quit whining. You've been hurt worse." With that, Dooley turned and preceded us into his room.

As he went to work, I poured three glasses of whiskey. Sharp swallowed his down in a single gulp. I kept my questions to myself until Dooley had finished wrapping Sharp's ribs and had cleaned up his bruised face.

As Sharp examined himself in the commode mirror, I opened with, "I guess you haven't learned how to conduct a civil conversation."

"It was civil enough until this mean son of a bitch decided to introduce himself. I just asked a couple of braves how much a guide might cost. I spotted our man sittin' under a shelter, eyein' me, but I ignored him. Pretty soon, he marched right over an' proceeded to pummel me. No reason other than meanness that I can figure."

"Did he overhear?"

"Too far away."

Dooley was washing his hands at the basin and said over his shoulder, "What the hell were you doing up there?"

I answered for Sharp. "A miner told us about an ornery Indian encamped up there. The way he described him, we suspected he might be Bane's go-between."

"So you sashay up the hill and start asking questions?" Dooley turned from the basin, shaking his hands dry. "Jeff, I thought you were smarter than that. Maybe you deserved a beating."

Sharp sat on the edge of the bed and rubbed his chin. "I gave that Ute no cause to pay me any mind. I only asked to hire an Indian for a couple of days to guide me around the local claims. Figured if I got him away from his brothers an' plied him with whiskey, I could ask questions without raisin' a fuss. All I was doin' was barterin' a price."

"Did he give any clue as to why he went after you?" I asked.

"No. Just beat on me an' told me to get back to my own people. Vrable might've described me to him, but I doubt it."

"Why?"

"Because Bane probably told Vrable not to go near his man until he had somethin' important. 'Sides, Vrable wouldn't call attention to himself by traipsing up to that Indian encampment."

"Maybe he's not Bane's go-between," I offered. "Maybe he's just an angry Ute who doesn't like white men."

"Could be, but I don't think so. We know Bane is a killer, and anyone he used would be tough as nails. Ya shoulda seen the Indians fade away when he came out of that shelter. They're scared of him … and he ain't scared of nothin'. If we're right about a go-between, I'm bettin' this is our man."

I paced the room. When I stopped in front of Sharp, I asked, "Do those Indians on the hill have money?"

"Money?"

"Do they have enough money to buy things in shops?"

"Yep. Those Indians do. Most are flush from playin' guide for every saphead that wanders into Leadville. Probably take 'em all on the same route. Why?"

"Would this Ute go-between buy supplies before he left Leadville to meet up with Bane?"

"Probably." Sharp straightened a bit and rubbed his wrapped ribs "If not for himself, then to resupply Bane an' the girl. What're ya gettin' at, Steve?"

I pointed at my new coat. "When I bought that coat, I thought about buying the store that sold it."

"What the hell for?"

"I paid twenty-four dollars for that coat. Twice the steep price we paid in Durango. Seems there's more profit in selling dry goods than in digging silver."

"Steve, that's the same in any minin' town, but our purpose ain't investin' anymore."

"Seems our Ute's skittish around white men. Were you thinking about taking a daily trip up that hill to see if he's still sitting in that shelter or has bolted camp for the mountains?"

Sharp's eyes showed comprehension."Smart thinkin', Steve. We buy that store an' wait for him to come an' get provisions for the trail. Hell, we'll be partners. I'm in for half. Ya can teach me the shopkeepin' trade."

"Not that store. It caters to people with money. We need to find the store where prospectors and Indians go." I paced the room again to think. "When I complained about the cost of that coat, the clerk tried to send me to a cheaper emporium."

"Probably several general stores 'bout town." Sharp nodded

toward the whiskey bottle, indicating he wanted me to pour him another drink. "Too late tonight, so we might as well put a dent in that bottle. Tomorrow morning—we go shoppin'."

Chapter 28

The third general store we visited had the feel of a shop that catered to the bottom layer of Leadville's citizenry. The store was located at the end of State Street, a thoroughfare where the pleasure houses were quarantined from respectable society. Within arm's reach of passersby, prostitutes displayed their wares in cribs that lined both sides of State Street, but the location—just below the Indian encampment—made the store perfect for our purposes. When I stepped through the door, I saw no expensive mining equipment, only implements appropriate for crude prospecting. Likewise, the dry goods tended toward the shoddy, and the foodstuffs didn't extend beyond wilderness basics. The disheveled and dusty appearance told me that the owner was lazy.

The gaunt, ill-groomed man behind the pine counter didn't offer us a greeting as we approached.

"Good day, sir," I offered.

The shopkeeper made a guttural noise in response.

"Is the owner about?"

"I'm the goddamn owner." He gave us a nasty look. "Ya got a complaint?"

"No, a business proposal."

He pointed at the door. "Get the fuck out."

"Excuse me?"

"Get the fuck out of my store. Now, ya goddamn fraudsmen. I don't need yer kind in here. Go sell yer damn cheatin' schemes someplace else. I ain't no sucker."

"We're honest men ... with money to buy whatever we want."

"Then buy something."

"What's the most expensive item in this store?"

Without hesitation, he said, "An army model Colt. Thirty dollars. Guaranteed new from the factory."

The Colt .45 cost seven dollars mail order, so prices remained outrageous even in this woebegone shop. "May I see it?"

The man looked dubious. "Show me thirty goddamn dollars first."

I removed my wallet and fanned out more than three hundred dollars in currency. "I have more. Enough to buy this establishment if you're inclined to sell."

"It'd take a hell of a lot more than that," he sniffed.

I took it as a good sign that he didn't dismiss my casual offer. "I have a hell of a lot more. Are you interested in selling, because I'm interested in buying."

I finally had his attention. "Why should I? This is my livelihood."

"There's a long winter in the offing. Denver can be warm and comfortable with a fat bank account."

"Why're ya interested in this shit hole?" He laid both hands flat on the counter and stared for a moment at the currency I still held in front of him. "Don't make no sense." He raised his head until he met my eyes. "Why?"

"We arrived too late to buy a decent mine, but with a store we can still get our share of the silver." I made a point of looking around. "We want a shit hole, as you called it, so we can fix it up over the winter. There's plenty of money to be made from the greenhorn prospectors that'll crowd this valley early in the spring." I made my voice firm. "If we can't buy this store, we'll open one across the street."

"Is that a fucking threat? I don't take to threats. I've a mind to throw ya outta here."

"How much?" I asked evenly.

Without hesitation, he said, "Twenty thousand. Stick that in yer hat."

"Ten."

The man roiled in laughter. When he got control, he made a little wave with his hand and said, "Leave. Ya ain't got no business here."

"Ten, and you retain fifty percent ownership. We'll do all the work and send you half the profits."

The storekeeper slowly pulled a gun from somewhere below and laid it on the counter. "Just as I thought, goddamn fraudsmen. Now I'm not asking, I'm telling ya—get the fuck out."

"Fifteen … for everything." This time Sharp made the offer.

He looked queer at us and then laid his hand across the pistol. "Who sent ya?"

"Who do you fear sent us?" I asked.

"There's some about that want me outta here."

"We're not with them. You can stay or you can go. We don't care. We're just looking to buy a business."

"If ya show me eighteen thousand in cash, ya got yerself a store."

Sharp spoke up. "Do ya sell to Indians?"

"I sell to anybody with the damn wherewithal. What the hell difference does it make? Give me eighteen thousand dollars, and ya can either sell to Indians or not. I don't give a shit."

"Sixteen," I said. "That's my final offer."

"The dickering ended five minutes ago. The number is eighteen."

"Not cash. I can transfer the money in your name to any bank. It's safer."

The store owner pulled out a sheet of paper and used scissors to cut off a small piece. He wrote for a second and then handed me the tiny piece of paper.

"That's my bank in Denver. Deposit eighteen thousand in that bank, and then we'll go to my lawyer so he can draft a sales contract. One more thing: I insist on two hundred additional in cash so I can leave this godforsaken piss hole."

He had just increased the price by two hundred. I was about to argue but realized it had been my mistake to show him how much cash I carried. I said, "The money will be transferred to your name after you sign the sales agreement. Your lawyer can hold it until you confirm the deposit."

He smiled. "Figured that." He held out his hand. "I'll take the two hundred now as a sign of good faith."

I smiled in response. "If you want the two hundred, close up and have your lawyer draft the contract now."

Sharp added shrewdly, "Our offer is good for today only."

After we got the lawyer's address, we stepped outside, and the cold bit me. I cinched my coat collar tight against my throat and glanced up at the Indian encampment. "I sure hope this works."

"It should," Sharp said. "He trades with Indians. I saw pelts on the floor behind the counter."

"Could've been from white men," I said.

"Not nowadays. The old mountain men are long dead, an' younger men ain't made of hardy enough stuff to traipse around these mountains on their lonesome. Nope, those pelts came from Utes."

"Let's get to the telegraph office. I want to close this deal before McAllen arrives tonight."

"Yep. He'll surely enjoy hearin' that yer a shopkeeper again."

Chapter 29

The transaction went smoothly. Within hours, our banks had made deposits at the Denver bank whose name the gaunt shopkeeper had written on the piece of paper. After we met in a lawyer's office and signed the contract, another telegram transferred the funds to the seller's account, and a later telegram confirmed the transfer to the seller. I handed over two hundred in cash to complete the transaction. Sometimes the speed of the modern world astounded me.

My first act after leaving the lawyer's office was to hire two young boys to sweep, dust, and arrange the store. I wouldn't own the store long, and a tidy shop might even put off some of the normal customers, but I couldn't own a shop in such a mess. Besides, when I sold it, I wanted a higher price than I had paid. Getting the better end of this deal shouldn't have been important, but my nature forced me to look at every business transaction with an eye on potential profit.

I spent the rest of the day cleaning the store, while Sharp waited at the hotel for McAllen. In the late afternoon, Sharp appeared and gave a low appreciative whistle. "Steve, I thought I'd wandered into the wrong shop. Ya sure spruced up this damn hellhole."

"McAllen here?"

"It's polite to say howdy before jumpin' into business."

"Howdy… is McAllen here?"

"Yep. He gave us a little errand. Can ya close up?"

I untied my apron. "Never opened. Boys, come collect your pay."

The two boys stopped what they were doing and scurried over with their palms up. I had picked them randomly on the street, but they had both proved to be hard workers who knew how to follow directions without my having to keep an eye on them. Neither of them had ventured toward the hard-candy jar either.

I dropped several coins in each outstretched hand and said, "If you want to earn more, come back tomorrow."

Both boys smiled at each other and ran out.

"What does McAllen want?" I asked.

"We're to tell Grant that he's arrived and McAllen will meet him for dinner."

I reached into my pocket for the latchkey to the shop. "Let me lock up. Any sign of Red?"

"Nope."

"Did you tell McAllen about the store?"

"Yep. Thinks we lost sight of our task. The captain ain't a patient man. After we talk to Grant, we better try to calm him a bit."

As we started walking the three blocks to the Wells Fargo office, I said, "Jeff, I've been thinking: The shop's location's not bad for general business. Since we're on the corner, people can walk down Chestnut Street and avoid the brothels. The trick is to give them a reason to traipse down here."

"Steve, don't make McAllen right. We don't need to git him all agitated at us."

"Absolutely agree."

The Wells Fargo office was busy with end of the day mining business. Grant sat behind the same desk, ignoring the clutch of people at the counter.

Sharp edged in alongside the wall and said, "Mr. Grant, may we have a moment?"

Grant looked up with an annoyed expression, but then recognized us and smiled like we were the most welcome sight he had seen that day.

"Gentlemen, I've been expecting you. Let me get my coat, and I'll escort you to the property."

What property? Then I realized the reference to a property was a ruse so we could go somewhere private. If nothing else, Grant was quick-witted. Whatever we planned, we needed to take into account that our adversary was clever and not easily fooled.

After we stepped out to the street, Grant's demeanor immediately turned surly. "What the hell happened to McAllen the other night?"

"He arrived in town only an hour ago," Sharp said.

"Where was he? And why the hell didn't you inform me he wouldn't meet me for dinner?"

"We ain't his servants," Sharp said. "McAllen takes care of his own business."

"You're his friends."

"In case ya haven't noticed, there ain't any telegraph stations on the road from Durango. How the hell were we supposed to know when he'd arrive?"

"What held him up?"

"Goddamn it, ask him yerself."

"I will. When?"

"He'll meet ya tonight for dinner."

"Alone?"

"We'll be at a table where we can keep an eye on things."

Grant seemed to consider that and nodded before asking, "What's McAllen's mood?"

"If he don't kill ya on first sight, ya just might get through dinner."

"Tell him he needs to hear me out first. If he gets too riled, he'll regret it."

"You think you can win a fight with the captain?" I asked.

Grant looked at me for the first time. "I won't fight McAllen with guns, knives, or fists. I have another weapon that'll hurt him more. Just tell him to stay calm until he hears what I have to say."

"We'll tell him," I said. "But you two must have some history, because he thinks you had something to do with the Utes grabbing his daughter."

"He's guessed more."

"If he has, he ain't shared it with us," Sharp said. "If ya know McAllen, ya know he don't talk a hell of a lot."

"Gentlemen, I'll see you at dinner." Grant turned to go but then swiveled back to face us. "But stay a couple of tables away. If you get within earshot, I'll leave. This is private business."

Chapter 30

The three of us entered the Carbonate dining room about an hour before the appointed time. McAllen wanted to arrive ahead of the dinner crowd so we'd have a broad choice of tables. Only two tables were occupied, and those were filled by elderly couples.

The captain scanned the room. "Nobody looks suspicious."

"We do," I offered.

McAllen threw me a nasty look. "Then take care of it, Steve," he said with an irritated tone that I had come to expect. "Tip the staff generously and tell 'em to leave us alone unless we call 'em over."

I approached the dining room steward and, with a folded banknote in my palm, shook his hand. When I withdrew my hand, the banknote no longer belonged to me.

"Good evening. My name is Mr. Dancy, and I'm a business associate of that gentleman over there." I pointed to Captain McAllen.

He nodded slightly.

"We need two tables for the night: one for my associate to discreetly discuss a business arrangement, and another for myself and another associate. We'll pick our own tables. Please ask your staff not to disturb us unless we call them over." Still no reaction from the steward, so I added, "Have I made myself clear?"

"Not quite clear enough," he said as his eyes flitted down to his closed fist.

I shook his hand again, and another banknote passed between us. "I'm sure we're clear now," I said firmly.

"Enjoy the evening," he responded.

After I returned from my errand, McAllen said, "You two take the table to the left of the door. If anyone comes in, their back will be to you. I'll sit at that table in the rear corner." Before leaving us, he added, "Drink beer or wine. And not much of that. I want you to keep a sharp eye out."

I restrained a *yes, sir.*

After Sharp and I took a seat at our designated table, I called a waiter over and ordered an expensive French Bordeaux. McAllen told us not to drink a lot, so we might as well drink well. After the waiter uncorked the bottle and I tested it, I looked over to see McAllen scowling a warning at me.

As the waiter poured, Sharp said, "Captain ain't too happy about ya disobeyin' his orders."

"We'll only be disobeying if we order a second bottle." I hooked a thumb at the dining room steward. "Besides, that steward's happy, and one happy man per room is plenty."

After testing the Bordeaux for himself, Sharp smiled appreciatively. "Good choice, Steve." After another taste, he added, "Yep … a mighty fine sippin' wine."

"We have an hour before Grant arrives," I said. "Maybe we should order oysters to wile away the time. I heard they transport them here live."

"You're paying, of course."

Damn it, I was too slow. "Of course."

"Then let's make the captain nervous by enjoyin' ourselves."

I started to wave the waiter over, when I heard, "Mr. Steve Dancy, I suggest that you take every opportunity to enjoy yourself while you can."

The woman's voice came from over my shoulder. Out of the corner of my eye, I had seen a rotund woman get up from one of the two occupied tables. When we came in, the woman had sat with her back to me and I hadn't paid any notice to the matronly diner. A mistake. When I turned my head, I saw my worst enemy hovering just over my shoulder.

"Mrs. Bolton, a pleasure. I assumed that you were still in San Francisco."

"I had business in Colorado that my assistants couldn't handle."

That gave me pause. "Was that business here or in Durango?"

She smiled sweetly. "My interests move around."

I was the one that had moved, and I didn't need a reminder that her matronly flowered dress cloaked a thoroughly demented woman. Mrs. Bolton had a huge swollen face that seemed far too large for her squat, corpulent body. Despite a less than attractive personage, she carried herself with a haughtiness that demanded toadying attention.

Now here she stood before me, acting coy. She knew that I knew she had sent the two men to kill me in Durango. It was a measure of her malice that she wanted her enemies to plainly see her connivances while she pretended wholesomeness and innocence.

"Cliff and Pete weren't good ranch hands," I said. "They were worse gunmen."

"For goodness sake, I haven't the slightest idea what you're talking about." She paused dramatically to bestow one of her excessively sweet smiles on me. "Dear Mr. Dancy, do I understand that someone tried to shoot you?"

"You know full well what happened in Durango. You hired those men."

"Cliff and Pete? You're mistaken. I would never hire misfits for serious work. And Mr. Dancy, I assure you that I take our little disagreements seriously."

I suddenly grew interested in her dinner companion. He was dressed in respectable dinner attire and looked a full twenty years younger than Mrs. Bolton. Trouble. It would be just like her to flaunt a hired assassin in front of me. Damn her. I already had enough on my plate.

"How're you doing financially?" I asked to needle her. "I hope you can live comfortably with the stipend your son left you."

"Oh, that trifle. You must know I ran the ranch while my son ran the state. The ranch's banking affairs were quite complex—far too complex for my son to fully understand." She rewarded me with another of her sweet smiles. "Thank you for your concern, but money is the least of my worries."

Damn. The old biddy had skimmed her son's profits from the ranch. That meant she could afford to hire professional killers. I gave her dinner mate another appraising look, but he ignored me. I didn't have time for this right now.

"Mrs. Bolton, when Sean Washburn hired assassins to kill me, I went directly to the man himself and killed him." Now I paused for dramatic effect. "If you send any more men, I will also deal with you directly." I paused. "Do you understand?"

"I haven't the slightest notion what you're talking about."

"Yes, you do."

"Dear Mr. Dancy, Cliff and Pete worked for my daughter-in-law. Perhaps you should be threatening her."

"I'm not playing your games. Please return to your table."

"Goodness, your ego astounds me. I have a full life to live, and it does not revolve around you."

"Who's your dinner companion?" I demanded.

"A gentleman friend. Perhaps you've heard of him." Now her too-sweet-smile turned into a triumphant sneer. "His name is Bat Masterson."

Chapter 31

Mrs. Bolton returned to her table, but Sharp's worried expression bothered me more than her unexpected visit.

"Have ya heard of Bat Masterson?" he asked.

"Of course, but I didn't think he was a killer for hire."

"Me neither."

"Do you know him?" I asked.

"Nope."

"Jeff, you know everyone."

"Never ran across Masterson." He looked in their direction. "Sure would like to know what she told him. If he took her employ, it had to be a pack of lies."

"You're right. I should go over there and set the story right. If I do it right in front of her, it'll make her mad as hell. Maybe I can get her so angry, she'll spew spittle all over Masterson's dinner."

Before Sharp could respond, Grant strolled right by us. I watched carefully as he approached McAllen. No immediate gunplay. No handshakes either. The two men just looked warily at each other, and then Grant slowly sat down across the table from McAllen.

It looked like the two were just going to talk, so I glanced over at Masterson. "Stay put," Sharp said. "We gotta keep an eye on Grant and the rest of this room. I'll talk to Masterson tomorrow."

"Why you?" I asked.

"Because Mrs. Bolton didn't hire him to kill me. I'll talk to him and find out what that shrew told him. Don't worry, I'll make sure he's got the story straight."

It made sense. I took a sip of wine and looked around the room. "I don't see anyone suspicious. Do you think Grant came alone?"

Sharp didn't answer at first. After his own inspection, he said, "Steve, I'm not as good as you with a handgun ... why don't ya take a look around an' make sure there ain't no nasty lookin' men hangin' about outside?"

"Good idea."

I got up and left the dining room. Nobody lurked in the lobby, and a check of the indoor privy didn't reveal anyone hanging around there either. I hesitated and then decided to take a peek outside—without returning to my room for my sheepskin coat. I walked fast, and my outside tour took less than five minutes.

When I walked back into the dining room, Sharp asked, "Why are your teeth chattering?"

"Took a look outside. Didn't see anyone I wouldn't trust holding the reins of my horse."

"Steve, when I said outside, I meant the lobby."

I took a good swallow of wine. "I figured that, but I thought a look outside might be wise." I nodded in Grant's direction. "I think he came alone." I swept the room with my eyes again. "Damn. Unless he's in cahoots with Mrs. Bolton." The thought frightened me. "Do you think that's possible?"

"Shit. Maybe. She's got reason to hate ya, but she might also be angry at McAllen for helpin' ya. I can't imagine how Grant would get together with her, but we better keep a close eye on her an' Masterson."

Over the next hour, we ate pheasant, drank wine, and watched the two tables. Nothing untoward happened. Bolton and Masterson left first. I couldn't tell anything from their demeanor, but just as Mrs. Bolton passed our table, she winked at me. Damn her.

A quarter of an hour later, Grant got up from McAllen's table and walked out wearing a self-satisfied expression. As soon as he left the dining room, McAllen came toward our table but stopped when a hapless waiter crossed his path. He practically grabbed the man by the scruff of the neck and turned him back toward the kitchen. I heard him bark, "Bring us a bottle of good Kentucky bourbon."

McAllen plopped down at our table. "I was right." He looked around, as if the waiter should already be at his elbow. "He wants to take a shipment from the Carbonate Kings . . . before the Rio Grande finishes the train line to Leadville."

"What part does he want you to play?" I asked.

"The main villain . . . but that's not what he said. If I take care of the Pinkertons and the transport after the heist, then I get twenty-five percent and my daughter." McAllen pounded his knuckles against the table. "He conveniently forgot to explain the double cross he has in mind."

"Did ya tell him ya already quit the Pinkertons?" Sharp asked.

"Yep. Told him the story we agreed on. He said if I can't handle the Pinkertons, he'll kill my daughter. Gave me two days to get my job back."

"Do you believe him?" I asked.

"Bane's nature is to kill. Anyway this goes, Bane'll kill her." McAllen shook his head. "There's nothin' even Vrable can do to change that."

"What about the letter?" I asked.

"I decided not to bring that up yet. After a day or two, I'll demand proof that he has her and she's still alive. I'm going to wait until Red gets here and you boys set up shop in that store."

"Sounds reasonable," Sharp said.

"Steve, one more thing." McAllen gave me a hard stare. "Get rid of that Mrs. Bolton ... and I mean now. I don't know what she's doing here, but there ain't no good in it. You take care of her before she messes up our plans."

"How do you propose I get rid of her? I can't just throw her on a train again."

"I don't give a shit how you do it. Kill her, for all I care. Just take care of her ... and do it before Red arrives."

Chapter 32

As I scrubbed my face the next morning, I worried about how to handle Mrs. Bolton. Despite what McAllen had said, I was not about to kill her, but she wouldn't go away on her own. I also didn't want to tangle with Bat Masterson. How the hell was I going to rid myself of this threat?

Someone knocked on my door. I picked up my Colt and moved to the side of the door frame. "Yes?"

"Open up, Steve," Sharp yelled.

When I opened the door, Sharp burst in with more energy than a youngster released from school. "What's keepin' ya? I already ate, an' I'm ready to learn the shopkeepin' trade."

"It's not even seven. Let me at least get a cup of coffee."

"Damn, Steve. Ya don't know squat about miners. Ya already lost half yer trade. These ain't gentlemen bird hunters. Miners start as soon as there's enough light to see. Let's go. We can brew coffee at the store."

"Jeff, what's got you so anxious? I thought shopkeeping would bore you."

"Nothin' bores me. Specially nothin' I've never done before. Come on. Get yer coat and gloves, and let's go."

As we approached the store, I saw my two young helpers waiting by the locked door. "Need help today, Mr. Dancy?" they asked, as they patted their sides to keep warm.

"Yes, boys. I'll figure out something for you to do." I unlocked the door. "Do either of you know how to make coffee?"

"Yes, sir. Make it every morning for my pa."

"Good. Get that stove started and make us a pot." Mostly out of politeness, I asked, "Where's your pa this morning?"

"At his diggin's. Been there since sunup."

I didn't need to look at Sharp. I could feel his smug expression on the back of my neck. Partly to get by the moment, I turned to the second boy and handed him a silver dollar. "Run to the bakery and buy a loaf of sourdough. You can buy a sweet roll for yourself and your friend. Bring back the change."

As the boy ran out, Sharp yelled, "Get apples too." Sharp turned to me. "Now what?"

I opened the shades. "How are you feeling?"

When I turned around, Sharp looked puzzled. "Oh, ya mean the beatin'. Hell, I've been beat up before. I don't want nobody to poke me in the ribs, but otherwise I'm fit enough."

"Then how about you nose around the other general stores and get their prices. I want the lowest prices in town, but I don't want to give merchandise away either."

"Lowest prices? Hell, I've been paying outrageous prices for gear all my life. I thought it was time to even up the tally."

"Did you see any customers waiting at the door? Word will get out about our low prices, and we'll get all the business we can handle. Speaking of that, we need more stock." I checked to make sure the boy had our coffee going. "As you drink your coffee, make me a list of merchandise miners and prospectors buy. While you're checking around town, I'll leave the shop in the boys' hands and send a telegram order to Denver."

"Steve, we aren't really in the shopkeepin' business. Remember, this is a ruse."

"The better we run the store, the better the ruse. Besides, I don't know any other way."

Sharp thought a minute. "Might as well do the job right. I'll add to my list stuff Indians buy."

"Don't worry about cheap whiskey. Seems we got plenty of rotgut under the counter."

"How 'bout knives, used rifles, cornmeal, wool yarn, beads . . . ?"

"Plenty. Seems the former proprietor catered to our friends on the hill."

"Probably did right well with that trade. Prospectors right off the stage too, I suspect."

"Jeff, how do you think that Indian who beat you up will react when he sees you in this store?"

"Coffee's ready," the boy yelled from the stove in the back of the store. About the same time, his friend came bursting through the front door clutching a burlap bag with a loaf of bread peeking out the top.

"Looks like breakfast's here," Sharp said.

After we had filled coffee cups and sliced apples, Sharp tore himself a section of sourdough and ripped a good chunk off with his teeth. Around a mouth full of bread, he said, "I've thought about it, an' I don't believe that Indian knew who I was. I think he was just angry, an' I was handy."

"Could give away our plan if you're wrong."

"I weren't askin' questions, I was hirin' guides. And I don't think that dandy Grant talks regular with Indians."

"He talked to Bane."

Sharp shrugged. "What choice do we have? You got another plan?"

"Not now. I suppose we've got to play this one out." I sipped my coffee. "But this plan, if you can call it that, sure relies on events going exactly as we hope."

"Well, if ya remember right, until we came up with this shaky plan, we had no plan at all."

"I'll think about an alternative."

"I'll tell ya what ya better think on: gittin' somebody to run this store. We gotta be free to git up an' go. McAllen's gonna keep givin' us errands, an' when the time comes, we gotta skedaddle after that Indian. Those two boys ain't gonna cut it."

That brought me up short. "Damn, you're right." I walked over to the stove and refreshed my coffee. I stood by the warmth and took a couple sips. "I need to think on it some more, but I might know someone."

"Bullshit, Steve. The only person ya knew in Leadville was Doc, an' he's left town."

"Not Doc."

"Who?"

"Not now. Finish your breakfast. We've got work to do."

Chapter 33

By the end of the day, we had a handle on pricing, we had finished organizing the store, and I had ordered a wagonload of merchandise from Denver. Customers were rare, but those that came in were surprised by our newly reduced prices. Hopefully, they would spread the word fast. The two boys had shown themselves to be good workers with a surprising maturity. I guessed children grew up fast on the frontier. No Indians had entered the store, but Sharp said they probably already had their stores for the winter.

After we closed, I left Sharp at the hotel door and walked on to the haberdashery. Several customers milled around, and I pretended to examine pieces of clothing as well. When the senior clerk noticed me, she nodded curtly in my direction and then continued to advise a tall, skinny man about the advantages of a tailored suit.

When she finally came over, she looked wary. "Good evening. I hope you find your coat satisfactory."

"It keeps me warm. Or at least as warm as a person could expect in these mountains."

"How may I help you?"

"I'd like to talk to you in private."

"In case you haven't noticed, I'm the only clerk working."

"When do you close?"

She looked irritated. "I'm busy. What do you want?"

Before thinking, I blurted, "I want you."

"Go to hell. Please leave the store. Immediately."

"I'm sorry. Poor choice of words. I meant, I want to hire you."

She stiffened her back and cocked her shoulders. "Get out. I'm not for hire. I believe you can find what you're looking for on State Street."

I had inadvertently made her furious, so this time I paused to think before I spoke. "Excuse me. This is a complete misunderstanding. Will you give me a moment to explain?"

"No. Last time you spewed a bunch of lies so I'd give you a discount on that coat. I won't be taken again. Please leave."

I tried a smile. "You always seem to be trying to get rid of me. The last time you kept sending me to an emporium down the street."

She tilted her head and examined me. "You speak like an educated gentleman, but you dress and lie like a guttersnipe." She glanced around. "You'll have to excuse me. I have other customers."

"Wait. I didn't lie to you about having enough money to buy this store. In fact, I bought a store, and I intend to make it the most profitable in Leadville. I came here to hire you to run it for me. I pay well, and I'll give you an ownership position."

"Why? You don't know me." She sounded dubious, but I had captured her attention.

"That's why I want to talk in private."

"Please go. You people are so tiresome."

"What people?"

"Con artists. People who work to take advantage. You're no different than all the rest, and I'm weary of your kind."

"You're mistaken. I'm not conning you. A friend and I bought the general store at the end of State Street. My partner is much more rustic than me, but I assure you, we're both gentlemen."

"That's an Indian store." Her eyes narrowed as she took half a step away from me. "You expect me to give up a position where the very best people shop to wait on Indians?"

"No ... not if you feel that way about Indians and people that may not be the very best. I'm sorry. My mistake." I turned to leave.

"Wait." She looked thoughtful. "How do you intend to make this store the most profitable in Leadville?"

"First, we cleaned the store up. I've ordered a huge shipment of new merchandise from Denver. Today we set our prices below every store in town. I'm a shopkeeper by trade, and I know how to make money. We'll do what's necessary."

"That's a bad location."

"Miners go where they can get fair trade for their dollar. We're on the corner, so respectable folk never need tread on State Street. It's also handy for Indians ... and we do intend to trade with the Utes."

Her interest appeared to grow.

"If you will come under my employ, I'll pay you forty dollars a month and ten percent of the profits." The last sentence obviously appealed to her.

"Why? Why me? Not because I gave you a discount on that coat?'

"Because you held your ground. I couldn't knock you off balance. My store isn't for gentlemen. It will attract tough men, and I need someone that won't fold."

Now she looked hesitant. "Are you saying I'd be alone in this store... on State Street?"

She caught me off guard. I hadn't really thought this through. "At times... possibly." Then I had a thought. "I have two boys that will be around if my partner or I need to leave."

"Boys?" She turned away and then whipped around to face me again. "How much do you want me?"

I stammered. "How much... I guess... why, what do you want?"

"Fifty a month, paid in advance. Ten percent ownership, not ten percent of the profits. An additional ten percent in the second year if we double the profits of the first year. Last, you get someone to teach me how to handle a gun."

"That's a stiff set of demands."

"What's your name?'

"Steve Dancy."

"I'm Mrs. Baker." She held out her hand and we shook. "Mr. Dancy, I came here with my husband. He was a mining engineer and was killed in a tunnel collapse. Unfortunately, he incurred debts before his death. So far, I've repaid all but thirty dollars. With fifty from you, I can be debt free and still have twenty dollars. I run this store. Mr. Cunningham hardly bothers to come by. I'm a good storekeeper, and you know an attractive woman will draw as many miners as your low prices. *That's* why you want to hire me. So if I double the profits, I want my ownership doubled. Last, your store is in the worst part of town, and you offer me *boys* for protection. I want someone skilled to teach me how to use a pistol."

"You came up with all that on the spur of the moment?" She didn't respond, so I added, "I'll agree to the rest of your demands, but I don't pay in advance. I will, however, give you fifty dollars to sign an agreement to work for me for one year."

"If I quit?"

"If within the first year, you owe me fifty dollars."

"You'll pay me sixty dollars to sign the agreement, and it goes down five dollars each month."

"Deal." I laughed. She was audacious. "Where're you from?"

"Philadelphia."

"Family?"

Her expression became defiant. "My father disowned me when I married Paul, because his family failed to qualify for a listing in the social register." Her eyes held mine with a steady gaze. "Don't worry, Mr. Dancy, I won't run home to Papa."

I nodded. "If you come over to the store tomorrow, I'll have papers ready." I examined her maroon dress. It flared from the hips but was tight above the waist. Her hair was pulled back in a modest bun, but stylishly to show off her graceful neck. Altogether, she looked alluring yet refined. "If I may, your dress will be impractical for my store."

She sounded wary when she asked, "What do you have in mind?"

"A gingham dress, perhaps. Something with more color."

She stiffened her back and cocked her shoulders again. I think she meant it as a defiant pose, but it had the effect of thrusting her breasts at me. "I won't show cleavage."

"No need." I glanced down at her chest and smiled. "A tight bodice like you're wearing will be quite sufficient."

I left while she was still blushing.

All in all, it had been a tiring day. As soon as I returned to the hotel, I ate a quick meal and retired, because Sharp insisted that we open at six in the morning. I missed the idle-rich bird hunting customers that I was used to in New York. They seldom came in until they had enjoyed a leisurely breakfast.

I unhooked my holster and was about to undress, when I heard a knock. I opened the door to see a pasty boy. "A gentleman in the lobby wants to see you," he said.

"Did he give a name?" I asked.

"Nope, but I knows him."

"Would it be inconvenient for you to tell me his name?"

"Do ya have two bits?"

"I do." I kept my hands at my side.

After a puzzled moment, he said, "If you gives me two bits, I'll gives you the name."

"Two bits is a lot of money. If I give it to you, I want you to let me know if any strangers ask about me or my friend, Mr. Sharp, in room 207."

"Two bits *ain't* a lot of money. If ya want me to keep an eye out for ya, it'll cost ya four bits ... every day."

"How do I know you're worth four bits a day?"

"You see me in the lobby. All the times. I'm always there, and I keep a keen eye out." He shuffled his feet. "Listen, Mister, I don't work for the hotel. I hang around and do favors for guests. I'm a professional."

"A professional?" I laughed. "Well, I'm a cheap. I'll pay you two bits a day."

"How good a job ya want done?"

I laughed again. I liked this enterprising kid. I reached into my pocket and held out a silver dollar. "For two days, but it includes giving me the name of the man downstairs."

He grabbed the coin. "His name's Bat Masterson. I'd bring my gun if I was you." A sly smile took over his pasty face. "I'll see you in two days for the next dollar ... if yer still around." He scurried away before I could respond.

Bat Masterson? Shit. Why would he want to see me? Should I avoid him? I decided it was better to see him in the lobby rather than on the street. He couldn't mean to shoot me in a high-toned hotel. After thinking it through, I decided to go unarmed. No sense in provoking a famous gunman.

I walked downstairs and saw Masterson in the quiet corner by the fireplace that Sharp and I had used earlier. He spotted me as I walked up, so I extended my hand and said in a friendly voice, "Mr. Masterson, pleased to meet you. I'm Steve Dancy."

He stood to shake my hand and simply said, "Likewise."

After the preliminaries, we sat in chairs facing each other in front of the welcoming fire. I guessed that he was in his mid-twenties, and he was smaller than his reputation. His custom-tailored suit fit perfectly, and his white shirt was clean and pressed. He had the look of a dandy but sported a short-barreled Colt.

"I thought we'd better talk," he said. "I don't know you or anything about you, but I believe in giving a man fair warning until I learn he doesn't deserve it."

"Mrs. Bolton hired you?" I asked, getting right to the point.

"Mrs. Bolton tried to hire me, but I'm otherwise engaged."

That stopped me for a second. Finally, I said, "I'm glad to hear that. I wouldn't want you after me."

"Don't take it as good news. There's plenty of idle men in this town. My take on Mrs. Bolton is that she doesn't give up easy. She'll find someone. Unlike me, he'll probably be a back shooter." He gave me an appraising stare. "What'd you do to piss her off so much?"

"I helped her daughter-in-law with the execution of her son's will. Her husband left almost everything to his wife." I paused. "To her way of thinking, I helped steal the ranch she built with her husband and managed for her deceased son. A large ranch, by the way. The largest in Nevada."

"Her daughter-in-law may've got the lion's share, but Mrs. Bolton has enough ready cash to hire anyone in this town willing to take on the work."

"You said you were otherwise engaged. May I ask how?"

"No secret. I work for the Santa Fe Railway . . . and I'm still sheriff of Ford County in Kansas."

"The Santa Fe? How did you come to be employed by them?"

"Long history. I helped them lay the tracks into Dodge City back in '72 when I was only eighteen."

"You're not laying track now, I hope."

"No, security. We're having skirmishes with the Denver and Rio Grande line. Miners are hauling fifty tons of refined silver a day out of these hills, and they haul the ore out by wagon surrounded by a heavy guard. The canyon along the Arkansas River has room for only a single pair of rails, so whoever gets here first will have a highly profitable monopoly."

"I heard the Carbonate Kings hire Pinkertons to ride alongside the Wells Fargo guards."

Masterson looked quizzical. "That's right. What's your interest?"

"Cost. I'm trying to gauge the profit in hauling a trainload out of these mountains. Shares in the winning line should do well on Wall Street." I tapped the arm of my chair in thought. "These skirmishes you mentioned, are they shooting skirmishes?"

"On occasion. Mostly moving survey stakes, man-made avalanches, and tearing up each other's tracks."

"Can I help? I own Santa Fe *and* Rio Grande stock."

Masterson gave me another appraising look. "Are you the gent that had a shooting in Durango?"

"Yes. The first of Mrs. Bolton's hired guns. Thankfully, they were just cowpokes looking for easy money. Not so easy, as it turned out."

Masterson shook his head. "People like you and me build reputations off no-accounts with shaky hands."

"I understand you faced some dangerous men in Dodge City."

"Drunk men for the most part. The secret to a long life as a sheriff is to approach danger stone sober. I learned that from Wyatt Earp."

"Is it true he's a teetotaler?"

"He takes a drink on occasion but never when he might face trouble. A sober man facing someone in his cups always has the edge. I'm giving you good advice. Don't drink in public until you deal with this threat."

"Thanks, I'll keep that in mind. May I ask a question?"

"You can ask. I'll decide whether I want to answer."

"I have a friend who's acquainted with Doc Holliday. He says he's only dangerous when drunk. How does that fit with your advice?"

"Doc's a strange one, and your friend's right. His hand shakes when he's sober and gets steady when he drinks. He also gets mean as hell sometimes, especially if wronged. But Doc's different than most men. Don't be fooled into believing you get better with a couple drinks under your belt. You just think you're better."

"Don't worry. I won't discard advice from you and Wyatt Earp."

After a pause in the conversation, Masterson asked, "How much stock do you own in the Santa Fe and Rio Grande?"

"I'd have to check my records, but if memory serves, about ten thousand shares of each."

Masterson sat upright. "That's a hell of a lot of money. Are you wealthy?"

"Yes. How long has this contest gone on?"

"Almost four years. It started with the line into New Mexico. The Santa Fe won that one, but the Rio Grande had the upper hand on the Leadville line. I think the Santa Fe hoped that enlisting someone with my reputation would encourage the Rio Grande to back off, but they didn't. Just got more aggressive. To tell the truth, my fee is substantial, so I'm not all that eager to see this contest end."

Since I held large investments in both rail lines, I did want to see this conflict brought to a reasonable conclusion. "Speaking of your reputation, I came west to write a book about the frontier. Would you be open to an interview? I have a contract with a New York publisher, and I promise to give you a prominent position."

"No, I'm sorry, but I'm writing my own book."

"How's it going?"

"Slow. Been busy."

"You know, if my book's a success, it'll give yours a boost when you get it finished."

"Thank you, Mr. Dancy, but I'm not in a hurry." He smiled. "I'm a young man, and the story is not near complete. I've been approached by many writers, but I'm determined to write my own story."

I reached into my pocket and pulled out a carte de visite that I had had created for me before I left New York. I realized this was the first calling card I had used since I had ventured west. I supposed Masterson's impeccable attire made me assume he wouldn't consider it pretentious.

I held the card out between us. "If you change your mind, please contact me first. I'll do you justice, and as you mentioned, I'm rich, so I can make it worth your while."

He accepted the card and put it into a vest pocket without looking at it. "You may be wealthy, but you're also building your own reputation with a gun. I suggest you rely on *your* experiences."

"With any luck, I won't have enough adventures of that type to fill an entire book. Keep me in mind."

He gave me yet another appraising look. "Put me out of *your* mind. I didn't like Mrs. Bolton, so I decided to warn you about her intentions. That's the only reason I came to see you. Good night."

With that, Masterson got up and left the Carbonate Hotel. I hoped that wouldn't be the last time I saw him.

Chapter 34

The next couple of days, we concentrated on running the store and stayed away from McAllen, Grant, and the Indian encampment. Townspeople had to believe we took our enterprise seriously, or Grant might guess our purpose. In the evenings, I went to bed early, but Sharp visited saloons and spread the word around town that he had discovered better profit in shopkeeping than in mining. Despite first approaching Grant as friends of McAllen, we hoped this would make us look like another couple of money-grubbers with our own interests.

Mrs. Baker slowly adjusted to her new position. She obviously felt out of her usual social class, but she gamely tried to fit in with us and our customers. She wore a woolen day dress with a murky paisley pattern that outlined her figure perfectly. When Sharp met our new senior clerk for the first time, he thought she was an odd choice—until he noticed how miners lollygagged until she was free to wait on them. Further down State Street, passersby saw all sorts of lurid displays by prostitutes in their boardwalk cribs, but none could compete with the attractions of the demurely dressed Mrs. Baker.

Word about our new pricing spread, and each hour we saw more business. I wondered if lower prices were a good idea, after we began to run low on stock. I sent the boys around to other shops, and they scavenged some second- and third-rate goods that the other stores couldn't sell. I followed up on their visits and convinced a couple of store owners to transfer more of their slow-moving stock to me on consignment. We didn't sell much of the shoddy merchandise, but it helped fill the empty shelves. Another advantage to these arrangements was that the other shopkeepers came to the conclusion that we only sold inferior goods. I was pleased to keep our real intent hidden until our Denver shipment arrived.

Masterson's warning kept me alert. I wore my Colt at all times and kept a shotgun under the counter. When Sharp and I made the ten-minute walk between the hotel and the shop, we both carried Winchesters. Sharp always preferred a rifle—even for close work—and I wanted to look as intimidating as possible. Sharp also slung a bag over his shoulder with enough coins to jingle so that people would think we were heavily armed to protect our till receipts instead of my life.

My biggest worry remained Mrs. Bolton. She had taken up residence in the Carbonate Hotel, and I saw her on occasion in the lobby or the dining room. She always nodded pleasantly, like we were old friends, but I took it as a reminder to follow Mr. Masterson's advice and have only a single glass of wine with my evening meal.

On her second day, Mrs. Baker approached me in the mid-afternoon. "Mr. Dancy, you have not met all of our agreed terms."

"Excuse me?" After we had both signed her agreement, I had handed her sixty dollars.

"Is Mr. Sharp an expert gunman?"

I remembered. "Mr. Sharp is partial to rifles. I'll teach you how to use a handgun."

"Mr. Dancy, my husband taught me how to fire a pistol ... I intend to be skillful. I overheard you tell Mr. Sharp about a conversation between you and Bat Masterson. Are you friends? Can he teach me?"

"No and no. I'll teach you."

She looked dubious. "Perhaps ... this is the slow part of the day. Shall we see if you know any more about guns than I do?"

"We should wait for our new merchandise. I don't have a decent handgun in stock."

She reached into the folds of her dress and withdrew a small pistol. "I have a gun, Mr. Dancy. I just need someone to teach me how to use it properly."

"May I see that?" She laid it flat in my outstretched palm. "This is a new Colt Lightning .38. Where'd you get it?"

"My husband. He felt a woman needed protection on the frontier."

"This is a double-action pistol. All you do is squeeze the trigger. There's not much to teach."

"Aim, Mr. Dancy, aim. I want to hit what I want, and only what I want." Despite her attempt to disguise it, I saw that I had won a bit of her confidence by recognizing the model of her pistol.

I walked behind the counter and pulled out two boxes of .38s.

"Let's go to the livery and rent a buggy." As I came out from behind the counter, I yelled, "Jeff! You got the store."

It was damn cold, so I didn't drive too far out of town. Mrs. Baker had put on a heavy full-length wool coat, which she buttoned up against her neck, raising the collar. With gloves and hat and myriad undergarments, she was dressed more warmly than I. I snapped the reins and drove until I saw a hill we could place behind our targets to catch any errant shots. After helping Mrs. Baker down from the wagon, I took a burlap bag of bottles over to a flat rock about twenty feet away and started setting them up in a line. I glanced back to see Mrs. Baker taking practice aim with her small Colt. At least, I hoped it was practice aim.

"Put that gun down!" I yelled. She lowered the pistol and looked embarrassed. "Never point a gun at someone… unless you plan to shoot them. Damn."

"My husband said that. I apologize. I forgot."

I walked to the buggy and held out my hand. "May I see your gun?" She handed it over. I emptied the chamber and dry fired it several times. It had not been modified. The pull was long and hard. I never liked double-action pistols because the trigger finger had to do all the work, which made it hard to shoot straight—especially for a second shot. A single-action pistol distributed the burden between the thumb and the trigger finger, making the actual firing so easy that a cocked pistol became dangerous—too dangerous for Mrs. Baker. Her husband had been a wise man.

After I reloaded the Colt, I handed it back to her and said, "Let's see how you do. Take it slow. Hold the gun with both hands, aim, and squeeze the trigger."

She looked at the line of bottles, raised the gun with both hands, and fired almost instantly. Before I could tell her to take it easy, she had emptied the gun. All the bottles were still safely intact.

I reloaded the Colt for her and handed it back, "This time, slow down. Focus on the front sight." She took the gun and slowly brought it up on the bottles. "Take a deep breath."

She inhaled slowly, but as soon as she expelled the breath, she fired all six shots in rapid order. She missed every bottle, but I had discovered her most serious problem.

"You're closing your eyes," I said.

She gave me a condescending look. "I am not."

"You are. You're scared of the gun. It won't hurt you: It's meant to hurt others. Relax. Shoot once, and count to three before you fire again."

"I'm not scared. I've carried this pistol for six months. I'm as comfortable with it as I am with my fountain pen."

"That's a lie, Mrs. Baker. I've seen your penmanship. You write straight, and you stay on the piece of paper. Pens don't make loud noises. You're afraid of the bang."

"Mr. Dancy—" She thrust her shoulders back again. "You put those bottles too far away, and I've shot only a few times. I'll get the hang of it. I learn fast… and I'm *not* scared."

"I apologize. I'm just irritated that I collected so many bottles. I didn't know I'd need only a couple."

"You have no cause to be impolite."

I handed her the loaded pistol. "Please try again."

We were into the second box of cartridges before she had hit two bottles. Finally, I asked, "Why do you want to learn to shoot?"

"To protect myself. I may be in that store alone, and I'll certainly walk home alone at times. Men in this town believe that every unattached woman can be bought or simply taken."

I examined the distance to the line of bottles. "Excuse my brazenness, but a man must be close in order to take advantage of you."

She followed my eyes. "I told you that you put those bottles too far away."

"I agree. My error. I was thinking like a man."

I grabbed the burlap bag by a bottom corner and shook out the bottles. Then I tucked the edges of the bag into the rough bark of a nearby tree. I stood back and assessed the height—just about right for a man's chest.

"Come here," I said. "I want you to stand close—arm's length. Put the gun in your coat pocket." I pointed at the bag. "Pretend this is the hairy chest of an ugly brute that wants to rape you." Her head snapped back at my use of the word *rape*. "Don't use two hands, just pull the gun out of your coat and thrust it into his chest and pull the trigger—three times. Understand?"

"Perfectly." She became calm but then looked hateful as she drew the pistol and put three bullets into the exact center of the bag. The burlap smoldered from the gun flash, but what I noticed was the grin on Mrs. Baker's handsome face. "I told you I wasn't afraid of guns."

"No, you're not." I'd found something she feared more. "My error. Let's do that again."

We spent the next half hour practicing very close-range shooting. Mrs. Baker became increasingly proficient. She even asked to shoot at the bottles again and did better.

As I was about to assist her into the buggy, she said, "See, you placed those bottles too far away. No one can hit them all the time."

I couldn't resist. My Colt .45 filled my hand before I whirled around to blast all three remaining bottles in an eyeblink.

As the echo died away, I heard her whisper, "Oh, my God."

Without a word, I took her elbow and helped her climb into the buggy.

Chapter 35

On the fourth day, our first Indian entered the store—it was Red.

Mrs. Baker was out, eating lunch with a woman friend, so we ignored Red until we finished serving other customers. Red wandered to the back and pretended to be interested in ropes and canteens. Once the other customers left, I sent my two young helpers to exercise Chestnut and Sharp's horse. I had done this on most days and knew they would be gone for well over an hour. After they left, I closed the shade, locked the door, and put up a closed sign. When I turned around, I was surprised to find Red right on my heels. I hadn't heard a footfall.

I opened with, "When did you arrive?"

"Two days ago."

Sharp had joined us by this time and demanded, "Why didn't ya let us know?"

"No need." He turned toward the stove. "Got coffee?"

"Cold," Sharp snapped. "Ya could have let us know without makin' a big show of it."

"Heat some." Red made a sweep of the place with his eyes. "Not much stock."

"We lowered prices and ended up selling more than we expected." I led the three of us away from the door and toward the back of the shop. "We still have some basic necessities, and we'll get a shipment from Denver in a couple of days."

"Too late. We'll be on the trail."

"Somethin's happened?" Sharp asked excitedly.

"No."

We both waited for Red to elaborate, but he just glanced at the stove again. I hurried over and moved the morning coffee remains onto the hot stovetop.

When I turned around again, Sharp asked, "Have ya seen McAllen?"

"Yep."

"Come on, Red," Sharp prompted. "What did McAllen tell ya? Talk to us, for God's sake. Words ain't half eagles, ya know."

For the first time since I had known him, Red looked taken aback. It had probably never occurred to him that his taciturn nature frustrated us. When he was on the trail, he was alone or with the almost equally terse McAllen. In settlements, he probably had learned the easiest way to get along with townsfolk was to keep quiet.

After a moment, he said, "Last night, McAllen told Vrable he hired on again with Pinkerton and demanded a letter from his daughter before he would go one step further." He gave Sharp an intent look. "Ain't got no more news. Like I said, nothing's happened."

"Hell, Red," Sharp said lightly, "that's news enough. It means we're still workin' the plan. That damn Ute might enter our store at any moment."

"Bad plan."

"Why?" Sharp demanded.

"Indian might go to another shop or already have what he needs for a short trip into the mountains."

I jumped in. "No other shops cater to Indians, and our prices are the lowest. If he needs supplies, he'll come here. Besides, he'll probably need a pencil and paper."

"Maybe... maybe not."

Sharp shook his head. "Got any better ideas?"

"I'm encamped on that hill. I'll keep an eye on him."

"Figured out which one yet?" I asked.

"Yep."

"Then we got two ways to know if he leaves," I offered.

Red shrugged. He obviously didn't care for my scheme.

"Are you ready to ride?" he asked.

"Everything's already at the livery," I said.

Red walked to the stove and poured himself a cup of boiling coffee. We both watched him gulp it down as if it were cold. Then he snapped the empty cup on the counter and walked toward the door. With his hand on the latch, he said, "If you got any more stock in the back, haul it forward and spread it around. You look like you're goin' out of business."

"Any other words of advice?" Sharp asked.

"Nope, but your coffee tastes like bull piss."

"Wouldn't know," Sharp answered. "Never tasted bull piss."

The doorbell tinkled as Red opened and closed the door on his way out. We stood there for a second and then both burst out laughing.

Chapter 36

The next day, Bob Grant sauntered into the store. I was alone because Sharp had gone to the bakery to buy a loaf of bread for lunch, the boys were exercising our horses again, and it was Mrs. Baker's day off. We hadn't seen Grant since that dinner when he had met with McAllen. I felt uneasy about his visit, although I was glad our supplies had arrived, and we looked like a prosperous enterprise.

After glancing around a bit, he walked over to where I stood and leaned against the counter. "How's business?"

"Better each day," I responded casually.

"Seen the captain?"

"No. And it's just Joseph McAllen now. He quit the Pinkertons."

"Rejoined, I hear." He gave me a queer look. "Thought you were friends?"

"He was in my employ once. My partner's known him for years, but he says McAllen keeps to himself these days."

"You friendly with other people in town?"

I didn't like that question. "Only Jeff Sharp."

"Mrs. Bolton?" he asked, with an arched eyebrow and menacing grin.

I used a rag to wipe the counter. "She slipped my mind."

"You haven't slipped hers."

Where was this leading? I decided to take a cue from Red and remained silent.

After Grant saw that I wasn't going to respond, he added, "I'm surprised to find a man of your talents tending a general store. I'd heard about that Durango killing, but I didn't know about your gunplay in Nevada until Mrs. Bolton told me."

I remained quiet and continued to wear what I hoped was a blank expression.

Grant leaned all the way over the counter until he rested on his forearms. "Don't worry, I'm not in cahoots with that old battle-axe." He winked. "She asked, but I got my own plans."

"Glad to hear it. Otherwise, I'd have to shoot you where you stand."

Grant jerked upright and looked a bit frightened. "I'm unarmed. That'd be murder."

I pulled my gun and cocked it in his face. I tilted my head to the side as if contemplating whether to shoot him. After a moment, I said evenly, "I got plenty of guns under the counter. One of them would be fired and warm in your hand by the time the law showed up."

He stared down the gun barrel as if he could dodge the bullet if he saw it coming. "You'd never be able to explain why I'd come after you, a known gunfighter."

"I don't know *why*, some damn feud with McAllen, I suppose. You probably thought I was on his side."

He finally met my eyes, but his voice was a bit shaky. "Are you?"

I slowly holstered my Colt while I kept my eyes riveted on his. "If I was, I'd have shot you. Now, get the hell out of my store."

Grant visibly relaxed. "Shooting me wouldn't be doing McAllen a service. We're partners."

"Great for you. Now, get out… and when you see Mrs. Bolton, tell her you've reconsidered, and you won't be doing her bidding."

"I already told you I said no to her."

I drew my gun again, but this time I laid it carefully on the counter. "For your sake, you better not be lying. I've killed a lot of men, and adding you to the list wouldn't bother me in the least."

"I'm not lying… I'm partnered with McAllen, not Mrs. Bolton."

"I don't give a shit about McAllen, but if I see you with Bolton or hear about you talking to her, I'll find you and I'll kill you. And don't try to wear McAllen like some kind of damn shield. He's Sharp's friend, not mine… and lately he hasn't been too friendly to Sharp either."

Grant turned his back to me and nearly sprinted out of my shop.

Had I handled this situation properly? I wasn't sure. Grant took me by surprise, and I had gone with my instincts. He sure didn't come in to tell me he had turned Mrs. Bolton down. Bat Masterson had warned me, but Grant didn't have scruples. He had another purpose, and putting my cocked gun in his face diverted him from where he had wanted to take the conversation. The tactic had left me in the dark, but my threat had, I hoped, convinced him that Sharp and I were no longer connected to McAllen. Although he might have bought my attempt to jigger the truth, I reminded myself that the man was clever as hell.

A little later, Sharp returned with a loaf of bread and a block of cheese as I was bundling in brown paper two pairs of Levi's, two shirts, and four pairs of socks for a customer. The boys came right behind, out of breath, jostling each other to see who got through the door first. Before leaving for the bakery, Sharp had done his magic with a can of beans, so we had enough food to feed the four of us.

As we ate, I told Sharp about Grant. He guessed that, despite what Grant said, he might be weighing the offer from Mrs. Bolton and had come in to size me up. If so, he thought my aggressive response might dissuade him from partnering with her. I certainly hoped so.

Close to seven in the evening, I sent the boys home. We were about to close, when a mean-looking Indian came into the store. I hadn't noticed him at first because I had been in the back getting the stove and coffeepot ready for the morning. As I walked up front, my heart pumped faster when I spotted Sharp and this Indian in some kind of staring duel.

"Can I help you?" Sharp finally asked, with a challenging edge.

"Thought you was prospectin' in the hills."

"Ya beat on me in front of the only guides willing to leave town in autumn ... ya kinda discouraged 'em."

The Indian returned to staring. When he spoke again, his tone said he was not joking. "I don't like you."

"I gathered," Sharp retorted.

For an instant, the Indian looked confused by Sharp's lack of curiosity about why he didn't like him. "Perhaps you didn't gather well enough. You're still hangin' around."

Without a word, Sharp ripped off his apron and marched around the counter. "Perhaps ya'd like to try again. This time I'll see ya comin'."

Another damn staring duel, but before I could intervene, the Indian simply said, "Not today. Got things to do."

"Ya got money? If not, get outta my store."

The Indian slid a double eagle onto the counter. "Will that do, storekeep?"

"What'd ya need?"

"Canned food, coffee, blankets, matches ... four blankets."

"Any particular canned food?" Sharp asked.

"Beans and fruit. Any kind of fruit. Twenty-eight cans of beans, fourteen cans of fruit."

"Cornmeal, flour, sugar? Dried meats?"

"I'll get corn and meat from my people. Got no use for sugar. Get me twenty feet of rope and fish hooks."

I stepped up to the counter. "Jeff, you round up the supplies, and I'll tot up the numbers." I turned toward the Indian after getting Sharp out of the way. I pointed at the gold coin with my pen. "That may not be enough."

He decided to try his skill at staring with me. After winning the contest, he said, "I got more. Get me what I asked."

I nodded. "Need a hand carrying?"

"No. I'll make two trips."

"One of my boys can bring the goods up in the morning. No charge ... other than a small tip, of course."

"You don't listen good, do you?"

I feigned indifference. "Make two trips then, but we close at seven. If you haven't returned by then for the second load, you'll find the rest of your order stacked inside the door in the morning."

"You wait. I need those goods first light."

I stared now. After I thought I had made my point, I said, "Don't dally, or you'll find the door locked."

"If I find the door locked, I'll burn this store to the ground."

"No, you won't. The law's probably already looking for an excuse to lock you up." A subtle flinch told me that I was right. I hesitated. "We'll wait a reasonable time, but I have an important dinner engagement."

"Go. I'll deal with your shopkeeper."

"That's my partner ... and you can't come in here when either of us is alone. Ever. You beat Mr. Sharp for no reason. Now you can do business in this store only if both of us are present." I let my right hand drop alongside my Colt. "We wear guns. If you enter this store and see only one of us, stay by the door until the other can come out front. Otherwise, we shoot." Another pause. "*Do* you understand?"

"I ought to kill you for talking like that."

"You got that backwards, you son of a bitch. I ought to kill you for beating my friend. And before you do something foolish, ask around about me. Now, move back toward the door until we gather up your order."

"You ask around about me, shopkeeper. I've killed men with a knife—men that thought they were good with a gun."

I told myself to get control of my emotions. If we were right, this Indian wasn't going to take this challenge too far, because he had been given a mission. We also weren't going to start a fight with him, because for our plan to work, we needed him to complete that mission. It occurred to me that I had threatened two men today. With Grant it was mostly theater, but I had almost lost it completely with this Indian. In both cases, I had used my reputation—a reputation I told myself was an accident of circumstances. I needed to think about that. Civilized men don't normally get into verbal spats that end in gunplay.

I pointed toward the door and, controlling my voice, said, "That's why I want you by the door. A knife's as dangerous as a gun at arm's length."

The Indian glared and then sniffed dismissively. I felt relief when he walked over to the door and leaned against the wall with both arms crossed against his chest. He yelled out, "Add a pencil to my order."

"Paper?"

He stared at me and then ripped a handbill off the wall by the door. "This'll do."

In a few minutes, Sharp returned with an armload of food and sundries. He dropped them on the counter and immediately returned to the back of the store. After two more trips, he said, "That's it. I'll be back in a minute with a couple of boxes."

By the time I had totted up the merchandise, Sharp had returned with two sturdy wood crates for the supplies.

I waved the Indian over and said, "That'll be twenty-three fifty, plus a dollar deposit for the boxes."

Without a word, he reached under his coat and withdrew another double eagle. He slid it onto the counter and then hefted the heavier of the two boxes and started toward the door.

"Wait, your change," I yelled.

Without breaking stride, he yelled back, "When I return. I'll be bringing this box back, so have sixteen dollars ready."

After he left, Sharp said, "That's an educated Indian. I wonder what made him so angry."

"I'm not sure I care. Nothing we can do to make his anger go away." I looked at Sharp. "He's leaving at first light."

"Yep, an' he thinks this whole affair will be over in two weeks."

"Two weeks?"

"That Indian's got a handle on 'rithmetic, an' he wanted twenty-eight cans of beans an' fourteen cans of fruit. Two cans of beans an' one can of fruit per day. Two weeks."

I thought a moment. "Is that enough food for two?"

"Don't know. Depends on how much fresh an' dried meat Bane's got. He'll catch fish too."

"Jeff, he ripped a Tabor Opera House handbill off the wall."

"So?"

"It went up yesterday. If Maggie writes her note on the back side, it'll prove she's alive as much as her pen hand."

"She's alive. Otherwise they wouldn't agree to get a note from her."

"But once they've given us the letter, do they have any reason to keep her alive?"

Sharp took a long time answering. "My bet is Bane can live in those mountains all winter with nothin' from this store. Those supplies are for McAllen's daughter."

"I hope you're right."

Sharp looked at the door and then back to me. "Steve, they'll kill her. I'm just guessin' about the timin'."

As soon as the Indian returned for the second box and his change, we locked up and headed directly for the stable. It took about an hour to make certain that we were prepared to leave in the morning. I had been arranging my saddle and gear outside Chestnut's stall when I jumped at discovering Red standing directly behind me.

"Damn," I said with an exhale of breath.

"The captain has instructions," Red said, ignoring my surprise. "We don't grab his daughter until after Raven has left for Leadville with the letter. He wants the robbery plans to go forward. We take his daughter to the Inter-Laken and hand her over for safekeeping to a couple named Schmidt."

Sharp stood up from his work and walked over to us. "Raven the name of my Indian friend?"

"Yes."

"Who're the couple?" Sharp asked.

"Pinkertons."

Red turned to leave. "Be ready by seven. We give Raven at least an hour start."

I couldn't resist. "I was right. He came in for supplies."

"I already knew he was leaving." And Red was gone.

Chapter 37

By seven the next morning, Sharp and I were dressed, fed, and saddled up. No Red, so Sharp smoked a cigar, and I puffed on my pipe while our horses pawed at the dirt on the stable floor. Chestnut seemed especially eager to go, and then I remembered that lately the boys had exercised the horses because I was busy. I rubbed Chestnut's neck and was rewarded with a head nuzzle. I realized I was looking forward to the ride, at least the first few hours. After that I would probably just feel cold. I walked over to the barn door and peeked outside.

"Clear skies," I said.

"Good. A heavy snow covers tracks."

"I'll bet Raven left hours ago. Where the hell is Red?"

"Here." Red appeared from around the side of the barn, as if he had been waiting there to surprise us when we called his name. "Mount up."

"Aren't we giving him a long head start?" I asked, as I stepped into the stirrup.

"We follow his trail. Minutes don't matter. If he sees us, the captain's daughter is dead, so we stay well back."

"Sentences, paragraphs," Sharp said. "Yer right, we better stay well back if yer gonna get all chatty on us."

Red ignored him and disappeared around the corner of the barn. By the time we had swung into our saddles and spurred our horses out of the barn, Red was waiting for us on his own horse. He was holding the reins of a packhorse.

"I thought we were traveling light," Sharp said.

"This is Maggie's horse."

"How'd it get here?" I asked.

Red shrugged. "Followed her scent, I s'pose."

Would I ever quit asking dumb questions? Obviously, Red had brought the horse with him. On second thought, maybe I was making progress with Red. Even if it had been at my expense, he had used humor for the first time that I could recall.

Sharp raised a more practical question. "Since you're bringing another horse, is there anything in those bags to make the trip more comfortable?"

"Dynamite."

"In that case, Steve an' I'll hang back a bit so we don't trample the tracks."

Red handed the reins to Sharp. "Captain says you know about dynamite."

Red actually grinned. As I spurred Chestnut forward, I hoped nothing would happen to dampen Red's mood. Even if tracking Raven presented no problems, getting the girl back would require good fortune. Evidently, Captain McAllen thought it might also take explosives.

It made no sense, but the temperature seemed to drop a few degrees as we left Leadville. Red must have watched Raven ride out, because he didn't wander around to pick up the trail. We were dressed warm and had plenty of blankets for the nights, but I knew there would be no fires to help us keep warm. Hopefully, McAllen was right, and Bane was only a day's ride out of Leadville.

When we started the climb into the surrounding mountains, I looked back to see that Sharp was falling behind. I wheeled around and trotted up to him. "Horses okay?"

"Yep. Just bein' careful. Don't want Maggie's horse to stumble carryin' this dynamite."

"I thought dynamite was safe unless lit."

"Depends on the age, how it was stored, an' how it's packed. If McAllen wanted dynamite on this trip, I wish he had asked me to buy an' pack it. Damn that man."

"Red probably knows how to handle dynamite safely."

"Yep, that's why he handed over the reins. What the hell do we need dynamite for anyway?"

"Maybe the captain believes a mere bullet can't kill Bane."

"Steve, ya gotta get close to use dynamite. How do we get Bane to sit still until it blows? This makes no sense." Sharp rode on for a minute. "Red doesn't need us on his heels, so I'd just as soon ride careful."

After three hours, Red came trotting back. As he reached us, he swung off his horse and came around to the pack on Maggie's horse.

"Did ya lose the trail?" Sharp asked.

"Nope. Clear markings. I came for lunch."

With that, he pulled a couple of cans out of the saddlebag and threw them to me. I swung down from Chestnut and drew my knife to open the beans. As I worked, I saw Red draw out a cotton bandanna from the saddlebag and unwrap it. He threw each of us a biscuit, wound the bandanna around the remaining ones, and stuffed them back into the saddlebag. Sharp moseyed over to the packhorse and examined the contents of the bags.

"Damn it, Red, there's no dynamite here."

"Musta forgot it. Let's eat."

"Shit." Sharp looked at me. "Food an' clothes for Maggie. That's all."

"Captain thought she might be cold." Red took the can of beans from me and poured them into his mouth right from the can. After he wiped his face with the back of his hand, he gave the can back to me. I went to my saddlebag for a spoon.

"When did you develop a sense of humor?" I asked Red.

"When I was a youngster. Don't have one by then, doubtful you get one."

"How far ahead is Raven?" Sharp asked, trying to ignore the practical joke.

"'Bout three miles. Slowed down, so I decided to give him some room. Might be doubling back."

"If ya didn't want us to ride with ya, why didn't ya just say so?"

Red grinned. "I'll leave shortly. You two hang back. I'll find you after I locate Bane."

"What if it's more than a day's ride?" I asked.

"Set up camp at dark. I'll find you."

Sharp talked around a mouth full of beans. "Are we part of this plan, or do we just escort the girl back to Twin Lakes?"

"Don't know yet." Red grabbed the bean can and poured another serving into his open mouth. He mounted and walked his horse away from us while chomping on his biscuit.

After he had disappeared over a rise, I started laughing. My mirth lasted until I spotted the look on Sharp's face. To get past the moment, I went to Chestnut for my canteen and washed down my biscuit with several swallows of water. When I turned around, Sharp was smiling.

"Damn Red. He got me good. I have to think on a way to get even."

"After we get Maggie," I offered.

"After we get Maggie."

Chapter 38

We had seen no sign of Red by nightfall, so we veered off and set up a crude camp. We didn't need to gather wood to prepare a hot meal, so it took less than ten minutes to settle in, unsaddling the horses and throwing our bedrolls and saddlebags onto the ground. We took awhile to groom the horses, and then Sharp went for the stash of biscuits. He threw me one as he started eating.

"Sure could use a cup of hot coffee," I said.

"Yep, got downright chilly after sunset. Sure hope I don't have to drop my drawers to do some business. Might freeze my pecker in the diminutive position."

I laughed as I threw one of my bedroll blankets over my head and shoulders and tucked the ends under my butt to give me some protection from the cold and hard ground. "Do you think Red can find us in the dark?"

"Don't see that it matters. This piece of ground is just as hard and cold as any on this mountain. Red'll find us in the mornin'... or when he needs us."

"Or a biscuit," Red said from behind us.

Both of us whirled toward the voice. I made a clumsy move for my Colt, but I had bound myself up tight with the blanket. Sharp, on the other hand, was free, and he leaped to his feet.

"Shit, Red!" Sharp exclaimed. "Quit sneakin' up on us like that, or I'm gonna bell ya like a goddamn cat."

"Bad idea. Wouldn't be able to sneak up on Bane."

"Did you find him?" I asked, pretending that I hadn't been caught where I couldn't protect myself.

Red nodded. "'Bout two hours away. Camped in a box canyon."

"Ya see the girl?" Sharp asked.

"Nope, but I heard her curse at Bane once. She's further up the canyon, further than I could go without being spotted."

"Can we sneak her out after Raven leaves?" I asked.

"Raven already left," Red said. "Passed by this way right after dark. Surprised he didn't hear you two gabbing" He turned toward Sharp. "Gimme one of those biscuits."

After Sharp threw him one, Red sat on a rock and gnawed on it a bit. Then he held aloft what he hadn't eaten and waggled it at us. "There's some white man's food I like. Biscuits are good on the trail for a couple days."

I tried again. "Red, can we get her out?"

He didn't answer until he had finished the biscuit. Then, as he picked crumbs off his jacket and popped them into his mouth, he said, "No." He harvested a couple more crumbs. "We gotta kill Bane first. She's deep in a narrow gorge, and I saw no way to slip around. Probably tied hand and foot too."

"Can we get enough of a sight line on Bane to use a rifle?" I asked.

Red grunted and shook his head. "Nope. He stays sheltered. He picked a good spot." He looked off into the distance as if he could see something new in the dark. Then he shook his head again. "Couldn't find a spot for a clean shot, at least not one I could climb to without being seen or heard. Too much loose shale. No... he'd hear me for sure."

"Does he come out for water, game, or his toilet?" Before Red could answer me, I had another thought. "Wait. Raven took him fish hooks. Where can he fish?"

Red swept the last biscuit remains off his coat and stood. After pacing our little encampment for a while, he said, "There's a tiny stream in the canyon, so he has water. Too small for fish, but it joins a good-size creek just below the mouth of his hideout. He could fish the creek and keep an eye on the canyon at the same time."

Sharp jumped up as well. "Can we set up for an ambush... tonight? He might just do a little fishin' in the morning."

"I'll go. You stay put," Red said, as he started to walk away from the camp.

"No." The firmness of my voice surprised even me. I hadn't traipsed up here in freezing weather to watch over a young girl after she had been rescued. "We all go."

Red pivoted to face me full on. "The captain put me in charge. Do as I say."

"I thought all three of us had an equal voice."

"Pinkertons *never* work that way. Somebody's always in charge. Today, it's me."

"Okay... you're in charge of all the Pinkertons on this expedition."

Sharp laughed and stepped up to us so that we made a rough triangle. "Red, the captain forgot to tell us ya was the leader, so let's just talk this through before one of us gets too het up."

"We can help," I added.

Red didn't normally show emotion, but he looked angry now. "We're in the wilderness, not some city saloon."

"Jeff's damn good with a rifle, and I'm even better. I'm sure you're an expert marksman as well. If you remember, lots of men have tried to kill Bane. The man's careful, and he's got a hide as tough as a grizzly. If we spread out along different lines, then we'll have a better chance of getting a clean shot... and if we all shoot, a better chance of killing him. You know, it might take three bullets to kill that son of a bitch."

Red flicked his eyes between us. "If I agree, will you follow my instructions once we leave this camp?"

"If all three of us go, yer the boss," Sharp said, slapping Red on the back.

Red's face tightened even more. For a moment, I thought Sharp had gone too far, but eventually a grin slowly grew across Red's face. "Then my first orders are to never slap the boss on the back."

Chapter 39

I discovered that in the mountains, dawn didn't break; light just seemed to seep from the eastern skyline until it was day. The two-hour ride had taken most of the night because we had led the horses on foot and then tethered them a good twenty minutes' walk away from our hiding position. The three of us lay in an arc on the far side of a creek that ran down a sloping valley facing the entrance to the box canyon. Red had arranged us on the far side of the creek, assuming Bane would cross over to our side to watch the canyon mouth in case Maggie tried to escape.

I was in a swale about seventy yards from the creek, and as I lay in the wet grass, I hoped Bane liked trout for breakfast. I had wrapped one of my blankets around my shoulders as we walked the last part of the way. I now used it as ground cover, but it had soaked through and provided little comfort. Despite four heavy layers of clothing and the blanket, I could not remember being colder. I was shaking so much, I wondered if I could aim and squeeze the trigger with accuracy. I took out my flask and took a long sip. Perhaps the sun would bring a little relief from the chill, but I doubted it.

Shortly after looking through my field glasses, I spotted Bane peeking around an outcropping. I watched him examine the terrain for a full ten minutes before venturing out from behind cover. He was big and cruel looking. Raven might have projected meanness but not raw evil. Bane looked like an ogre eager to kill anything found breathing. He was huge. My guess would be only a few inches over six feet, but he must have approached three hundred pounds—all of which appeared solid. His pockmarked and scarred face would frighten a child, but his dark, challenging eyes moved men out of his way.

Holding the field glasses over my eyes with one hand, I fumbled beside me to make sure I knew exactly where my rifle lay. The plan was to wait until he crossed the creek to our side, but I wanted my rifle ready in case somebody took a hasty shot. Just as Bane got to the stream, he stopped and stared off to his left. I followed his line of sight with my glasses and eventually spotted a buck grazing no more than one hundred yards from Bane. While I trained my glasses on the deer, I heard a shot and saw it stumble onto its forelegs and then rear up and bolt in the opposite direction. I dropped the field glasses from my eyes and saw Bane run after the mortally wounded deer. Damn, now what? I raised my rifle and sighted on the running figure but held my fire. A long-distance shot at a moving target was too risky. I decided to wait for Bane's return when he would be burdened with deer quarter. Since no one else shot either, I presumed Red and Sharp had come to the same conclusion.

After a few minutes, I saw Red scurry around the mountainside toward the canyon entrance. Just before he entered the canyon, he pointed at my position and then at Sharp's, and then held up the flat of his hand at us. The message was clear. Sharp and I should stay put while Red went in to bring Maggie out. How much time did it take to gut, skin, dress, and quarter a deer? I wasn't sure, but I focused my field glasses on where Bane had run after it. If he reappeared while Red was in the canyon, I would have to take the shot. After verifying that Bane was still gone, I looked around, but the low grass in the meadow didn't offer a better vantage for an ambush. After checking again for Bane, I glanced over to where Sharp was positioned. I couldn't see him, which was as it should be, but I hoped he would be ready to shoot with me if it became necessary.

The longer Red took, the more my heart pounded. The only good thing was that either the sun or my shaky nerves had warmed me enough that my hands were relatively steady holding the field glasses. After what seemed like forever, I heard a cry of pain and interrupted my vigil long enough to see that Red was hurrying Maggie away from the canyon. Thank God. I returned my attention to where Bane had disappeared around the ridge of a slope. Still not seeing him, I chanced a glance back at Red and his charge, and it was obvious that Maggie was having difficulty moving. Hurry, I thought.

I was concentrating on watching for Bane, when I heard the kind of splashing that meant Red and Maggie were wading across the creek. As I looked toward them, Red called Sharp and me over with hand signals. I didn't like leaving my blind, but Red's hand waves were insistent. I picked up my rifle and ran as fast as I could. Sharp and I arrived at about the same time, and we all knelt down in a tight circle.

"Take Maggie to the Inter-Laken Hotel and then let the captain know she's safe," Red said. "Go. Now! And hurry in case I fail."

"Fail to kill Bane?" I asked.

Red gave me a look that said I still asked stupid questions. "Go. I maimed Bane's horses, so he'll be on foot. When you get to our horses, take them all. I'll walk out."

I started to protest but realized I didn't have a better plan. In fact I didn't have any alternative except for all four of us to lie in wait for Bane, and my gut told me that counting on surprise could be dangerous. I looked at Maggie for the first time and saw that she was not in good condition to make a hell-bent flight down the mountain. Her face was bruised and anxious. She was pretty and—unfortunately—looked to be a delicate young girl.

Then she spoke her first words. "Let's go. My legs will work better the further I walk." Then instead of waiting for a response, she stood and started walking to the south.

Her father's daughter, except the captain would never have headed in the wrong direction. "This way," I said as I pointed east.

Without another word, she reversed her direction and limped along between Sharp and me. We each took a forearm and hurried her as fast as possible. Unless she could get her legs back, it would take us at least a half hour to get to the horses. I was more concerned about the five minutes hiking across the open meadow to the tree line. If Bane came upon the scene now, we would have no choice but to trade long distance shots.

"How long will it take Bane to quarter that deer?" I asked between breaths.

"Depends on how far he had to chase the animal before it died. Hopefully, the deer had a good run before it collapsed."

I took a quick peek back, but I could see no sign of Red or Bane. I hoped he would find a swale on the other side of the creek so he'd have a surer shot. When I turned around, Sharp was offering Maggie pieces of rock candy, but she shook her head and pointed to his canteen. She grabbed it when offered and guzzled swallow after swallow.

As we approached the first trees, Maggie handed the canteen back and said, "I'll take that candy now."

As she popped a couple of pieces in her mouth, I asked, "Did Bane give you food and water?"

"Some. When I asked for more, he said he wanted me weak."

"Here." I offered her some jerky. "You need more than sugar."

She nodded in agreement and started gnawing on the jerky with a mouth full of rock candy. I started to feel more comfortable now that we were hidden within the forest, but I kept my ears perked for the sound of gunshots.

By the time we arrived at the horses, Maggie was moving faster and showing almost no limp from being bound up for days. She had made a great improvement in a short period. Youth is the best healer. When she spotted her horse, she yelped with glee and ran to embrace the horse's neck. Sharp and I both went *shush* at the same time. She nodded understanding and put her finger across her lip, but she couldn't wipe the beaming smile from her face.

We had left the horses saddled in case we needed to make a quick escape, so it was just a matter of slipping our rifles in the scabbards and untying the reins. I turned to help Maggie up but discovered her already in the saddle. Sharp tied the reins of Red's horse to his rear saddle ring and then used his own reins to gently whip his horse across the neck as he swung into the saddle. His horse had bolted to a full gallop before Sharp's butt touched leather. Without instruction, Maggie chased after Sharp, and I took up the rear. All of us wanted to get down the mountain and back to civilization.

After fifteen minutes of hard riding, we slowed to a walk to give the horses a rest. I thought Chestnut could go another ten minutes or so, but we wanted the horses fresh enough for a burst of speed if needed.

"Are you taking me to my father or my mother?" Maggie asked.

"Neither," Sharp answered. "Do ya know where ya are?"

"Free," she answered.

Sharp laughed. "That too, but yer four days ride from yer ma, and the captain's gotta take care of some loose ends. The men that ordered you snatched are still walkin' the streets."

"Then where are you taking me? That Indian said Laken something."

"Twin Lakes," I interjected. "Your father arranged for a couple at the Inter-Laken Hotel to care for you until he cleans up this mess.

They're both Pinkertons, so you'll be safe, and Twin Lakes is far away from the bad people that did this."

"I don't know anyone at Twin Lakes. I want to see my pa. If I can't see him, I want to go to Durango to see my ma."

"If we take ya home, someone might grab ya again," Sharp said. "Ya gotta give yer pa time to sort this out proper."

She rode quiet for a few minutes and then surprised me by saying, "I'll go. It won't take long for my pa to kill those men." She rode a few more strides and then added, "That man who stayed behind—he's going to kill that bear-man, isn't he?"

"Bear-man?" I asked.

"That's the way I thought of him. A big, ugly bear that wore clothes."

"I'm sorry," I said. "That must have been frightening."

"I was never afraid."

I found that hard to believe. Then she turned in her saddle and looked at me before she said with pride, "My pa is a Pinkerton. He hunts bad men and kills them. I knew he'd rescue me."

"Did ya pray?" Sharp asked.

She returned her attention forward, toward Sharp. "I left that to my ma's husband. I'm sure he prayed plenty, for all the good it did."

"We talked to your ma and pa ... I mean your ma's husband ... before we left Durango," I said. "There's something you need to know. They think you're dead. The townsfolk even had a funeral for you. And as much as you'd like to, you can't send them a telegram saying you're all right. The men who ordered this might hear about it, and that would ruin your pa's plans to capture these men."

"He ain't going to capture them. My pa will kill them for taking me."

"Ya want revenge?" Sharp asked.

"I just know my pa. He's got grit, not like that squirrel my ma married."

"The preacher worked awfully hard to get a posse out looking for you," I offered.

"But he didn't leave his pulpit, did he?" She swung around again to look at me. "Did you know the right reverend doesn't even ride a horse? If he goes anywhere, which is seldom, he uses a buckboard."

"So does Wyatt Earp, I hear."

She whirled around in her saddle again. "Why are you defending him? That man back there said my pa sent you."

"Yes, we're friends of Captain McAllen," I said. This was getting too complicated for me. "Sorry. I don't want to get in the middle of any family squabble."

"It's not a family squabble. I haven't spoken a cross word to the reverend in nearly a year."

Chapter 40

The Inter-Laken Hotel looked beautiful in the late afternoon glow. It also looked warm and welcoming. Maggie had been sucking rock candy and chewing jerky all day, but I hadn't eaten a thing since the night before. My mouth started watering when I remembered the meal I had eaten here with Captain McAllen. We had rescued the girl, got back safe, and now were about to enjoy exceptional hospitality, a warm fire, good food, and top-notch Kentucky whiskey. I loved expensive hotels.

"Pull around to the stables," Maggie said. "That way you won't need to tip the stable boys."

"My treat," I said. "Let's get you warm and fed. Someone else can look after the horses."

"Suit yourself," she said, "but I do my own grooming."

With that she spurred her horse into a canter and circled around the side of the hotel's main building.

"Damn. You think she's related to anyone we know?" I asked Sharp.

"She's a McAllen all right," Sharp said, shaking his head. "Better catch up. Her dad won't be pleased if we let her out of our sight."

We both spurred our horses after Maggie. After a full day's ride over rough country, Chestnut responded like he hadn't been exercised in a week. He loved to challenge other horses, and he had been snorting ever since Maggie galloped away. If Chestnut had been faster, I might have considered taking him to Denver to race. He ran with enthusiasm and could run forever, but most thoroughbreds would arrive at the finish line first. No, Chestnut could take almost any other horse in a long-distance race, but those kinds of races didn't occur at fancy racetracks, or in mining towns, for that matter.

We threw up a cloud of dust as we pulled to a stop in front of the livery. Maggie had already dismounted and was leading her horse by the reins into the barn.

A stable boy ran up from the back of the barn. "Hey, hold on there, girlie. Where do ya think yer goin'?"

I realized she looked scruffy as hell. She wore buckskin pants and shirt with a coat roughly made from an Indian blanket. Her makeshift clothes were torn and dirt embedded, sweat had streaked her filthy face, and her matted hair hung in limp strands that stuck together as if glued. Despite her appearance, she threw her head and said, "I'm putting my horse away. Do you have any good brushes? She's been worked hard today."

"Excuse me, sis, but are ya stayin' at this hotel?" He looked around for the livery boy that should have brought the horse around for a guest. "I'm afraid these stables are for guests only. If yer here fer the evenin', ya can put yer horse in that there corral."

This was the type of problem I enjoyed solving. I handed the boy a silver dollar and said, "This young lady is checking in, and she prefers to groom her own horse. Now... do you have a good brush she can use?"

"Of course, sir. There's a clean stall about halfway down on the right. I'll go get a set of grooming brushes." He looked at Sharp and me. We must have looked a sight. "Are ya guests as well, sir?"

"We're only escorting the young lady, but we'll stay for dinner." I handed him another silver dollar. "We need to return to Leadville tonight, so can you groom our horses, feed them oats, and have them ready in an hour or so? You can put them in the corral afterwards."

The boy bounced the two heavy coins in his palm and then shoved them in his pants. "Of course, sir."

Funny how—in some situations—a single dollar can get a person the same service a governor or a famous stage actor might expect. I'm relatively tight when negotiating a business deal, but I always spend a little extra when I can get the absolute best service by giving a generous tip. Service, like bourbon, is something for which spending a few more dollars lets you live as well as a king. Of course, I have enough money, so a few extra dollars never gives me pause. I suppose someone who scraps for coins in order to eat has a different attitude.

I took Sharp's elbow and led him out of Maggie's earshot. "I'll help with the horses. Why don't you see if you can find that Pinkerton couple that'll look after Maggie?"

Sharp handed the reins of his horse to me. "Don't think that tip means I'm buyin' dinner. Yer the one that's particular about that horse. Mine coulda done just fine chewin' on some of that straw in the corral." He smiled to show he was ribbing me. "Meet ya inside."

After we finished, Maggie and I walked around the building to the front of the hotel. Sharp trudged out the entrance and pointed behind us. "The Pinks want her to come in the back way—directly up to her room, number 204."

Maggie squared her shoulders. "McAllens don't sneak in the back."

"'Fraid so," Sharp said. "Those are yer pa's orders."

She put her hands on both hips. "After being tied up for over a week, I ain't staying cooped up in a hotel room."

"No need," Sharp said. "They're goin' to cut and bleach yer hair and dress ya up in a pretty dress."

"I want a riding skirt." She stuck her lower lip out. "I don't like fancy dresses."

"That's why yer gonna wear one," Sharp said. "Pa's orders ... so no one'll recognize ya." She opened her mouth to object, but Sharp interjected, "If ya do like yer pa says, ya can ride every day."

That did it. You could tell by the expression on her face. All three of us reversed direction and marched to the rear entrance. When we entered room 204, the first thing I noticed was that a bathtub had been brought into the room and filled with steaming water. The second thing I noticed was the Pinkerton couple. I don't know what I expected, but they surprised me. Attractive and dressed expensively in tailored clothes, they fit in perfectly with this romantic hotel. They even looked to be the right age to have a fourteen-year-old daughter. To a casual observer, they were a handsome, rich couple rekindling their relationship in an isolated and exclusive hotel. Only the daughter looked out of place, but Maggie's separate room and her penchant for horseback riding would make her presence acceptable.

"Hello, Maggie," the woman said.

She gave the woman a defiant look and asked in a dismissive tone, "You work for my pa?"

"Yes. But let's be clear. We work for your father, not for you. We have our instructions, and we'll *all* follow them. Do you understand?"

Maggie pressed her lips together in a straight line and glared at the woman. Then, "Is that bath for me?"

"Yes."

Maggie turned to us. "Gentlemen, please excuse us." Then she looked at her pretend father. "You too, of course."

"Of course," he said. "Gentlemen, may I buy you a drink?"

"Is the captain payin'?" Sharp asked.

"He is."

"Then you can buy us dinner and a drink."

When we were seated in the dining room, Sharp immediately ordered a bottle of expensive Kentucky whiskey. Sharp enjoyed coercing others to pay for his expensive habits. Since I was the usual victim, I was glad to see the captain take a turn.

Our dinner partner reached out his hand and introduced himself. "I'm Carl Schmidt, half of a special team with the Pinkertons."

After handshakes and introductions, I asked, "What kind of special team?"

"My wife, Mary, and I investigate swindles. Mostly we set ourselves up as a rich and callow couple. We're pretty good at getting con artists to see us as a likely target."

"Who employs you?" I asked.

Schmidt laughed. "Rich men don't like to be suckered. They get angry, and they have enough money to hire us to get even."

"There much work out there for ya?" Sharp asked.

"Too much. We work the entire nation, but for the last couple of years, it seems we've spent most of our time in mining camps."

"Gold and silver swindlers?" Sharp said in mock surprise. "My God, who can ya trust?"

I began to wonder about this couple. Keeping my voice neutral, I said, "These men we're dealing with aren't swindlers… they're killers."

"Don't misjudge," Schmidt said. "A cornered swindler can be dangerous. We're experienced and capable of handling dangerous situations."

"Do you carry a gun?" I asked.

Schmidt lifted his coat enough for me to see his gun—a Smith & Wesson .44, just like Captain McAllen carried. "Mary always carries a pocket pistol and a derringer. In close quarters, we can handle the situation, but, as always, our main protection is to stay undetected. That's our best skill." He stood. "Gentlemen, the two of you stick out like a sore thumb in this establishment, and you're the ones who can be linked to Maggie. The sooner you leave Twin Lakes, the safer she'll be."

With that, Carl Schmidt walked briskly out of the hotel dining room.

Chapter 41

After a hasty meal, Sharp and I were on the road to Leadville. Just before we left, we spotted the perfectly groomed Schmidt family descending the central staircase. McAllen's cleaned-up daughter looked almost unrecognizable to us, with straw-colored hair and feminine clothes. She wore a pretty yellow dress and looked like the offspring of a society couple from the East out here on holiday. Taking Schmidt's admonishment to heart, we didn't acknowledge them.

Unless we ran into something unforeseen, we expected to arrive in Leadville shortly after dark. We'd only been gone two days, so hopefully nobody had noticed that we had left town. Maggie was safe. Raven should have returned with Maggie's letter on schedule and without suspicion. Neither Bane nor Red had a horse, so both should still be in the mountains. As we rode hard toward Leadville, it appeared that our plan was working.

Few things in my life have looked as inviting as the Carbonate Hotel. By the time we pulled up, I was chilled to the bone. In fact, for the first time, I fully realized the meaning of that expression. A stable boy took our horses as we lugged our saddlebags up to our room. Trudging up the stairs, we met McAllen coming down. All three of our heads whipped around to see if there was anyone within earshot. When we saw no one, Sharp said in a quiet voice, "Maggie's with the Schmidts."

McAllen actually smiled before he said, "Silverado," and quickened his steps down the stairs.

After we reached the second-floor landing, I whispered to Sharp, "Step into my room a moment." When we got behind closed doors, I asked, "What's Silverado?"

"A miners' saloon on the north end of town. A place Grant would never go."

"When?"

Sharp laughed. "I thought we were talkin' about the captain."

I plopped my saddlebags on the floor. "Let's go."

In a few minutes we were in a rowdy saloon that did a good business peddling three staples: liquor, prostitution, and gambling. Liquor them up, let the girls get a piece of their bankroll, and then separate them from the rest of their week's pay at the gambling tables. This formula worked in every mining encampment, cattle town, and rail head.

McAllen sat at a table tucked into a corner at the front of the saloon. We could see everyone as they entered and, since most men surveyed in front of them, few would notice us until they were well into the saloon and turned around. McAllen had a bottle of Kentucky whiskey and three glasses on the table.

Sharp poured as he said, "We got yer daughter away from Bane an' escorted her to the Schmidts at Twin Lakes." Sharp shoved a full glass over to McAllen. "She's safe an' in good hands."

"Jeff, Steve." He saluted us with his glass. "Thank you. I owe you my daughter's life and a good deal of money for your expenses. I don't know how I can repay either."

"Forget the expenses," I said. "Money's just a tool to get what you want, and Jeff and I wanted to help a friend."

Sharp nodded and then made eye contact with McAllen. "Joseph . . . Bane was still alive when we left. Red stayed behind to kill or delay him so we could get down the mountain."

McAllen used two fingers to twist his whiskey glass back and forth by quarter turns. When he looked up, he said, "Red ain't back yet."

"He couldn't be back yet," I said quickly. "He ordered us to take his horse down the mountain. He's on foot."

"Bane?" McAllen asked.

"Red maimed his horses." I hesitated. "One of the two of them will eventually hike out of those mountains."

McAllen nodded. After he swallowed his whiskey, he said, "That Indian made it back with Maggie's letter late last night. It was written on the back of a Tabor Opera House handbill that's posted all over town."

"Yep," Sharp said. "Raven left before we rescued Maggie, so he shouldn't be suspicious. That damn Indian ripped that handbill off the wall of our store to save buying paper."

McAllen indicated he wanted his shot glass refilled by wiggling with his fingers. As Sharp poured, he said, "Vrable wants to rob the next silver shipment. The rail line and winter are closing fast on Leadville."

"What do you want us to do?" I asked.

"Get back to your store. We can't have any suspicions that something's amiss. When I get the specifics for the robbery, I'll tell you what to do."

After an uncomfortable silence, I asked, "Do you still think they want to see you hang for this crime… or just shoot you during the robbery?"

"Both." McAllen downed his second glass. "I've thought about this. If I were doing it, I'd shoot me a couple times at the scene so I'd be captured easy. Nothin' lethal, just enough to slow my escape."

"What's your plan?" I asked.

McAllen gave me a direct look. "Steve, if you don't mind, I'll keep that to myself. Benjamin Franklin said three men can keep a secret if two are dead."

I stiffened. "Captain, have I ever violated a confidence?"

"No, Steve, but if you'll remember Carson City, you also didn't share your plans with me."

For some reason, Sharp found McAllen's comment amusing. After he quit chortling, I said, "All right, Captain. But in the spirit of being aboveboard, I intend to stop this war between the Santa Fe and Rio Grande railroads. I can hold off a week or more if my actions will interfere with your plans."

"How do you plan on stopping it?"

"I'll send a telegram that'll get attention in New York."

"New York?" Sharp asked. "Hell, they're shootin' at each other here."

I turned my attention to him. "The men in Leadville solve problems with guns, but the moneymen in New York talk. I've been thinking about this for the last couple of days, and I'm sure this can only be resolved two thousand miles from here."

"Why do you care?" McAllen asked.

"I own a substantial stake in both railroads. It's my money they're wasting with this feud."

McAllen waved off Sharp from refilling his glass again. "Then go ahead and send your telegram. I think my business will be over in a few days anyway."

"Bat Masterson runs security for the Santa Fe Railway. He's not involved in Grant's or your plans, is he?"

McAllen's brow furrowed. "Not that I know of, but that's worth thinking about."

Chapter 42

Sharp and I left the hotel first thing in the morning to open the store. When we arrived, Mrs. Baker had already opened up, heated the store, and brewed coffee. Further surprises awaited us. It took me a minute before I figured out why the shop was brighter. Mrs. Baker had arranged six lanterns to chase away the gloom. Previously, only a single lantern had provided illumination in the rear to supplement the small windows in front. Why hadn't I thought of this? We stocked lanterns, so it was only a matter of using our inventory. If we ran out of stock, we could sell the lanterns hung around the store.

"Hell, ma'am, looks like a different store," Sharp exclaimed.

"Jeff!"

"What?" Sharp looked at me, puzzled.

"Watch your language." I faced Mrs. Baker. "I apologize for his rudeness." I threw a grin at Sharp to show I was kidding. "He's an uncouth barbarian—only out of the caves a couple years."

"Tunnels... I've only recently surfaced from the tunnels." He took off his hat, and with a flourish, did a respectable European bow. "My apologies, ma'am. The store looks tidy an' bright as a spring day."

"Thank you, Mr. Sharp." She turned toward the stove to pour us coffee. "We did over four hundred dollars in business while you two were off doing whatever you were doing. I could see we would soon be running low on supplies again, so I sent off another order to Denver." She paused. "Three thousand dollars' worth."

She was testing our business relationship. I accepted the mug of coffee she held out to me. "The merchandise better sell."

She smiled. "It will. I've learned a lot in the last two days. A lot about this store... and a lot about you."

Now I was on guard. "What do you mean?"

"I learned about Durango and Nevada." She faced me square. "You're a gunfighter."

"No, ma'am... I'm a man who got pulled into a couple of bad situations."

"And shot your way out of them."

"What's your point?" I was getting angry.

She walked over to the counter and fumbled until she pulled out the shotgun and Colt .45 we kept hidden from sight and laid them gently on the pinewood top. "I want you to teach me how to use these."

"Why?"

"Because I don't know how."

"I already taught you how to use your pistol. Why do you need to know how to use these?"

"I don't want to be afraid anymore."

"I'm sorry to disillusion you, but knowing how to use guns won't keep you from being afraid."

"Are you telling me that being handy with a gun doesn't help?"

That stopped me. "It helps until you get into a situation. Then the fear comes flooding back."

"I can live with that. What I can't live with is being afraid all the time."

I realized Mrs. Baker was a brave woman. Overcoming fear defines bravery and controlling your fear separates the brave from the foolish. "If you keep running this store the way you have, I'll teach you how to use a revolver and a rifle." I picked up the shotgun. "You don't need lessons with this … unless you're going for birds. For men in close quarters, just point, cock the hammer, and pull the trigger." I laid the shotgun back on the counter. "If you fail to kill them, you'll make them deaf. Now, please put these away."

After she had replaced the weapons below the counter, I added, "By the way, Jeff is an expert with a rifle, and he can teach you a lot more about survival on the frontier than I can."

"Is that true?" she asked Sharp.

"Well, the part about a rifle's true enough. I'm twenty years older than Steve, so I guess the part about survival also holds some truth."

She looked like a youngster at the candy jars. "Ever been in a shooting?"

"Steve's the one to teach ya how to kill; I'll teach ya how to avoid being pulled into bad situations."

"Good enough for me," Mrs. Baker said.

"Me too," I said. "I think I need a few of those lessons."

Chapter 43

After we had opened the store the following day, the liveryman where we boarded our horses came rushing in, looking distraught. He stood in the center of the floor and just breathed hard for a minute.

"I got terrible news." He was looking at me. "Mr. Dancy, come with me to the livery."

"What news? Tell me."

He looked even more nervous. "I'm sorry, but yer horse is dead."

"What? Chestnut?"

I didn't wait for an answer. I charged out of the store and ran to the livery. When I got to Chestnut's stall, I gasped. I knew instantly that Chestnut was dead. My horse lay prone with lifeless eyes, slack features, and, most alarming, a frothy mouth. I laid my hand on his chest but felt no lifting or falling. The stall was as quiet as a funeral parlor. But it hadn't been. The dividing walls had been kicked so severely that they leaned into the adjacent stalls to crowd the horses on either side.

How had this happened? What had happened? Chestnut was a strong, healthy animal. Animal? As soon as I thought the word, I wanted another: a word that came close to *friend*. Chestnut and I had been together since St. Louis and had traveled thousands of miles together. Even in towns, I saw him nearly every day. Guns didn't dampen my fears of the frontier, Chestnut did. As long as we were together, I felt confident roaming around a raw country that was eager to teach city dwellers how much they didn't know. I didn't need a word close to *friend—friend* was the right word. I had just lost a true and faithful friend—one that I would miss terribly. With that thought, I collapsed on top of Chestnut's neck and cried.

"I'm sorry."

The voice came from behind me. I pulled myself together, used my sleeve to wipe my face, and turned toward the liveryman. "How did this happen?"

He raised both arms, palms up. "Ya want the animal doctor?"

"Go get him."

My voice must have sounded angry, because he didn't hesitate. After he left, I examined the stall and then Chestnut. I could find nothing dangerous in the stall and no wounds on my horse, which didn't make sense. Chestnut had been his strong, sure-footed self all the way down the mountain. No hint of illness. Heart attack? Occasionally, a horse had been known to run until its heart gave out, but I had never heard of a horse having a heart attack while at rest. No, not a heart attack. Chestnut had suffered severe convulsions. The damage to the stall told me that the convulsions had not been short. I couldn't look at him anymore. Chestnut had suffered an agonizing and slow death.

Not finding anything in Chestnut's stall, I searched the rest of the barn. I found nothing unusual and nothing out of place. The liveryman ran a tidy business. But where had he been? His room was connected, and the noise must have been earsplitting.

I walked out of the barn and into the frigid morning. I wanted my pipe, but I had left it at the store. I was thinking of walking back for it when I saw the animal doctor walking toward me. He wore a hostile expression.

When he stood in front of me, he asked, "Are you the one that insists I stop my treatment of live animals to look at a dead horse?"

"Yes." I turned and went into the barn. I didn't want an argument; I wanted a professional opinion.

As soon as the doctor saw Chestnut, his demeanor softened. He immediately kneeled over my horse and pried open his mouth. Then he stood and looked around the stall. Eventually, he leaned over and picked up a twig of weed the size of a small piece of tobacco stem. After he sniffed it, the doctor handed it to me.

"Do you have any enemies?" he asked.

"A few." I didn't elaborate.

"Your horse was probably poisoned. That's water hemlock, sometimes called snakeroot. The most poisonous plant hereabouts. It will kill a horse in two to three hours. A human quicker. Eat that tiny piece, and you'll be in my care for a week."

"Why do you say probably?"

He turned to the liveryman. "Any chance of snakeroot in your feed?"

"Absolutely not. No, sir."

The doctor turned back to me. "Then your horse was definitely poisoned."

I nodded toward the liveryman. "You believe him?"

"Clyde? Hell, yes. Best man with animals I've ever seen. If he says there's no snakeroot in his feed, then somebody brought it in and fed it to your horse."

I turned to Clyde. "Why didn't you hear Chestnut kicking his stall apart?"

"Musta happened last night when I was playing faro at the Gemstone."

"Fits," the doctor said. "This horse has been dead for over ten hours."

"You don't lock up or check the animals before you go to bed?" I wanted to blame someone, so I took my anger out on someone close at hand.

"The big doors are locked, but I leave the side door open for owners. Everybody knows that."

"I didn't."

"Well, ya shoulda asked. I can't be here twenty-four hours."

"And you can't be bothered to check on your charges after you come home drunk from some saloon."

"I give a listen. No noise, no problem." He suddenly shed his compassion. "Listen, I didn't kill your horse, and I'm not payin'. Ya oughta think about who mighta done it and quit blamin' me."

Now I really got angry. I pulled two single eagles from my pocket. I gave one to the doctor and said, "Thank you. Sorry to interfere in your work."

I flipped the other coin in the air at the liveryman. He caught it deftly. "And as for you, I don't want your goddamn money. That's for the splendid care you gave my horse. It should settle our account with enough left over to bury him properly. Now, if you'll excuse me, I've got to go find a woman."

I started to stomp out when the doctor said, "Good idea, young man. Release some of that anger with a woman."

I hesitated only momentarily. "I will, Doctor. But I don't intend to fuck her; I intend to kill her."

Chapter 44

I marched out of the livery, intent on finding Mrs. Bolton.

Thinking her name made my teeth grind. It had to be her. Her nature was evil to the core, and she hated me with the passion of a wronged woman. She knew that killing Chestnut would hurt me. I entered the Carbonate Hotel intent on murder. Then I suddenly stopped. Vrable? Could he have done it? If he believed I still worked with McAllen, he might think killing my horse would keep me in town during the robbery. Damn. Now I wasn't sure. It had to be one of the two, and they might be working together. I decided to talk to Sharp and cool off before I did something stupid. I sure didn't want to spend my time out West locked up in prison.

As soon as I stepped into the store, I waved Sharp over. He knew something was wrong from my face, so he hurried to meet me at the door.

"Mrs. Baker," I yelled. "You got the store. We'll be back shortly."

Without another word, I turned and walked away.

When Sharp caught up with me, he asked, "What happened?"

"Somebody poisoned Chestnut. He's dead."

"Damn ... I'm sorry."

"I need you to help me figure out if it was Vrable or Bolton."

"What do ya know?"

"The doctor confirmed it was snakeroot, and they convinced me that it wasn't mixed in the feed. Somebody knew the liveryman's routine and entered an unlocked side door after he left the barn late last night to play faro. That's it. I looked around the barn and saw nothing out of the ordinary other than my dead horse."

"Snakeroot's not hard to find." He walked a ways before asking, "Do ya know if Mrs. Bolton is still in Leadville?"

I pointed around the next street corner. "No. That's a good place to start."

"They could be workin' together. Vrable told ya she'd tried to hire him."

"I already thought of that." I put a hand on Sharp's forearm to stop his progress. "Jeff, I hope Vrable's not involved. I want revenge, and McAllen will be furious if I take action against Vrable. I want it to be Mrs. Bolton."

"What will ya do if it is? Ya can't just walk up and shoot a woman."

"Half hour ago I would have just shot her. I've had enough time to figure out that would be a bad move, but not enough time to figure out a good move."

"If she's still here, let's talk to McAllen."

"He won't like it. He doesn't want to be seen with us."

"Stealin' or killin' a horse is a lynchin' crime in this state. The captain will know how to get evidence."

"They'll never hang a woman."

"Maybe not, but if they throw her in prison, she'll stay put better than she did in San Francisco. If she's still registered at the hotel, let's leave a note with the desk clerk that we want to meet McAllen at the Silverado."

"All right, but we'll seal the note and have the kid I hired as a watcher slip it under his door. Vrable might have bribed the desk clerk."

"Shit, yer right. Let's go."

We quickened our pace as I slapped my chest with both arms to get back some of the feeling that the morning chill had stolen from me. When was this robbery planned? Soon? We hadn't heard any news from McAllen, but that didn't mean anything. Ore shipments were kept secret to make it more difficult for bandits. The Wells Fargo and Pinkerton protection teams would be the first to know, but even they might have only one day's notice. For all we knew, it could be happening right now. Because McAllen's daughter was safe, he could forewarn his team of Pinkertons. He probably didn't feel like he needed our help. In his mind, we had already done our bit by rescuing his daughter. Besides, McAllen wasn't the type of man to ask for help, especially when he had his Pinkertons around him.

The lobby of the Carbonate Hotel looked quiet, so we went up to the desk clerk. Like many small men put in a position of minor authority, he pretended to be busy for several minutes before he looked up at us with a quizzical expression.

"Is Mrs. Bolton still a guest?" I asked.

"Yes, Mr. Dancy. In fact, I think she's in the dining room having breakfast."

"Thank you." I walked away from the desk and said to Sharp, "Let's sit down and surprise her. Gauge her reaction."

"Ya want me to come with ya?"

"Yes, I don't trust myself alone with her. Watch and tell me what you see."

Mrs. Bolton sat at a table in the middle of the elegant room with two waiters hovering at her shoulders. I bet she drove the staff mad with her endless demands. That woman could terrorize a battle-hardened general. I looked around and spotted McAllen in a corner with his back against the wall so he could watch the entire room. For a moment, I thought about asking Sharp to talk to him but decided that would violate McAllen's orders. I had already learned something though: the ore shipment robbery was still at least a day in the future.

I waited until Mrs. Bolton was engrossed in giving instructions to the waiters before I approached. I wanted to surprise her. When it looked as if the waiters were about to leave to do her bidding, I plopped down beside her. Sharp slid into a third chair.

"Coffee, please. And if your biscuits are fresh from the oven, bring a couple of those as well."

Not the slightest flinch. In fact, she smiled sweetly as she told one waiter, "You can put those on my tab and bring these gentlemen their coffee immediately. You have our orders; now show me your backsides."

The two men scurried away as if she held a bullwhip.

"I see you have the hotel staff properly intimidated."

Again the sweet smile: "It only takes a day." She folded her hands on the table. "Why do I have the honor of your company?"

"Two men told me you tried to hire them."

And again, not the slightest flinch. "I hope you're properly intimidated."

"Intimidation is not your objective. You're looking for men to kill me."

"How do you know I'm still looking?"

I hated this woman but not as much as she hated me. She was fat, in her fifties, and had a huge, broad face that dominated the rest of her corpulent body. With her flowered dresses and pearl jewelry, she looked matronly and innocent. Until she opened her mouth. Then she revealed her insides, which were unseemly and repellent. She had warned me in Nevada that she wanted to kill me, and she had almost succeeded in Durango. I knew how to challenge a man, but how should I deal with a grandmotherly looking woman who hired people to do her dirty work? Make her angry so she made mistakes? She was already angry. Poison? I couldn't—even after Chestnut. But unless I did something, I would face an unending string of hired gunmen.

"You're the one that ought to be careful," I said. "One day, one of your hired hands will testify against you, and you'll spend the rest of your life in prison instead of in your lovely house in San Francisco."

"Mr. Dancy, be realistic. No jury will find me guilty. You're a killer, and I'm a ranch woman with no idea how to do the things you accuse me of." She smiled. "I can be quite sweet when I set my mind to it. The jury will feel sympathy for me as a poor woman who's been falsely accused by a despicable killer."

"You're right, I have killed people. Perhaps you should be the one who's worried. I might decide to attack the head of the beast, like I did with Washburn in Nevada."

"What? Are you going to mount your trusty steed and charge off to slay the evil dragon? I don't think so, but just in case, the hard-looking brute at the next table protects me." Again, that damn smile. "He has a gun pointed at you this very minute."

I looked over at the next table and saw a nasty sort with his hand below the table. He nodded at me. A man with a drawn gun on me. I first felt relief that this was something I might be able to handle, and then I remembered that she would just hire another. I tipped an imaginary hat at her guard and returned my attention to her.

"Mrs. Bolton, this feud will end soon…and you will not be happy with the outcome." I rose. "Good day, and you may eat our biscuits when they arrive. The waiter probably glazed them with spit anyway."

When we got to the lobby and found a quiet corner, I asked Sharp, "What did you see?"

"Beyond a reprehensible woman? Not much. She's protected, an' she's still out to get ya."

"She also killed Chestnut. Her comment about a trusty steed was her way of telling me."

"Ya sure?"

"I'm sure. That woman revels in bragging about the ill she does others."

"Well, ya gotta put that aside for the time bein'."

"Why should I?"

"McAllen gestured that he needs to talk to us. Somethin's afoot."

Chapter 45

McAllen met us at the Silverado in less than an hour. He gave us a nod and then got a beer from the bartender before joining us. We had kept the chair in the corner open for him, and he sat down with a sigh and took a long swallow of beer before starting the conversation.

"We have problems."

Both Sharp and I stayed quiet, so he continued. "First, last night someone killed that Indian that worked with Bane."

"Raven?"

"That was the name he used."

"Do they know who killed him?" Sharp asked.

"I do. I've seen Bane's cruel handiwork before ... probably killed him because he led you men to his camp."

Suddenly I felt a swelling of sorrow that I hadn't expected. Obviously, I had avoided thinking about the possibilities. Fearing the answer, I asked. "Red?"

McAllen's expression turned sad. "Only one man was gonna come out of those mountains." He sighed again. "Appears it was Bane."

We sat silent, and then Sharp raised his beer mug. "To Red—a loyal friend an' a dangerous enemy. It was an honor to ride with him."

McAllen and I muttered agreement, and we took a slow sip to commemorate a capable but troubled man. A man, I suspect, none of us really knew.

After we set our mugs back on the table, I asked, "Does this mean that Vrable knows we got Maggie back?"

McAllen shook his head. "I saw Vrable this morning, and he still acted like he had the upper hand. I'm not sure, but I don't think he knows.

That didn't make sense to me. "Why wouldn't Bane alert Vrable?"

"Maybe 'cuz he's tryin' to get her back," Sharp offered.

"That'd be my guess," McAllen kept his voice low. "Vrable surely told him to stay away, and Bane's probably not ready to admit failure… so he'll look around town a bit and try to locate her. Bane doesn't need to stay occupied long: the ore shipment leaves at four tomorrow morning."

"Four?"

"Security. We want to be long gone before the town even wakes up. If Bane spends the day looking for Maggie, my plan may still work."

"Ya feel like sharin' yer plan?" Sharp asked impatiently.

McAllen looked irritated—never a good sign. "Jeff, why the hell do you think we're meeting? Losing Red changes things. We need to all play from the same sheet music… and before I finish this beer, 'cuz I gotta get my team ready."

"Are we part of your plans?" I asked, confused.

"Of course, what'd you think?"

"That with Maggie safe, you'd rely on your Pinkertons."

"I wish I could. Vrable may have bribed one of my men, so I haven't said a word to either of them. They think it's routine guard duty. It doesn't matter anyway; when the robbery starts, if they're loyal, they'll follow my orders. If they don't, I'll kill them."

"Only two men?" Sharp asked.

"Three counting myself. Same as Vrable's team of Wells Fargo agents. Normal security detail of six. Besides the roadmen, Vrable may have one of my men and probably both of his in on the robbery. It's gonna be hard to sort out the loyal men from the bandits." He looked at me. "I tried recruiting Masterson to help you boys, but he has his hands full with the Rio Grande mischief."

"What about the teamster?" I asked. "If I were Vrable, that's the first one I'd bribe."

"Good thinkin', Steve. Control the wagon, and you control the fight. Instead of using the bullwhip, the teamster could pull up and let the wagon get surrounded."

"What's Vrable tellin' ya to do once the robbery starts?"

"Order my men to drop their guns. Vrable says he'll do the same for his agents. The shooting will probably start as soon as my men's guns hit the ground."

"What's our job?" I asked.

"I want you to leave this morning and scout out the terrain along the shipment route. Pick out the likely spot as best you can. Red would've been better, but you'll do fine. Stay within two or three hours of Leadville. That'll position you on the road after daybreak. I think it will be close to town so Vrable can bring the ore back to Leadville. He bought a played-out mine a year ago, so I figure he'll pretend to find a new vein and claim that the stolen silver has been freshly dug out of his own mine."

"Smart," Sharp said. "Once he's deposited most of it in a bank, he can use the remainder to salt the mine. With healthy production records an' showin's, he can sell his worthless mine at top dollar. In some ways, ya gotta admire the man."

"Bullshit!" McAllen exclaimed. "There ain't nothing to admire. He's a confidence man, that's all. I'll see him dead or behind bars. Then you can go visit him and see how smart he is."

Neither of us responded, so McAllen continued. "You're staying the night, so bring appropriate gear." He looked at each of us to make sure we were listening. "I need you to ambush the ambushers."

"What about your team?" I asked.

"If you can kill the roadmen or pin them down, my team'll take care of Vrable's men." Another look between us. "Can you handle it?"

Jeff and I looked at each other and then nodded to McAllen. "I need to buy a horse before we can leave," I said.

McAllen gave me a puzzled look. "A horse? Why?"

"Someone poisoned Chestnut last night."

McAllen looked even more puzzled and then said in an unsure voice, "Bane?"

"I suspect Mrs. Bolton."

"Red could have talked," McAllen mused. "If he did, Bane might've done it to draw you out so he can get you to tell him where Maggie is."

"Red didn't talk," Sharp said immediately. McAllen gave him a hard look, so he explained. "Red understood Bane's nature. He would've fought to the death."

McAllen pondered that a minute and then asked, "Steve, can you put Mrs. Bolton aside until this is over?"

"This isn't over until she's taken care of, but, yes, I can wait until after tomorrow."

That seemed to satisfy McAllen. I didn't mind waiting a couple of days because I didn't know what I was going to do. If I could tie her into Vrable's plot, maybe I could get her thrown behind bars. Somehow, that didn't feel like a satisfactory answer. The woman was malicious as hell and probably crazy. She had attacked me with hired guns, tried to enlist Bat Masterson to shoot me down, sidled up to Vrable, and murdered Chestnut. Damn her. This was a personal feud, and I didn't want impersonal revenge. Sending her to prison was not enough. A night in the wilderness would give me time to think, and I needed to approach this problem calmly.

"Joseph, any chance Bane'll think of Twin Lakes?" Sharp's question brought me back to our current predicament.

"Maybe, but he'll search here first. The man acts more threatening than a starving mountain lion. He'll have a hard enough time asking around Leadville. Even if he thinks of it, he'll hesitate before going to the Inter-Laken. The man looks like an ogre, but he's not stupid. He knows he'll look like a buzzard in a canary cage at that hotel." McAllen took another swallow of beer. "Did you see Maggie after the Schmidts cleaned her up?"

I said *yes* simultaneous with Sharp's *yep*.

"Think Bane will recognize her?"

"Not from a distance. She looked like an eastern debutante," I said. "I don't believe the Schmidts would let him get close."

McAllen looked into his beer a moment, and then he shook his head as if coming awake. "Doesn't matter. I must proceed on the basis that Maggie is safe."

Chapter 46

We made an excuse about checking a claim that had come up for sale and handed the store over to Mrs. Baker again. She actually seemed pleased. I remembered that she had been proud that she ran the haberdashery without interference from Mr. Cunningham. She was definitely an independent woman, and the thought occurred to me that she might bristle under my daily supervision. That shouldn't be a problem. After this affair had run its course, I would either sell the store or let her run it.

We were on the trail in less than two hours. It helped that we had never gotten around to stowing our gear after our last foray into the mountains. We could have gotten off a half hour earlier, but I felt the liveryman owed me a bargain on a new horse. He didn't agree. After some hard bartering, I bought a fine-looking horse at a slight discount from the original asking price. The horse was spirited and nervous, and I already regretted my choice.

"What are ya gonna name him?" Sharp asked as we rode down the trail that led to Denver.

I didn't want to name him at all. This was not my strong and steady Chestnut and, at least at this point, I intended to sell him when I returned to town. Nothing felt right. My saddle felt different, and the gait didn't feel right. When I looked down at his head and neck, the dark brown color seemed unnatural. To be fair, the horse also had no feel for me. Well, we'd see.

"Ya thinkin' or ignorin' me?" Sharp asked.

"Brown."

"What?"

"I'm naming him Brown."

"That's an awful name."

"So far, I think he's an awful horse."

"Steve, that's a fine animal. Ya'll get used to him."

"I'm new to the frontier. I need a horse that knows more about the backcountry than me."

Sharp laughed. "Well, that's an easy mark to pass. I believe Brown just might have the edge."

I wanted to change the subject. "Jeff, have you ever been robbed?"

"Yep, in South America. I was just twenty-two an' sinless as all get out. Banditos grabbed my haul." His face took on a faraway expression. "On a mountain road, just like this."

"Did you fight?"

"Hell, no. The gold I carried wasn't worth my life. I handed it over, just like they demanded."

"Ever catch them?"

"Not to my knowledge, but that sort always ends up bad. Taught me a lesson, though. Always had good security after that."

I remembered Belleville, Sharp's Nevada mining operation. He had situated it deep in a canyon with natural fortifications and numerous guards. It struck me that Sharp seldom made the same mistake twice. I also realized that I couldn't be on the trail with anyone more capable of handling the situation in front of us. Sharp must have sent dozens of shipments by wagon and knew how to protect them. Red might have been a better tracker, but Sharp had studied the threats to slow-moving ore wagons.

"What type of terrain will they pick?"

Sharp didn't answer at first. Then he said carefully, "They've had lots of time to plan this, so they'll have picked the best spot to surprise the caravan. The shipment leaves at four, an' first light isn't until around six, so between two to three hours out of Leadville makes sense. However, ore wagons move at a crawl—lots slower than a horse. We'll start lookin' an hour away from Leadville."

"How many?"

No hesitation this time. "Vrable's a careful man. Even though he has McAllen in his pocket, he'll want too many rather than too few. Bad men come cheap, so my guess is six or seven. Maybe more."

"Okay, the bandits rob the shipment, and the agents don't put up a fight. Do they take the wagon? How does Vrable make sure they don't keep the ore, and how does he keep ten or more men quiet after the robbery?"

"Ya gotta take those questions backwards to forwards. For this plan to work, the scheme has to remain secret, and the robbers can't blackmail Vrable when he starts depositin' the silver. Vrable and his men ain't gonna throw down their guns—they're gonna fight. The robbers are told to kill the Pinks, an' the Wells Fargo agents kill the outlaws. Nobody expects the double cross. Everything neat and tidy."

"It can't go perfectly."

"It can go good enough. There's only two Wells Fargo agents other than Vrable, an' I bet he's confided in only one. The other won't survive the gunfight. He can do it with one agent an' the teamster. All that's left is to drive the wagon to his mine an' hide it. When he rides back into town, he'll claim that there were more outlaws than corpses, an' they hauled off the shipment. He'll say they shot at them as they rode away, but there were too many."

"McAllen?"

"Dead. Only safe way."

"McAllen thinks Vrable wants to see him hang for the crime."

"I know, but I don't see it. Too complicated. Easier to put the blame on him when he's dead."

"What about those who return with him? Won't they have a hold on him?"

"Probably partners in the mine scheme. My guess is that he's worked with them before, an' he hired them on as Wells Fargo agents. Unlike other criminals, confidence men have a strict code of honor. An' if he's bribed a Pinkerton, the poor bastard'll get a surprise bullet as a final payment."

"Bane?"

"Cash. Vrable'll pay because he's afraid of him, an' he may want to use him again someday."

"That's a lot of shooting and a lot of dead men."

"Three Pinks, six or seven outlaws. Yep. Lots of dead, but his story'll hold unless they find the shipment."

"Something bothers me. That shipment can't be worth enough money to justify all the killing."

"Forty, fifty thousand dollars. An' he gets revenge on McAllen. More important, he'll use the silver to get hundreds of thousands for that useless mine. It's a confidence man's dream.

"You've been pondering this awhile, haven't you?"

"Just figured out how I'd do it. But I got one fear."

"What's that?"

"Vrable's smarter than me."

Chapter 47

By my pocket watch, we found the ambush spot an hour and twenty minutes outside of Leadville. There was a sharp turn in the road and good cover from either side. Sharp and I dismounted and walked the entire ground. On the uphill slope were boulders with an unobstructed view of the road, and a ravine on the downhill side provided ample cover for shooters. The shipment convoy would be in a deadly cross fire.

"Shit."

I looked at Sharp. "Bad, huh?"

"We'll have to split up." He pointed to either side of the road. "One on each side." He shook his head. "Ya gotta get high in those boulders so ya can get a good line on both sides of the road. There's no place for me to hide on this side where I can get a clear shot." He shook his head again. "This is perfect for an ambush."

"I go into the boulders?"

"Steve, yer the better shot. Take the men in the boulders an' then shoot at the ones in the ravine. Ya gotta get me enough time to come up from behind after the shootin' starts."

"Makes sense. Let me go up there and see if I can find a spot where I have a clear line at both hiding places."

After a short climb, I saw boot prints behind two boulders. Somebody had already scouted out this area. I looked up and saw the rock formations extending all the way up the hill. In ten minutes, I had found my spot about twenty yards further up the hill. Close enough for an easy shot but also dangerously close if I made the slightest noise. I couldn't find my way in the dark, so I'd have to be in position by dusk and stay quiet. I shivered in anticipation of the cold.

After I climbed back down to the road, Sharp pointed and said, "See that tree?"

"Yes."

"It's half chopped down. They're gonna finish it in the mornin' so it blocks the road. They won't see it until they make the bend."

"I guess that confirms we got the right spot."

"Oh, it's the right spot alright. Did ya see that trail that led off the road 'bout a half mile back? I'm bettin' it leads to Vrable's mine. Gets 'em off the road real quick."

"I found a good spot for me. How about you?"

Sharp glanced down the ravine. "Nope. I'll have to stay in the thickets until the shootin' starts. Not good. They can get off a couple shots before I can get a bead on 'em."

"That won't work."

"I know."

We both stared down the ravine. There was no place to hide below where the ambushers would set up. Then we both examined the boulders. If two or three shooters sat in the ravine, all the Pinkertons could be dead before Sharp and I directed our shots at them. We might stop the holdup, but our friend would be dead or wounded.

"Can we take them before the caravan arrives?" I asked.

"In the dark? Red could, but not us. If we wait till light, they'll already be hidden."

"Damn."

"Damn," Sharp repeated.

"Let's ride down the road and find a place to fix a meal and think about it. We'll come back on foot before dusk."

As we swung into our saddles, I said, "They'll be here before dusk."

Sharp looked at me. "What do ya mean?"

"That tree. They won't want to finish cutting it down in the dark. I bet they're thinking like us. Get in position tonight."

"Damn, I believe ya might be right."

"Can we take them this evening?"

"They're not afraid, so they might get careless. After takin' care of the tree, they'll probably eat a meal. Maybe even build a fire." Sharp reached over and slapped me on the back. "Damn, Steve, we may get the drop on the whole load of 'em."

I looked around. "Where do you think they'll eat?"

Sharp grinned. "Right in the middle of the road. Flat ground an' nobody's on this road at night. Yep, warm themselves by a fire, eat a meal, an' then scurry to their hidin' places at the crack of dawn."

That sounded reasonable, but Sharp had already misjudged some aspects about this robbery. Could he be wrong again? What if they hid on either side of the road at dusk instead of gathering together for a meal? If we set up to take them on the road, we might not be able to get into position behind their ambush points.

I swung around in my saddle and looked to all sides. "How many do you think there'll be?" I asked again.

"I said six or seven, but now I think only four. Two to a side. They only have to kill three Pinkertons, an' this is perfect ground for an ambush. Vrable's smart an' cautious. He'll want to keep the number to a minimum."

I gave Sharp a hard look. "I don't think we should make the same mistake you suspect they'll make."

Sharp nodded. "I agree. Let's hide the horses down the road an' get in position. Hardtack for dinner."

We hid the horses about a mile down the road. Luckily, we found a small glade with plenty of grass about forty yards into the brush. We left the horses saddled in case we needed to leave in a hurry and picketed them with long ropes so they could graze over a wide area. As we hurried back on foot carrying our rifles, we chewed on hardtack and jerky. I didn't mind the wilderness except for the cold, the lousy meals, and sleeping on the hard ground. At least I had a flask that we passed back and forth to wash down the dry food.

Huffing a bit, I said, "This road is narrow. What happens when two wagons meet?"

"Stagecoaches gotta give right of way to ore wagons." Sharp laughed. "A teamster haulin' ore has gotta recover any spilled load, but if a stage goes over an edge, the driver just buries his load."

"You're joshing."

"Nope." Between mouthfuls, Sharp added, "When we get back, let's trace our path from the tree to our hidin' spots. If we can get to 'em without trouble, we can set up on either side of the road by the tree."

"What if we can't?"

"Then we got to decide if we're gonna try to take 'em tonight or get in position to take 'em in the mornin'."

The terrain wasn't that much different close to the tree because it was only a few yards away. I climbed the boulders and found a good spot to watch the area by the fallen tree. From there I tried to navigate over to the previous ambush point I had found. I had no problem in daylight. The smooth boulders made it easy to move quietly, and they were regular enough that my footing felt secure. I stood tall and examined the path between the two spots. Could I find it in the dark? I wasn't sure, but my bet was that if I did it three or four times, I wouldn't have a problem tonight.

When I climbed down, Sharp had already returned to the road. "I'm okay. How about you?" I asked.

Sharp rubbed his chin. "I'm better off up here. I could never get to the ravine without makin' noise, but I couldn't find a hidin' place down there anyway." He pointed. "I think I can position myself there an' surprise 'em from the side."

We both looked around, and then I descended into the brush and tried to move toward the ravine. Even with daylight, I couldn't move two steps without noisily crushing dry twigs under my boots. Wherever Sharp set up on this side of the road, he would have to stay put or alert the ambushers to our presence. It seemed that there was no way to surprise them from both sides at once—unless they gathered close to the tree before dusk.

I looked up at Sharp. "Jeff, I say we set up to take them by the tree."

Sharp looked the ground over again and then said, "Yep."

"How will the law take it if we kill these men before they rob the shipment?"

"Been thinkin' on that. If they fell the tree across the road, the law will stand behind the Carbonate Kings. The captain can tell 'em he had uncovered the plot an' he recruited us into the Pinkertons. We'll be fine."

"What if McAllen is killed?"

"I'd still take my chances with a jury if it comes to that, but I don't think it will—unless we lose the shipment. Besides, what choice do we have?"

"None. It's the only way to save our friend. I'll do it, but I don't like shooting men in the back."

Sharp laughed. "Then shout *howdy*."

I laughed as well. I guess that's what they call gallows humor. When I came west, I never anticipated getting into the type of gunplay that would haunt me. In the West, disputes were often settled with guns. Tycoons in New York destroyed opponents for sport, but their enemy usually limped away—albeit broken and friendless. I guess that is what people call civilization.

I pulled out my pocket watch. It was half past three.

"Yep," Sharp said. "We better get into our positions. They could come trottin' up that road any time."

Without hesitation, we both extended our hands and shook. We had some long, cold hours ahead of us that would be relieved in the end by violence. Our eyes met briefly, and then we each went to our respective sides of the road.

Chapter 48

In fifteen minutes, I was shivering from the inactivity. Damn. I dreaded the confrontation, but I began to hope they'd show up soon so we could get this dirty business over with. I kept completely hidden with my back against an ice cold rock because I assumed I'd hear Vrable's gang approach. What must the weather be like in the winter? Colder for sure, but it was hard for me to imagine. I kept my flask in my coat pocket. Bat Masterson's warning about staying sober in a gunfight played on my mind, but mostly I wanted to conserve the whiskey for after dark.

After an hour in hiding I heard ribald male voices. I was tempted to take a peek, but I had already determined that they would be the most alert on first arrival. Better to stay down. Shortly, I heard horse hooves and realized these men were bantering so loud that I heard them from a good distance. Careless? Overconfident? I hoped both. It took all my will to stay put because I was anxious to see how many were in their band.

The men got noisier as they approached. I began to pick up snatches of their conversation, which seemed to be about the relative merits of prostitutes they had all experienced. I began to question Vrable's cleverness. I wasn't an expert, but it seemed to me that a good crew would have approached quietly and perhaps even sent a single man forward to scout the ambush point. They were either none too sharp, or they had absolute faith that Vrable had rigged the robbery so well that they had no worries.

Suddenly the men's voices became clear, and I realized they had just rounded the bend in the road. One sounded to be in charge, and he ordered two of the others to fell the tree. When I heard the axe strikes, I decided to chance a peek. Only four. Sharp had been right. Would he also be right about them preparing a meal together? Would they gather or split up and get into position for the morning? Three of them were in view, and I could easily shoot all of them before they could swing a weapon around in my direction. The fourth was out of sight behind the tree, but if I was right about Sharp's position, he should have a clear shot. Without real contemplation, I decided.

I pulled off my gloves and laid them on a boulder and then rested my rifle on the gloves.

On a whim, I shouted "Howdy!"

Then the shooting started.

Instinctively, I aimed at the most difficult shot first. The bullet hit the man chopping the tree in mid-swing, and the impact sent his axe flying. When I shifted my sights to the two men in the road, I saw that they were still astride their horses. I chose the one who had turned toward me in response to my shout. I could actually see his bewildered expression as the bullet hit him center chest. My third target had his wits about him and spurred his horse to make an escape. Too late. My shot penetrated his arm, turning his body for a second shot that I was sure killed him before he hit the ground.

In less than two seconds, the three in sight were down. Shots from the other side of the road told me that Sharp had not hesitated to take his man.

Instead of clambering down the rocky slope, I found myself rooted to my hiding place. I grew disgusted at the sight of my handiwork and collapsed onto my backside with my rifle across my lap. Twice I had ambushed men I didn't know. This was not what I had expected when I came out West. I had heard the stories and expected to see more violence than in New York, but I was confident that if I used my head I could avoid getting embroiled in it myself. How had this come about? Bad friends? No, Sharp and McAllen were good men. I would have befriended them if I had encountered them in the city. Circumstances? If it were mere misfortune, then it seemed an unusually long string of bad luck. My character? Did some part of me crave this kind of excitement? Some things in my past made me wonder. Damn, I hoped not.

Suddenly, I heard my name. When I peeked over the edge of the boulder, I saw that Sharp was on the road making sure our targets wouldn't suddenly spring to life and return shots in our direction. I should have been doing the same instead of wallowing in self-recrimination. I stood and waved my rifle before making my way down the pile of rocks.

When I got to the road, Sharp said, "All dead."

"Sorry I went against our plan. I was afraid we wouldn't get a better opportunity."

"Hell, I was prayin' ya'd start shootin'. I had a clear bead on both of 'em. Surprised me ya took out one of my men first, though."

"I felt if I jumped early, I needed to make it easier for you."

"I was ready." Sharp gave me an odd look. "Steve, that was a joke about shoutin' howdy."

"I know, but it occurred to me that it was a good way to get them to swing toward me so I'd have a better shot."

"Good, 'cuz there ain't no gentlemen's rules in this type of engagement."

I looked around at the dead bodies. "I noticed."

"These men were goin' to do the same to McAllen an' his men."

"I know. It's just that this is the second time I've killed men without warning."

I'm not sure what I expected from Sharp, but what he said next took me by surprise. "Those back-shooters deserved to die. Probably already done worse. If ya want to feel bad about somethin', feel bad about them Utes. They hired on to snatch Maggie, but they only did it to get provisions for the winter."

He was right. "Thanks, you made me feel better and worse at the same time."

"Now I got company." He slapped me on the back. "My pa used to tell me that I didn't need to worry about right an' wrong as long as I continued to worry about right and wrong."

In an odd way, that made sense. As long as you let your conscience needle you, you wouldn't slide into that dark abyss.

I shook off my melancholy and asked, "How does this play out from here?"

"Well, Mr. Dancy, some would say we shoulda thought about that before we started blastin' away."

Sharp's comment wasn't that funny, but I laughed from nervous release.

"How 'bout we put our heads to it while we get these bodies out of sight."

We hauled the bodies deep into the ravine and piled rocks on top of the corpses as a crude burial. After we huffed back up to the road, we slowly led their horses by the reins to the glade where we had tethered ours. We talked through the alternatives on the mile walk and settled on a course of action. It was a risky plan, but if it worked, it would close this episode for good.

Chapter 49

After hours of shivering cold, I welcomed seeing a star wink out in the gathering glow of dawn. Sharp insisted that a fire could be smelled from miles away in the crystalline air, so we just huddled together with our backs against the fallen tree. We shared the flask until it was empty, and then we periodically held it upside down over our mouths, tipping it back and forth in the futile hope that a drop had miraculously eluded our prior efforts.

My pocket watch said it was about a quarter after five. If the caravan left on schedule, we estimated that the slow-moving ore wagon would arrive about six. Although we barely had enough light to see, we scurried to our respective positions. I began to worry that our plan was too simple. What had we forgotten? What if Vrable didn't act in the way we expected? Most important, what if we had completely miscalculated, and more people were in on the conspiracy than we had guessed? Too late. If events went awry, we would just have to make the best of the situation.

In less than ten minutes, I heard the type of squeaks that wagon springs make protesting their load. Listening carefully, I soon picked up a crackling noise as the wagon wheels crushed pebbles in their path. They were early. But how far away were they? There were no male voices this time. These men were professionals. We assumed there would be some type of shout when they completed the bend and spotted the fallen tree blocking their progress. That would be our signal to start shooting.

Sound travels far in the mountain air. They weren't as close as I had thought when I first heard them. As I strained to listen, I couldn't pick up a human voice, but the other sounds became louder and louder as the ore wagon relentlessly rolled toward us.

Then I heard a man yell, "Hold up there!"

Without lifting my head, I immediately fired five rounds into the air. There was enough shooting that I was sure Sharp was doing the same from the other side of the road. Before the echoes subsided, I rose and aimed my rifle down on the road.

I saw one Wells Fargo agent sprawled on the ground. McAllen had his rifle aimed squarely at Vrable.

Then I heard the captain order his team to aim their weapons at the other Wells Fargo agent and the teamster.

"Drop yer guns!" Sharp yelled.

"Now!" I shouted from the other side of the road.

Everybody looked around at everyone else with confused expressions.

I decided to clarify the situation. "Captain, we killed the outlaw gang last night. We have a bead on Vrable's men, and we shoot on your orders."

McAllen spurred his horse and came up next to Vrable, then put his rifle barrel under his chin and lifted his head a smidgen. "Tell your men to drop their guns."

"Drop your guns, men." Vrable's voice affected surprise. "It appears that Captain McAllen intends to steal this shipment."

When the guns noisily clattered to the ground, McAllen carefully lowered the hammer on his rifle. Then in a move so fast I didn't catch it, he drove the gun barrel into Vrable's gut hard enough to knock him off his horse. McAllen flew out of his saddle and used the butt of his rifle to hit Vrable alongside his head. He stood there in such a rage, I thought he might shoot him.

Suddenly, McAllen turned away and signaled us to come down. As I descended the rocky slope, I heard him give a brief explanation to his two men, and then he ordered the contrite teamster to turn the wagon around.

"Steve, sit up there on the wagon. Make sure he takes it slow and easy. Throw me your rifle and use your handgun. Shoot him if he snaps the reins on the horses."

McAllen slipped my rifle into his scabbard and went over to talk to Sharp. We finally got the wagon turned around. Slow but not easy. Sitting in the shotgun seat, I watched the difficulty in reversing direction and developed an appreciation for the driver's skill. I was happy the teamster had enough sense to avoid getting himself shot, because I don't think any of us could have handled the team on the narrow road, especially with the fallen tree restricting forward motion.

The whole time the driver worked his team, I kept my Colt out but along my right thigh so it was out of his reach. After the final jigging of the wagon, I raised my pistol and ordered the driver to pull up. Now what? I shielded the Colt with my thigh again and glanced over my shoulder to see Sharp approaching.

"Steve, use Vrable's horse to gather up ours and bring 'em back here." Sharp pointed at the teamster. "What's yer name?"

"Brad."

"Brad, get yer ass down here an' load that Wells Fargo agent onto the top of this wagon."

I waited until Brad had climbed down before I jumped from my seat. I walked over to Vrable's horse, but before I swung into the saddle, Sharp took hold of my shoulder to stop me. "McAllen approved of the way we handled this."

"That's because it worked."

We had shot a few rounds into the air, figuring the only way to expose the conspirators was to make them think the robbery was happening according to plan. We had assumed that Vrable would shoot at McAllen because he hated the captain and McAllen was a dangerous man in a fight. It was a gamble, but Sharp and I had agreed that McAllen would also go after Vrable. We knew the captain was fully capable of taking care of himself in that type of situation. Also, McAllen had forewarning, so his readiness would give him an edge. We hoped. We had taken this course because the feud had to end, right here on this road, and not in some courtroom with uncertain evidence that a crime had even been intended. We had never anticipated that Vrable would shoot the Wells Fargo agent. He must have relied on the ambushers to kill McAllen and the other two Pinkertons. In the end, there would be a trial, but several trustworthy witnesses had seen Vrable commit a hanging offense.

"Yep. Right about that," Sharp said. "If our little trick had failed, McAllen would've been mad as a hornet."

I laughed. "In that case, I intended to act like a dumb city dweller following your lead."

Sharp released my shoulder and slapped me on the back with a snort. "Ya'd probably got away with that one too … except for this." He showed me a folded piece of paper from his pocket.

"What's that?"

"Last will and testament. Wrote it out last night in case things went bad this mornin'." He smiled and snapped the paper against his other palm. "In here, I give ya credit for our ruse."

"Damn." I shook my head and pulled myself into the saddle of Vrable's horse. "Jeff, you sneaky son of a bitch. I guess I am just a dumb city dweller."

Chapter 50

I looked at my watch and saw that it was only a little after nine. Damn, the day seemed long already. As we rode back into Leadville, I remembered that the main thoroughfare was named Chestnut, and the troubles I had left in town leaped back into my consciousness. McAllen may have had his daughter and reputation intact, but I still had unfinished business.

McAllen ordered us to the town office of H. A. W. Tabor, the biggest, and some said the luckiest, of the Carbonate Kings. Tabor was also mayor of Leadville, which meant he was the town marshal's boss. The marshal, a man named Mart Duggan, was a notorious bully, and I had been lucky enough not to encounter him or any of his police thugs. It helped that I had stayed away from the brothels and the rowdier saloons. The police effectively kept the town reasonably peaceful, but the Carbonate Kings used Wells Fargo and Pinkerton to protect their property. The rich always trusted private police more than public servants on the taxpayer payroll.

McAllen went into Tabor's office by himself, while we kept an eye on our prisoners. Vrable and his enlisted robbers were subdued, but the Pinkertons still made a show of looking intimidating. After about a half hour, McAllen stuck his head out of the door and waved me in. Odd. Why would I be called into the ongoing discussions? I gave Sharp a glance, but he just shrugged.

Tabor's office was luxurious, even by New York City standards. I had heard idle talk in my store that he was worth several million and on the way to more. Much more.

As I entered, he approached with his hand extended. "Mr. Dancy, I've heard about you, and I'm glad we have this opportunity to meet." He shook my hand vigorously. "Thank you for all you did today."

"You're welcome, but I must admit, I did it for Captain McAllen, not you."

"Of course, of course. You don't even know me. But I still feel an obligation, and I think I can repay it."

"That's not necessary."

Tabor gave me an indulgent look. "Mr. Dancy, please listen to me a moment." He paused dramatically. "Mart Duggan accepted a contract to kill you. He's already deposited five hundred, and he'll get another five hundred when the deed is done." Now he looked a little too pleased with himself. "I presume you know Mrs. Bolton?"

"I know Mrs. Bolton, but how do you know about a deal between her and the marshal?"

"I have a man inside his police force. Mart is not the kind of man you allow to move around without a watcher."

"He's the marshal, for God's sake."

"Mart is a scoundrel and a killer. He once threatened to throw me in jail when I criticized the way he ran his office. Since then, the town leaders have let him run his petty rackets because he keeps a lid on the town."

I turned to McAllen. "Captain, it appears I need to pay attention to my own affairs. Let me know when the trial will be held, and I'll make myself available."

"Hold on, Steve. Mr. Tabor isn't just giving you a warning. He intends to resolve this issue… at least as far as Duggan goes."

My head whipped around to Tabor. "How?"

"He's doing this for money. I'll pay him more not to do it. He has it good here. He'll see reason." Tabor laughed. "The man doesn't have an honorable bone in his body. I bet he keeps the five hundred he's already got."

"That would be a mistake. Mrs. Bolton does not forgive, and she never forgets. But, I thank you. I'll repay you, of course."

"Not necessary. Captain McAllen says he owes you an enormous debt, and he has instructed me to use his share of the reward to remind our dear marshal that he is an officer of the court. Besides, this won't come cheap, young man."

I looked at McAllen. "Thank you, Captain, but that won't be necessary. I can afford it."

"Steve, you're going to let me help with this." The tone of voice ended that discussion.

I extended my hand to Tabor. "Thank you for the information and the intervention. It's appreciated." I turned to leave.

"Where do you think you're going?" McAllen asked.

"To my hotel to get warm and fed so I can think. I need to figure out how to end this feud with Mrs. Bolton."

"Steve, we didn't call you in just to tell you about her shenanigans. I wanted you off the street. Someone could've plucked you off that horse as easy as shooting that wooden Indian in front of your store. Stay here until Mr. Tabor returns and tells you he has convinced Duggan to double-cross that bitch."

I thought about it. My natural instinct was to ignore them and do what I wanted, but that was incautious. No, it was foolish. It made no sense to risk my life against yet another of her hired gunmen, and it made no sense that I resented help from Tabor. I needed to avoid trouble because, sooner or later, my luck or skill would fail.

"Will you do it now?" I asked Mr. Tabor.

"Yes. We need to secure the ore, but the captain has his instructions. The marshal will be sleeping in his room at this hour." Tabor smiled, as if he looked forward to interrupting the marshal's sleep. "He needs to be rousted anyway to take charge of these prisoners."

"Captain, this may take a bit," I said. "After you secure the shipment and prisoners, could you have one of your men order breakfast sent over to this office?"

"I'll do it on my way over to the marshal's room," Tabor said. "Help yourself to coffee in the meantime."

I wanted to object because I didn't want to be beholden to this man. Why did I feel competitive with him? I fought McAllen's enemies because the situation called for it, not because I felt a need to win a confrontation. Tabor was just being polite, and I bristled. I looked at Tabor and looked around his office, and I knew. This man competed in my arena—business. Those gunfights were someone else's arena, and I didn't care about winning; I cared about surviving. This realization made me enormously happy. I may have been in the West, but the West was not yet in me. Even though I had been thrilled—even euphoric—after surviving gunplay, the violence hadn't corrupted me. I needed to get back to my journal. It seemed that with a little thought, I could put together an interesting entry.

I was walking over to the stove to pour coffee for myself when I had a thought. "Mr. Tabor?"

"Yes."

I reached inside my coat and withdrew my wallet. "If you offered

Duggan another five hundred, do you think he'd testify against Mrs. Bolton?"

Tabor contemplated my question. "No, perhaps for a thousand, though." He made a dismissive wave of his hand. "I'll take care of it."

I pulled out a thousand dollars and held it out to him. "No, Mr. Tabor. You're taking care of breaking his agreement with Mrs. Bolton, and I'm eternally grateful, but I'll handle the bribe to get him to do his duty."

Tabor tentatively took the currency I held in front of him. "You own that general store at the end of State Street, am I not correct? With a partner, if I heard correctly."

"You heard correctly." The end of State Street was his way of saying in the low-rent district.

He held the bills up in front of him, but I noticed he had a firm grip. "This is a lot of money. Are you sure?"

"I *want* Mrs. Bolton in prison."

"You made this kind of money from that ramshackle shop?" Tabor sounded incredulous.

"I own other things."

Now he looked intrigued. "What other things, if I may ask?"

"Among other assets, I own shares of the Santa Fe and the Denver and Rio Grande."

Tabor actually took a half step back. I was having fun, but I noticed McAllen looked irritated. "Both lines?" Tabor asked.

"Yes. And I intend to stop this feud. I'm sure you'll agree Leadville needs a secure method of refined-ore shipment."

Tabor shook his head in disbelief. "Why is a person of your means running a shoddy general store?"

I signaled him to come over to the window. "See that gruff man on the black horse?"

"Yes."

"That's my partner, Jeff Sharp. Have you heard of him?"

"No. He's rough looking." He studied him. "Is he a gunman?"

I laughed. "No more than necessary to protect his property and his friends. No, Jeff's the largest independent mine owner in Nevada. We only got into storekeeping to help foil this robbery."

"I see." He left the window. "Now that you put the name in context, I have heard of Jeff Sharp, and what I hear is mostly good." He gave me an appraising look before continuing. "Mr. Dancy, you don't need to concern yourself further about the two lines competing for Leadville. My sources tell me a deal was struck in a meeting between the parties in New York. The Santa Fe gets the southern route into New Mexico, and the Denver and Rio Grande gets uncontested rights to Leadville. Thankfully, your intervention won't be required."

"That means my intervention has already worked. I sent a series of telegrams suggesting that same solution."

"Well, I'm sure—"

"Mr. Tabor, we need to get to our respective tasks." McAllen's tone would brook no argument. "You two can discuss business when we get this shipment off the road and these prisoners behind bars." He grabbed Tabor by the elbow and gently led him to the door.

After they had passed onto the boardwalk, McAllen stuck his head back into the room before closing the door. "Steve, sorry to spoil your fun, but for your information, a man's pecker is not measured by how much money he has."

I thought about the long-barreled Smith & Wesson that McAllen carried. "Nor is it measured by the length of his pistol barrel."

McAllen, a man who rarely smiled, gave me a grin. "Steve, I think you got it wrong there." His head disappeared, and the door closed with a solid click.

I laughed. This was one of the rare times that McAllen had made a humorous comment. At least, I assumed he meant it humorously.

I poured myself some coffee and sipped as I watched McAllen through the window. He briskly took charge and got the teamster to move the wagon down the street. I assumed they were taking it to the Matchless, Tabor's biggest mine. McAllen looked his normal brusque self, but I could see that he was happier than I had ever seen him. After all he had been through this last month or so, he must have felt enormous relief. I was happy for him, and I realized I was feeling pretty good myself. No family member of mine had been in jeopardy, but this whole episode had been scary as hell, and my nerves had been keyed up for far too long. Thank God it was over.

I was at the stove refilling my coffee when I heard the door open behind me. I turned, expecting to greet Tabor. It wasn't him.

"Can I help you?" I asked, from the other side of the room.

The huge man stood as still as a statue and just stared at me and then spit on the carpet in utter disrespect of civilization. His clothes looked solid and in good repair, but filthy. His face was so pockmarked and scarred, I wondered how he shaved. After a moment, a putrid stench wafted across the room and almost made me recoil. But the eyes were what grabbed me and held me like a taut lariat. Those eyes spewed hatred and told the world in no uncertain terms that this man was decidedly dangerous. His existence threatened all things living.

Bane was an apparition from a nightmare.

I knew only one of us would leave this room alive, but how did he intend to kill me? His hands were empty, and if he wore a gun, it was underneath his over-large coat. I decided it was foolish to analyze or finesse. I needed to react, not think.

Shifting my coffee cup to my left hand, I said, "Bane, if you twitch, I'll kill you."

He snorted indifference. "I want the girl." Nothing moved but his mouth.

"Didn't you see the commotion outside? It's all over."

"Give me the girl and you live." He remained still, like a cat ready to pounce.

Why? The girl meant nothing now. He must have wanted the pleasure of killing her to get even or because he wasn't right in the head. I held no illusions that if I told him where to find Maggie that he would let me live. It wasn't his nature.

"That half-breed on the mountain was a friend of mine," I said as casually as I could muster. "I'm going to kill you for what you did to him."

"Try, you puny shopkeeper." His voice was gravelly, like it wasn't used much. He said the next words with pride. "No one can kill me."

He lunged toward me as he slipped his hand into the pocket of his coat.

I instantly drew my Colt and shot him twice, center body. As he stumbled, I took more care with my aim and shot him two more times in the head. Bane still stood, but he was dead. I shot him one more time in the middle of his chest, and he banged his back against the door and slid down to the floor.

Before crossing the room, I ejected my spent cartridges and reloaded. I wasn't going to take any chances. Damn, this man was harder to kill than that bear. With my gun continually aimed at Bane, I crossed the room and stood over his body. He wasn't going to get up. Reaching into his pocket, I pulled out a knife with a six-inch razor-sharp blade. The mountain man had sewn a sheath inside his coat pocket. Damn. I wondered if he could have gotten within arm's reach if I hadn't shot him when he first lunged.

As I looked down at the bloody mess, I realized that this time I had no regrets. I took a sip of coffee from the cup in my left hand. I hadn't spilled a drop. "Sorry, Bane, you never had a chance. You're scary all right, but Mrs. Bolton is the one that terrifies me."

Chapter 51

It felt good to dress for dinner. I had taken a nap, been to the barber, and taken a long hot bath with a bottle of good Scotch whiskey at my side. I looked forward to excellent food, opulent, warm surroundings, and the companionship of friends. I had a lot to enter into my journal, but it could all wait until tomorrow. I had bought a copy of *The Last of the Mohicans*, and even though James Cooper wasn't one of my favorite authors, I was going to play hooky from the shop another day or two and just hang around the hotel reading and writing.

As soon as I entered the hotel dining room, Sharp waved me over to a table in the far corner.

I plopped into an available chair and immediately asked, "Are we drinking wine or whiskey?"

"Both. Whiskey while we wait for McAllen an' wine with dinner."

Sharp signaled a waiter and ordered Kentucky whiskey and three glasses without asking my preference. That was all right, because I felt so good I was going to make Sharp pay for the evening.

"Well, if my luck holds, McAllen will be late," I said.

"Good fortune has been followin' along in our footsteps. Maggie's saved, we rescued the ore shipment, Vrable's in jail for murder, an' Mrs. Bolton's locked up for tryin' to bribe an officer of the court." Sharp laughed. "Hell, we even made money with that damn shop."

"You forgot the truce between the Santa Fe and the Denver and Rio Grande. My holding went up three bucks per share in the last two days."

"Then dinner is on you."

"Not a chance. Jeff, you're paying tonight, and I can assure you the tab will be truly outrageous."

"Done," he said with a smile.

I had been had. Most people would probably find it odd that we argued over who would pay a bill that both could easily afford. They would probably find it even stranger that winning this contest at times meant getting the other to pay, but in different circumstances, winning meant paying yourself. It was so confusing, even I could get mixed up.

McAllen arrived before the whiskey and made a show of inspecting the empty table. "Hell, I need a drink. Are you men waiting to see what you order for dinner before selecting the wine?"

Just as he finished complaining, the waiter slid a silver tray onto the table with three glasses, our whiskey, and a crystal bowl of ice shavings.

"Thank you, gentlemen." McAllen poured as he waved the waiter away.

I reached across the table and used a spoon to add ice shavings to my drink.

Sharp grabbed his heart in a faux attack. "You're ruinin' fine whiskey, Steve. For the life of me, I can't understand you easterners."

"I'll drink it before the ice melts," I said. We had had this conversation before, but it seemed like ages ago. The last time I was served ice with whiskey had been in Carson City, Nevada. I turned to McAllen. "Any charges?"

"Just the opposite. There was a wanted circular on Bane. Five hundred dollars, dead or alive. Marshal says to come over in the morning, and he'll give you a draft." McAllen raised his glass. "Congratulations, Steve, I think you're getting the hang of it out here."

"What do you mean?"

"When I first met you, you'd have waited to discover Bane's intentions. Now you just up and shot him before he thought you'd act. His reputation and appearance halts most folks, so Bane kills people before they get their minds around how bad he is." McAllen took a sip. "Also, you didn't back off till your gun was empty. Five killing shots. Another smart move with that son of a bitch." Now he took a healthy swallow.

"He told me he couldn't be killed."

"Did he?" McAllen said. "Probably so many men have tried over the years that he believed it, but you set him right on that score." McAllen lifted his glass again. "Let's have another toast to Red, and then we'll call that nervous waiter over."

After we said some appropriate things and drank, I asked, "How long before Vrable's trial?"

"Week, hopefully two." McAllen actually grinned. "Since I can't escort Maggie back to Durango until after the trial, the longer it takes, the more time I get with her. I'll pick Maggie up from Twin Lakes in a day or two."

"What're ya doin' tomorrow?" Sharp asked.

McAllen's expression turned serious. "I'm going into the mountains. I'll get Maggie after I find Red."

"You think Red's still alive?" I asked, incredulous.

"No, but he deserves a proper burial. I know how Bane would've left him."

"Can I—"

"No. I'll take care of this myself." He used his tone that shut off further discussion.

I called the waiter over in the awkward silence, and we ordered. After he left, I said, "Jeff, this five hundred dollar reward changes our arrangement." I smiled at him. "I'll host this evening."

"By God, yer right. It'll be a pleasure to be yer guest this evenin'."

Damn, how did he make me feel like I always lost these jousts? I looked at him, and he smiled knowingly at me. I started laughing and gave him a salute, which got him laughing as well.

"Damn you two," McAllen said. "I can never follow your table contests, but one of you is buyin'."

McAllen said this with such irritation that Sharp and I laughed even longer. I was really enjoying the evening. Perhaps it had something to do with the whiskey during my soak, but I had been in a good mood earlier as well. It was such a relief to drink carelessly. Bat Masterson had admonished me to stay sober in the face of threats, and I hadn't had more than a single drink in a day since. Tonight I intended to have a good time.

Dinner was excellent. For two hours, we had a continuous stream of great food, better wine, and even better conversation. McAllen had refused any further liquor after the food arrived but stayed in a jovial mood—at least it was a jovial mood for Captain Joseph McAllen. He planned an early start in the morning and could not be convinced to down wine like Sharp and me.

I spotted baked Alaska on the dessert menu, so I asked to speak to the chef. A white-clad Frenchman sauntered over like he owned the place. Maybe he did.

"I hope you gentlemen enjoyed your meal," he said, in a heavy accent.

"Yep," Sharp answered. "Best meal since I left France."

"Of course." He wore a patronizing smile that immediately put me off.

"I noticed that you serve baked Alaska. How do you prepare it?"

"That is secret, but you must order it. It is exquisite. I prefer to call it omelette à la norvégienne, but Americans pronounce French so poorly, I decided to call it Alaska to avoid embarrassment."

"How considerate of you," I said. "Apportez trois ordres, s'il vous plait."

He looked as dumbfounded as I had hoped. "You speak excellent French, monsieur. When were you in France?"

"Never." I waved my hand dismissively. "It's a simple language. But I need clarification. I hope you prepare the omelette à la norvégienne like Chef Ranhofer at Delmonico's in New York City."

He lifted his chin and had to look down his nose to keep his eyes on me. "This Alaska, as you call it in America, was invented in Paris. I can assure you that it's superior to anything you may have encountered in New York."

"We'll be the judge of that. As I said, bring us three orders. And you may want to work on your English... your pronunciation is awful."

After he stomped off, McAllen said, "Steve, he's gonna spit in our food."

"I'm full anyway. I intend to take a single bite and send it back."

"Well, I'm eatin' it," Sharp said. "Spit or no spit. Let's get some cognac."

McAllen stood. "You gentlemen order after-dinner drinks. I need to use the privy."

I watched McAllen leave and grew envious of his steady gait. I wasn't too sure I could retain my dignity when it came time for me to walk out of here and to my room.

I was going to call over the waiter to order cognac when Sharp said, "I believe Alaska *was* invented in Paris."

"The French use pastry, Delmonico's uses meringue. I prefer our way."

"Sorry to disappoint you, Steve, I've had it both ways in France."

"Doesn't matter. He's an ass."

"Now we agree."

We both laughed like men in their cups, and I was about to tell Sharp about other things my family's French maid had taught me when I heard the most frightening sound I could imagine.

"Mr. Steve Dancy, you thieving swine."

Mrs. Bolton.

I turned slowly to see her leveling a shotgun at me. The restaurant had grown so quiet that I could hear guests casually talking in the lobby. She looked possessed, but her hand looked steady on the trigger. I had been in this situation once before with her and had escaped. Perhaps again?

I tried for a casual tone. "Mrs. Bolton, that language isn't befitting a lady of your stature."

"Neither are loud noises, but you're about to hear one."

"Mrs. Bolton, perhaps you should look around. You'll find—"

"Shut up. Your little whore tricked me the last time I had a shotgun pointed at you, but not this time."

"How did you get out of jail?"

I could see by her overly sweet smile that my ruse had worked. She was going to brag about getting released. I had to keep her talking.

"You think they would keep a woman locked up? You're a fool. They wanted to keep Vrable and his men separated, and they only had three cells, so my lawyer got me released by promising I wouldn't leave this hotel."

"What—"

"Enough! No more talking."

"Wait! Let Sharp move out of the way."

"Too late. Goodbye, Mr. Dancy."

I threw myself to the floor, but the shot I heard came from a heavy caliber pistol, not a shotgun. I flipped over but kept low as I reached for my gun. My head rolled over and I came eyeball to eyeball with Mrs. Bolton. She wore a shocked expression. The hair at her scalp was matted in blood, while the back of her head smoldered from the gun flash. She had been shot with a pistol shoved against the back of her neck.

I shakily got to my feet and saw McAllen through a blue haze of gun smoke.

"Thanks," I said weakly.

"You're welcome... now we're even."

Chapter 52

McAllen holstered his gun and stepped over the massive body of Mrs. Bolton. "Gentlemen, Ladies," he yelled. "Please excuse this disturbance. I'm Captain McAllen of the Pinkertons. Unfortunately, this crazy woman was about to kill many people. The marshal will want to ask questions, so please stay at your tables."

I had gotten to my feet, and McAllen asked, "Are you all right, Steve?"

"Better than if that shotgun had gone off."

"Then help me move her into the lobby. Bloody bodies tend to put people off their feed."

Sharp came up and grabbed an arm while McAllen and I each grabbed a leg. The restaurant manager, apparently anxious to get the body away from his customers, hurried over to help by lifting the other arm. We shuffled her into the lobby and dropped her around a corner where she would be out of sight of the restaurant patrons but in full view of the hotel guests. As soon as we plopped the body down, the restaurant manager scurried away as if whatever Mrs. Bolton had was contagious.

"Damn," Sharp said. "I'm sure glad ya pee straightaway. Takes me forever nowadays." Sharp laughed, as he always did when he found himself amusing.

I looked down at her and realized I was still drunk. "Well, Captain, I'm glad you didn't drink much. Even the slightest hesitation, and they'd be cleaning Jeff and me off those drapes."

"Not much chance of that. I saw her come down the stairs with that shotgun and kept an eye on her instead of going to the privy."

"You knew she was out of jail." I said this as a statement, not a question. "Why didn't you tell me?"

"Didn't want to ruin your evening."

A hotel clerk brought over a blanket, and we threw it over her corpse. After we had her covered, I asked, "Joseph, have you ever killed a woman before?"

"Not sure." McAllen didn't give the slightest hint that he was joking. "Anyway, Steve, you're free of her."

"Not quite yet."

"What do you mean?"

"I'm taking her to Mason Valley to be buried next to her son. Now she'll have a piece of that ranch forever."

"Well, I'll be damned," Sharp said. "Yer goin' back to see Jenny." Sharp used the toe of his boot to nudge Mrs. Bolton's blanket-clad body. "Hell, ya didn't need an excuse."

"Yes, I did."

"Well, ya'll need company too. I'm comin' with ya."

"All the way to Mason Valley?"

"Hell, no. Just to Carson City. Steve, my boy, the rest of the journey is yers alone to take."

Chapter 53

The next morning, when Sharp and I entered our store, we both stopped mid-stride. What the hell? The natural pine shelves had been whitewashed, the merchandise had been rearranged, and we didn't recognize the clerk behind the counter. As we stood there gawking, Mrs. Baker approached us wearing a bright floral dress that swooshed around her legs as she walked.

"Good morning, gentlemen."

"What have you done?" I stammered.

"Forget Steve's poor manners, ma'am." Sharp gave a little bow. "Ya look stunnin'."

"You mean my dress?" She did a complete swirl, sending her skirt billowing.

"Your dress, the whitewash, the merchandise." I pointed at the clerk. "And who's that?"

"One of our new clerks. With you two gallivanting about the countryside, you didn't expect me to run the store with two boys, did you?"

"One of our new clerks? How many did you hire?"

"Two … oh, and I still use the boys." She walked between us and hooked an arm around each of our elbows. "Come along and I'll show you some of our other changes. And don't look so worried—we did nearly a thousand dollars worth of business while you were gone."

My furrowed brow immediately relaxed. A thousand dollars this time of year was spectacular. Most people had started to burrow in for the winter. She led us to the back of the store, which had also been whitewashed and now displayed an oil painting of a flower-filled landscape full of sunshine. Below the painting hung a placard that said *Coffee 5¢*. The stove was stoked, and eight captain's chairs were scattered around a small table with a checkerboard and several copies of both Leadville papers.

"We sell coffee now?" I asked.

"And lunch. We get a good crowd."

"Can you make money at that?" I asked.

"Merchandise makes money, but you can't sell to people huddled against the cold in their rooms." She waved her arm across the back of the store. "This gives men a place to gather during the day, and they buy things after they get done chatting."

"They come here instead of a saloon?" I asked.

She smiled. "They like to watch me ... and if they get an urge, the establishments right down the street accommodate their needs." Her expression turned a bit wicked for the first time since I had met her. "I should demand a commission."

"Do ya ever get bothered?" Sharp asked, with concern in his voice.

"Nothing we can't handle," she said, throwing a glance at the new clerk. "Besides, we don't sell liquor. And Clyde sends the ones that come in drunk packing."

I took better notice of our new clerk. He was big. Tall and hefty. With her pocket pistol and his presence, I figured she was right: They could handle unruly customers.

"The place looks bright and cheery, ma'am," Sharp said.

"You haven't lived through a Leadville winter. It's depressing. The new decorations draw them away from their drab quarters and keep me cheerful."

"Well, I'll be damned," Sharp gave a low whistle. "Nearly a thousand dollars, ya say."

"Nine hundred and sixty four, to be exact."

"Mrs. Baker," I said. "Could Mr. Sharp and I have a private discussion?"

"Of course. You men take a seat right here and help yourself to coffee." She gave Sharp a fetching grin and used her hand to swish her skirt as she retreated to leave us alone by the warm stove.

"Damn, what the hell got into her?" I said as I plopped into one of the chairs.

"Purpose," Sharp answered.

"Purpose?"

"She ain't had a rudder since her husband died. Now she has a purpose in life. We were gone so much, she ran this store. Women need a family or somethin' else to keep their minds in joyful spirits."

"You got women figured out?" I asked.

"A damn sight better than ya'll ever understand 'em. That woman's ripe for a man. I just might see if I fit the bill."

"Jeff, she's too young for you."

"I may be too old for her, but she's not too young for me. 'Sides, ya got Jenny."

"Doubtful. She didn't return my letters." I got up and poured us coffees. I handed a mug to Sharp before I retook my seat. "I say we keep the store and let Mrs. Baker run it."

"Hell, yes," Sharp said. "If she can do a thousand dollars in a few days at this time of year, she'll fill this store with customers come spring."

"How big of a raise?"

"Ten dollars a month, plus ten percent of the profits."

"She already owns ten percent."

"Then give her an extra five percent. What the hell."

"Agreed." I could feel myself smiling. "I suppose you want to tell her."

Sharp glanced toward the front of the store. "Yep. Sure ya want to leave tomorrow? Mrs. Bolton ain't gonna rot in this cold."

"Jeff, you know winter's on the way. I'm leaving tomorrow."

"Damn." He glanced at Mrs. Baker again. "I sure hope her bed's empty when I get back in the spring."

Chapter 54

My butt hurt. Even using a pillow, a buckboard seat was less comfortable than a saddle. I had rented the wagon in Carson City to haul the pine box to the Bolton ranch in Mason Valley. I had been bouncing down the Carson Trail for nearly six hours, and no matter which way I shifted my weight, every bump punished my tender rear end.

Mr. Tabor had offered to load the coffin on top of one of his ore wagons heading down the mountain. I hadn't realized how fortuitous that was until I had ridden for nearly a full day on the hard plank that someone at the stable had generously called a seat.

We had gone through Denver to catch trains over to Carson City, but I took advantage of the city to sell the overexcited horse I had never bothered to really name. If I got nothing else at Jenny's ranch, I hoped to buy a horse. I'd already decided to pay someone else to return the buckboard to Carson City.

Sharp had been a great companion, reveling me with stories of the West for my journal. I had enough material for my book, but I felt no need to rush back to New York City. Besides, I could massage my notes into a book out here as easily as in the East. Maybe better.

As I approached Jenny's ranch, I grew increasingly nervous. The last time I had been here was only three months before, and I had asked if I could court her. Jenny had declined and sent me on my way. Since then I had written her two letters and received none in return. At least I could let her know in person that her mother-in-law wouldn't bother her anymore.

The ranch looked the same as the first time that I had seen it, except then it had been summer, and this was late autumn. The colors had transitioned from greens to brownish hues, but the ranch itself looked tidy, and all the structures seemed in good repair. The first place I visually checked was the porch. On my first visit, Mrs. Bolton had stood on that porch looking like a massive ogre, daring the world to displease her. This day, the porch was empty.

I saw one cowboy working a horse in the breaking pen, but no one else. I began to worry. In Carson City, I hadn't checked to see if

Jenny was in town. What if she wasn't at the ranch? I knew nothing about ranching, but I assumed that, unlike farming, it was a year-round enterprise. Suddenly, Jenny's foreman came out of the barn pretending to wipe his hands in a towel, but I could see that the towel hid a pistol.

"Expecting trouble, Joe?" I yelled.

Joe smiled and shoved the pistol in his waistband as he threw the towel over his shoulder. He signaled that everything was all right to someone in the barn and walked over to meet my lumbering wagon.

"Steve, good to see ya." Then he looked concerned. "What's in the wagon?"

I pointed at the gun in his waistband. "Is that the way you greet all your visitors?"

"All the unexpected ones. Ya never know. Once a gunman came traipsin' in here with a gang of Pinkertons, snarlin' demands at the owner." We both laughed, because, of course, that had been me. When we both regained control, Joe again asked, "Steve, what's in the wagon."

"You mean, who's in the pine box." I took a breath. "Joe, it's your old boss."

"Mrs. Bolton? John's mother?"

"Yes. I brought her back to be buried here."

"Who killed her?"

"What makes you think she was killed?"

"Who killed her?"

"The Pinkerton that was here with me a couple of times."

"We owe him, then." He gazed at the coffin like it was a gift. "That hag sent Cliff and Pete back here to cause trouble, but we ran them off. She also filed lawsuits in California that required Jenny to go there to defend herself." Joe looked away from the coffin and back at me. "It's not been peaceful since ya left."

Something he said worried me. "Jenny in California?"

"No, she's at a neighborin' ranch buyin' pigs to feed the men. Lost ours to a damn wolf, and the men are tired of beef." He smiled. "She'll be back soon."

I stood up and stretched before climbing down from the wagon. "Got a drink?"

"Yep. It's a bit early, but this looks to be a time to celebrate." Joe waved over a boy who looked about fifteen. "Chris, take this wagon and pull it into the barn. Leave the horse hitched. We'll probably bury this shortly." Then he turned to me before the boy could ask any questions. "Come on. I got a bottle in the bunkhouse."

When we got to the bunkhouse, Joe grabbed his bottle of whiskey and two glasses. He wiped the glasses with the towel that still hung over his shoulder. "Let's sit outside. Gotta take advantage of this weather while it lasts."

We sat on a long bench that was placed near the wall so we could rest our backs against the bunkhouse. The late afternoon air was brisk, not bone-shattering cold like Leadville. I took a tentative sip and was surprised to discover an adequate whiskey. I took another sip before saying, without preamble, "Cliff and Pete are dead."

Joe raised an eyebrow at me.

"I killed them in Durango. She sent them to kill me, and I got lucky."

Joe nodded and then said, "Ya get lucky a lot. Maybe ya can spare some for a poor cowhand with only three dollars to his name."

"Jenny gave you a raise."

He chuckled. "That she did, but I go down to Fort Churchill for poker. Love to play, just no good at it."

"Jenny lets you go?"

"We have an agreement. I never play with the boys in the bunkhouse, and she lets me go to Fort Churchill every Saturday night." He took a healthy swallow of his drink. "She's a smart boss."

I reached into my pocket and held up a coin for Joe to see. "Five bucks to return that wagon to Carson City on your next visit to Fort Churchill."

Joe looked puzzled as he started to pour us a second drink. "How do ya expect to get back?"

I put my hand over the glass. "Do you have a good horse I could buy?"

"Several." He thought a minute. "What happened to yours?"

"Mrs. Bolton poisoned Chestnut, and I'm not riding that buckboard back to Carson City."

Joe nodded his head. "That explains the saddle in the back of yer wagon. Freedom out here means owning a horse." Joe threw himself off the bench. "I think I got one to fit ya."

That was encouraging, because Joe was a phenomenon with horses. I followed him to a corral that quartered three horses. I immediately liked a light brown one. It was leaner than Chestnut but had similar coloring. I especially liked the way he watched us approach, in curiosity, not in fear.

"What about that one?"

"It's the one I had in mind."

Joe lassoed him while I hauled my saddle and harness from the barn, and I was riding around the corral in short order. After I felt comfortable, I nodded at Joe, and he lifted the gate so I could ride out into the fields. In ten minutes, I knew I would buy this horse. This was not Chestnut. He was faster, but he had none of the twitchiness of that horse I had ridden in Leadville. It's hard to explain after a short ride, but the horse felt sure-footed and confident. As Joe had said, we fit.

Over another drink, we negotiated a price, and I paid with paper money. After we completed the deal, I decided to take the horse out for another ride. No telling how long Jenny would be, and I needed to get to know the horse so I could pick an appropriate name.

I had just remounted when I heard shrill squealing. I looked over to see a two-wheel wagon full of pigs, being pulled by a mule. Jenny sat on the teetering seat, snapping the reins against the mule's back.

I sat nailed to my saddle until Joe reached up, took the reins out of my hands, and threw them around the corral rail. "Might as well say hello."

I dismounted and walked into the yard as Jenny pulled up on the reins. We both just stared at each other. She wore a blank expression and a dowdy housedress, but she still looked prettier than any woman I had seen since I had left this ranch. Then she smiled. I fell in love again instantly. Damn, I should never have come here.

"Steve, I can't believe it's you." She leaped off the wagon and threw her arms around my neck and hugged me. "Why'd you come back? No … I didn't mean it like that." She squeezed but did not kiss. "I'm glad you're here, whatever the reason."

I pushed her out to arm's length. "I came with what many would assume were sad tidings … but in your case, I think you'll be happy."

"My mother-in-law is dead."

I was confused. "How did you know?"

"Her death made the local newspaper."

"She's in the barn," Joe said from behind me.

Her smile disappeared. "You brought her *here*? Why?"

"To bury her in the dirt of this ranch . . . with her son. Those were the only two things she cared about. She wanted this ranch so bad she died for it, so I figured she ought to get a piece of it for a grave."

"Very poetic but stupid. Steve, take her away from—" She stopped, and I could see her think. Finally, "You're right. *I* need to bury her." She took a deep breath. "Now."

I understood but said nothing.

"Joe, get two shovels." Then she screamed, "Chris!" and he came running. "Put these pigs in the pen and give them some slop to shut them up."

"Yes, ma'am." He leaped onto the wagon and snapped the reins.

Joe came out of the barn with two shovels. "Cliff and Pete are dead too."

She turned and met my eyes. "You?"

I nodded.

"So much good news in a single day. I hope they died painfully." Her voice sounded bitter and she threw me an angry look before she marched off into the barn. Soon she was driving the wagon into the field that included the Bolton family graveyard.

I didn't go with her and Joe. Bringing Mrs. Bolton back here had been a mistake. Jenny was right. It was stupid. I didn't like her reaction, and I certainly didn't like her bloodlust. Had I fallen out of love ten minutes after I had decided I was in love? Jenny always seemed like at least two different people. She confused me. The travesties she had endured were unspeakable, and they would damage anyone, but most of the time she seemed untouched, or pretended to be untouched. And then anger and hatred would flash white hot. This was not the appealing Jenny.

I loved the joyous Jenny, the one full of life, the one with enough energy to make a room full of people happy to be alive. This Jenny's smile radiated good will and innocence. My Jenny's laugh made you believe you were the only one that could delight her.

The other Jenny hated. She could kill—she had killed. She was unbelievably stubborn—headstrong to a fault. She snarled and snapped out words like a bullwhip. And she was cold—colder than a corpse covered in ice.

These were the two Jennys I knew. I even think I understood them both. I always believed that my Jenny would one day emerge as the winner. But even my Jenny acted out roles she scripted as if for the stage. I was never sure if I was seeing one of the two Jennys I knew, or another disguised with good acting.

However many Jennys there were, they were all breathtakingly pretty and smart as hell. Too smart. She was calculating. At seventeen, she had already been manipulating men for years. Me? Yes, of course she had manipulated me. I took care of everything for her, and the only thing I received in return was the ire of her mother-in-law.

Damn it all.

I walked around the edge of the barn and saw Jenny and Joe throwing dirt into a grave about fifty yards away. She threw the dirt with relish.

I watched her lithe form as she wielded the shovel with the sure-handedness of someone accustomed to laboring in a field. The sun had baked her complexion a walnut brown that made her smile appear brighter than untouched snow. As she flung dirt and bile into the grave, her hair flew free and her breasts lifted and fell with a regular rhythm. Like the grand nature of the West, she was pretty, rugged, and dangerous.

With a new clarity I saw that she was the exact opposite of the women I had known in the East, and different was no longer enough. My Jenny might not win. At an impressionable age, she had been tutored and taunted by Mrs. Bolton. The things she had suffered had seared anger deep in her soul and I would be a fool to think I could now come along and coax her to a brighter outlook.

I went over to the corral and mounted my new horse. I was leaving. The last time, she had rejected me. I had ridden away with the sun against my back, feeling devastated. This time I was the one that chose to leave, and I would ride west, into the light of a setting sun. I guess I had to come back to take another look at her—with the distance of time to add perspective.

Now I could leave her and this ranch for good and not feel like I had left something undone.

Suddenly, I knew the name of my new horse: Liberty. I was finally free, and Liberty would carry me back to Carson City to rejoin Jeff Sharp.

I was only a quarter mile away when I heard a woman yelling after me. Jenny's screaming was unclear, but I believe I heard her yell my name. When I looked over my shoulder, she was standing alone outside the barn, hands cupped around her mouth. Then she dropped her hands and struck a defiant pose with feet spread and both hands on her hips.

I tapped my spurs into the side of Liberty and never looked back again.

I would like to express my appreciation to Jim and Marylu Allen, Richard Bigus, Mac and Sandy Castle, Barbara Cunningham, and all the wonderful people at Wheatmark. You have all made this a better book. Thank you.

Printed in the United States
151429LV00001B/129/P

9 781604 942385